Dark Salvation

Jennifer Dunne

Hard Shell Word Factory

Thanks are in order to a whole host of people: to my family,
who supported and encouraged me,
even if they can't understand why I want to do this....
to Tricia Bray, for critiquing above and beyond the call of duty,
and manning the 1-800-PLOT-HELP hotline
at all hours of the day or night....
to Gail Shelton, for her wonderful editing that uncovered the story
I wanted within the story I wrote....
and to Shirley Chan,
the geneticist who helped me develop the theory of neukocytes,
and who provided invaluable everyday details about genetics research.
Any mistakes are mine.

© 2000 Jennifer Dunne
ISBN: 0-7599-0401-4
Trade Paperback
Published November 2001
eBook ISBN: 0-7599-0367-0
Published October 2001

Hard Shell Word Factory
PO Box 161
Amherst Jct. WI 54407
books@hardshell.com
http://www.hardshell.com
Cover art © 2001 Mary Z. Wolf

Chapter 1

DAMN LACROIX for not telling her about the underground garage! But it would take more than an underhanded trick to make her give up now.

Rebecca Morgan pressed her back against the smooth steel wall of the elevator, letting the metal's cold touch seep through her suit jacket and the rayon blouse clinging to her skin. Gradually, she stopped shaking.

The elevator chimed, and the doors began sliding closed. She lunged for the control panel. Slamming her finger against the door open button, she pressed it again and again until the doors slid open, revealing the glass-walled vestibule separating the elevator from the deserted parking area. She was safe. She wasn't trapped. And when she was ready, the elevator would whisk her up above ground.

She braced her palms against the reassuringly solid elevator walls and took a deep breath of the cool air, so different from the scorching heat of the Arizona desert above, and focused on the job she'd come here to do. If she played her cards right, this interview could be her ticket to freelance work for a major paper. She'd be a success, by her own efforts and on her own terms. Bringing down a con-artist like Lacroix in the process was just the icing on her congratulatory cake.

But first, she had to control her emotions. Much as she hated being underground, she'd stay in the elevator until she restored her composure. Overcoming her childhood fear would be easier than overcoming a bad first impression.

Closing her eyes, she listened to the soft whir of air forced through vents hidden in the vestibule ceiling, and lifted her face to the bright fluorescent light streaming in the open doors. Her pulse steadied and she took deep, calming breaths of the slightly metallic air. She was ready to tour the mysterious Prescott Institute and meet its reclusive director who, according to her research, didn't seem to exist.

Her pulse and breathing sped up again, but not from fear or anger this time. Desmond Lacroix existed. After countless calls and letters to the Institute, she'd finally spoken to him on the phone. Sparred with him on the phone was more like it. She'd tried to pin him down about

Doctor Avram having worked at the Institute, Avram's alleged drug problem that he'd "narrowly escaped" having destroy his life, and his revolutionary new surgical methods that he'd said came to him in a "dream." Lacroix had sidestepped and dodged her every question, in a thick caramel voice that distracted her so much, she wasn't even certain what she'd said to prompt his invitation for a private tour of the Institute. But his invitation was burned in her memory.

"I suppose I've no choice but to give you a guided tour," he'd said. His soft chuckle had made her so weak she'd dropped her pen. "Or you'll sneak over my walls in the middle of the night. No telling what trouble you might get yourself in."

Even though she'd taken him up on his offer, she suspected she might be getting into trouble anyway. She recalled the way Avram's face had paled when she'd asked who he'd worked with in Arizona. After insisting once more that he'd done all the testing for his new procedure when he returned from Arizona, he'd ended the interview so quickly he'd practically thrown her out the door. At the time, she'd been too busy trying to follow up on his clues to wonder what had scared him. Now, when it was too late, she realized the narrow escape he'd referred to might not have been from drug addiction.

She glanced out through the glass-walled vestibule at her rental car, the only occupant of the underground visitors' parking lot. A sign indicated that employee parking was another level down, but she hadn't investigated further to see if any of the 730 people Lacroix claimed to employ were parked there. She'd preferred to go immediately to the oasis of safety promised by the open elevator. Had she made a mistake by coming here alone? How desperate was Lacroix to keep his secrets?

Bending down, she picked up her notepad and pen from the gleaming floor of the elevator. She felt half-dressed without her microcassette recorder and camera, something else for which she blamed Lacroix.

"You must come alone," he'd insisted. "And you may not use film or tape while on Institute property. Neither condition is negotiable."

She'd agreed because she needed the interview. Unless Lacroix himself gave her a clue, all she had was an intriguing mystery, not a feature story. She just hoped her knack for getting subjects to reveal more than they planned held out a little longer.

She turned her attention to the elevator panel. Aside from the usual "door open," "door close," "alarm," and "stop" symbols, only two buttons indicated floors. The bottom button read "P," as did the digital display at the top of the panel, so she pressed the button marked "M." The steel doors whispered shut, and a slight vibration carried through the soles of her dress pumps. In her notebook, she jotted the quick question, "Where's the employees' elevator?"

The doors slid open to reveal a marble foyer. Clusters of ferns and potted palms alternated with marble benches around a tinkling fountain, while even more plants lined the walls, blurring the edges of the room with green shadows. Her baked and heated skin absorbed the cool moisture of the fountain's spray as she inhaled the reassuringly familiar aroma of living plants.

The Prescott Institute continued to surprise her. She'd never expected to find such lush opulence concealed within the all but deserted farmhouse and windowless cinder block building she'd seen from outside. Of course, she also hadn't expected the dilapidated barn to conceal the entrance to an underground garage. She gripped her pen, anxious to discover what else the Institute concealed.

As her eyes adjusted to the room's diffused lighting, she made out the shape of a man in the shadows. Disregarding the benches, he lounged against the wall with one foot crossed in front of the other, like a GQ ad come to life. Shadows cloaked him, allowing her to see only his light linen suit that hinted at a powerful body beneath.

He stepped forward in silence, pushing away from the wall with fluid grace. Prepared to give him a single dismissive glance, her cheeks heated as she stared. The man's thick black hair fell in waves to his shoulders, and instead of the dress shirt she'd expected, he wore a dark green turtleneck that hugged his chest and made the linen jacket cling like a second skin.

Dragging her gaze up from his chest, she discovered him making a similar appraisal of her. A strange tingle of pleasure rippled through her at his half-smile of approval and the emerald sparks kindling in the depths of his eyes. Or maybe the chill air was making her shiver. Then he spoke.

"Ms. Morgan?"

Desmond Lacroix. She'd recognize that caramel cadence and timbre anywhere, even if she heard him reading the entries in a phone book. His resonant voice was even more devastating in person. It filled her mind with images of murmured endearments and passionate readings of Shakespearean sonnets.

Excitement coiled through her, quickening her pulse. She told herself it was because his measured pronunciation hinted at the remnants of a drawl. He'd probably taken voice lessons at some time in the past, hoping to disguise his origins. Another secret for her to discover. Another deception to expose. She looked forward to peeling away the layers of his disguise, and revealing the truth of the man.

She offered a professional smile and extended her hand.

"Mr. Lacroix. Thank you for taking the time to see me."

"My pleasure, I assure you." His words wrapped around her in a verbal caress, and he clasped her hand a moment longer than necessary. "Did you have any trouble finding the Institute?"

She thought back to the rutted dirt path she'd followed from the Interstate. She'd feared for her car's suspension with every bump, until the path snaked between two battered and faded farmhouses, and passed a bare cinder block building bigger than both houses combined. The path ended at the drooping red barn he'd told her to park in, and which concealed the entrance to the underground garage. "Your directions were quite clear."

Another half-smile touched his lips, acknowledging that she hadn't answered his question. Before he could exchange more pointed pleasantries, she flipped open her notebook, reminding him that she was here for business. His charm couldn't camouflage the fact that no records existed of a Mr. Desmond Lacroix, or that the Institute's paper trails ended with a holding company no one had ever heard of.

He gestured her toward the glass door on her left.

"The Prescott Institute is divided into three general areas of research," he began, sliding a plastic keycard through the reader beside the door. It hummed and released the lock with a loud click. He held the door open for her, letting her enter the sterile white corridor before him.

The corridor stretched for at least thirty feet before turning a corner, with doors on both sides. They must be in the cinder block building, then. But was the entire Institute contained in the one building, or were the three areas divided between the three buildings? They'd all looked equally lifeless from the road.

The air on the other side of the door stung her nose and throat with its antiseptic bite, and a heavy metallic taste clung to the inside of her mouth. Swallowing didn't help. A sudden whiff of spice pierced the hospital smell, and she turned to find Lacroix behind her. She'd overlooked the subtle, spicy-sweet fragrance of his cologne in the lush foyer. But it contrasted well with the sterile atmosphere of the hall, just as the warmth radiating from him contrasted with the overly-conditioned air.

"We research the blood and vascular system, blood-born contagions, and vascular applications, such as new methods to perform transplants and transfusions in greater safety," he elaborated, pausing to let her write everything down. "Because of the strict rules regarding sterile working conditions, I can't take you in to see any of the applications research. But your tour will cover the other two areas of the facility. Feel free to stop me if you have any questions."

He set off down the hall at a brisk pace, forcing her to scramble to catch up to him. So there were places she couldn't see. Were they manufacturing illegal drugs? That would match Doctor Avram's shady background. But illegal drug manufacturers were usually in it for the money, and wouldn't waste their profits on such an elaborate environment.

Maybe they were conducting illegal medical research, performing unsanctioned operations, or using unwilling test subjects. Kidnapped homeless people, perhaps. Or nosy reporters.

She shivered. No, it had to be drugs. She'd find a way to see those hidden areas later, after she'd taken the officially sanctioned tour. Forcing the issue now might jeopardize the concessions she'd already won.

He hurried her past featureless metal doors, each with a keycard scanner mounted in the wall beside it.

"What's in these rooms?"

"They're not part of the tour."

She couldn't pass up the chance to see one of the hidden rooms. Dropping a little ways behind him, she stopped and tested the door. The cold steel knob turned, but the door refused to budge. She pushed harder, and the scanner beside the door began squealing with a high-pitched repetitive tone more annoying than any car alarm she'd ever heard.

Lacroix stepped up and slashed his card through the scanner, instantly silencing the machine. "Leave the doors alone."

He turned to lead her back down the hall as the door unlocked with a loud click. It was the opportunity she'd been waiting for. She pushed open the door and stepped into the dimly lit lab.

A rough wooden table with brightly painted drawers filled the center of the tiny room. Narrow counters and desk spaces ran around the walls, with shrouded laboratory equipment stored neatly for their next use.

The door closed behind her with a bang, plunging the room into darkness. She started to tremble. She couldn't breathe.

Light. She had to have light.

Whirling around, she groped for the wall, half afraid of what her hands might come across in the dark. When her fingers brushed the cold, hard surface of the door, she slid her hands to the sides, but couldn't find a light switch. Desperate to get out, she grabbed the door knob with both hands, twisting and pulling. The mechanism refused to yield. The darkness closed in upon her, and she pounded on the door, slamming her fists against the rigid surface.

The welcome buzz and click of the scanner freed the door, and she wrenched it open. Rushing out, into the light, into the air, she practically tripped over Lacroix. He reached out a hand to steady her, but she batted it away. She needed space.

"The locks have a built-in delay feature. You have to wait a few seconds before they'll open again. What did you think you'd find in there, anyway?"

She could barely hear his voice over the pounding of her pulse. Pressing her back against the cool tile wall, she forced herself to take a deep breath. The antiseptic air burned her throat, but she swallowed it in welcome gulps. When she could trust herself, she looked at him.

His eyes narrowed. "Are you all right?"

"Yeah, I'm okay now." She grinned, trying to make light of her panic attack. "I don't do too well in small, dark places."

"I understand. I used to have a similar fear, of being buried alive."

His face blurred, and she imagined him being thrown into a shallow grave. She shuddered, the picture in her mind so realistic, she almost seemed to be there with him. Shovel after shovel of dirt fell on her helpless body, weighing her down, blocking out the light, cutting off her air....

"Ms. Morgan!"

The shout roused her, and she realized Lacroix was shaking her. He stopped, but his hands remained clamped on her shoulders, two points of concentrated fire. They were close enough that she could smell the musky aroma of the man beneath his cologne.

She looked up at him. The pallor of his face made his eyes seem twice as green. She must have given him quite a scare.

She shrugged her shoulders, but he didn't remove his hands. Their heat spread over her collar bones and up her neck, melting the last of her tension.

"We can end the tour, if you wish."

"I'm fine." She moved her shoulders again, and this time he lifted his hands away. The cold tile wall behind her absorbed the residual heat from his hands, leaving her at the mercy of the hallway's chill. She dismissed the feeling with another shrug and concentrated on her work. She'd only seen one room, and no researchers. "What do you do in that lab?"

"It's not currently in use. That's why it wasn't part of your tour. We have much to see, and a limited amount of time."

"Then let's get moving." She pushed herself away from the wall.

Lacroix nodded. "Stay close to me this time."

"No problem." Her flippant tone couldn't quite hide her shaking voice, but he didn't embarrass her by mentioning it. He also didn't seem upset at her attempt to breach his security system, making her wonder if the empty labs had been a setup that she was meant to find.

Leading her down the strangely empty corridor, he opened doors every so often to let her look at ongoing research. Each time, he gave her too vague a description of what they were working on for her to tell by looking if that's what they were really doing or not. She tried to get him to clarify his remarks, but his elaborations were masterpieces of noninformation. Work stopped whenever the researchers spotted them and Lacroix never entered any of the labs, so she had no opportunity to examine the labs in detail or question the researchers. They might be doing the research he claimed, or they might be synthesizing some poison more addictive than cocaine. The money had to come from somewhere, and drugs were still the best bet.

Her heart gave its traitorous vote for legitimate research, and Rebecca gritted her teeth in frustration. She knew the Institute was a setup. No one went to that much trouble to disguise a normal business. It had taken her the better part of four months to unravel the complex chain of interconnecting businesses that funneled money from dummy companies and institutional investment accounts into this mystery in the desert. But until she knew who was behind it, or what was being disguised, she knew nothing. Maybe the Institute did exactly what Lacroix claimed, but used its income and expenses to launder money from another source. She had to get more information from Lacroix.

After they peered into another room, she asked casually, "How many of the labs are in use?"

"Lab space is assigned based on the needs of the research projects. The different experiments require a variety of square footages and hardware."

Another non-answer. But this time, she wouldn't let go. "So how much of your space is being used?"

"We're currently operating at over 90% of utilization."

At last, something she could use! She noted the percentage in her pad, and scratched a quick reminder to look up utilization rates of other facilities.

He stopped and opened a door to another lab, then gestured her inside. After checking to make sure the lab was occupied and well lit, she hurried in, determined to find out if the lab was in use for its stated purpose. He followed her inside.

A young man in a wrinkled white lab coat sat at the counter, hunched over a microscope that was far more complex than the simple magnifiers she remembered from high school biology. A scattering of Twinkie wrappers surrounded him, perfuming the room with the odor of preserved sugar. It was sickeningly sweet, but a welcome change from the antiseptic air of the hallways. He must have heard the buzzing of the scanner, because he lifted one hand and made vague shushing motions at the door.

Lacroix frowned. "Dr. Chen."

The researcher bolted upright, almost falling off his stool in his haste. He swiveled to face them, speaking with a lilt more appropriate for a California beach bum than a brilliant scientist.

"I didn't know it was you, okay?" His face wrinkled as he tried to place Rebecca. "You're new."

"This is Rebecca Morgan. She's a reporter, taking a tour of the Institute. I thought she might be interested in your work. Ms. Morgan, this is Doctor Andrew Chen."

Dr. Chen beamed, and waved them over to the microscope.

"Dr. Chen is one of our sharpest researchers," Lacroix murmured to Rebecca as they crossed the lab. "His doctorate is in molecular biology. He's a brilliant scientist, but his interpersonal skills are a little...underdeveloped."

She nodded. Dr. Chen was a nerd.

Oblivious to their exchange, Dr. Chen began showing off his research. She didn't follow all of his technical jargon, even with the background research she'd done, but she grasped enough to understand he was researching DNA structures, trying to understand what the various sections of genetic code were responsible for. At least, that's what he said he was doing. She made notes of things to follow up on, all the while looking for a way to prove he did what he claimed to do.

"So, how would that work?" she asked.

"I'd start with a cell sample. Then I'd trap it on a slide, and inject proteins to flag the antigens I'm looking for. If they show up, I break apart the DNA to get more details. Get it?"

"No, I still don't see how you'd do it."

"I'd take a cell sample." He pronounced each word slowly and carefully, as if talking to an idiot. She saw her chance.

"A blood sample?"

"Maybe."

She stretched out her left hand. "Show me."

The researcher glanced at Lacroix, who shrugged. "If she wants you to poke her with needles, go right ahead."

"Well, okay. But it might hurt." Dr. Chen watched her carefully, as if he expected her to swoon at this revelation.

Her pulse quickened. Had she trapped him into exposing a lie? She kept her left hand steady, waiting for Dr. Chen to make his next move.

He shook his head, and pulled on a pair of latex gloves. Then he took two sealed paper packets from one of the primary-colored drawers. More packets filled the drawer.

He ripped the first packet open, and took out an alcohol wipe. He unfolded it and rubbed it briskly over the tip of her ring finger, then tossed it onto the gray Formica counter. The wetness evaporated immediately, chilling her skin. He opened the second packet and tipped a small metal lancet into his hand.

Glancing away, she found Lacroix studiously examining the far wall. She grinned. He'd certainly chosen an odd job for a man who was squeamish about the sight of blood.

The sharp prick of the lancet pulled her attention back to her hand, in Dr. Chen's tight grip. A bead of bright red blood welled up from the puncture. He wiped her finger again, cleaning the wound. A fresh spot of blood gleamed on the tip of her finger, and he touched it to a slim glass slide. He dropped an even thinner piece of glass on top of the slide, and the droplet of blood spread out between the layers.

She put her finger in her mouth, grimacing at the bitter alcohol residue. Lacroix's sharp intake of breath caught her attention, and she glanced over to see him staring at her, his emerald gaze fixed on her mouth. He swallowed, and she imagined that his sensuous lips imprisoned her finger. Her cheeks heated. Turning away, she focused all of her attention on Dr. Chen.

He fed the slide to the microscope. After taking a moment to adjust the focus, he beckoned her over. She put her eye to the foam rubber eyepiece and saw things that looked like giant soccer balls and tumbleweeds drift past. She backed away, suddenly sharing a little of Lacroix's queasiness.

Dr. Chen added drops of liquid to the edge of the slide.

"These compounds react with the antigens I'm looking for...." His voice faded, and he looked back and forth quickly between the microscope and a multicolored chart tacked above his desk.

"What is it?" Lacroix leaned over the researcher.

"This is very okay." Dr. Chen bounced on his stool. "I need to do another test."

He was already reaching for her hand. She nodded, not quite sure what was happening but sensing its importance to her story. If they really were doing research here, maybe it was the research itself that was such a big secret.

Dr. Chen wiped off her finger again, then forced a slim glass tube, not much wider than a piece of spaghetti, against the wound. It slowly filled with blood. He jabbed the tube into a block of Styrofoam to cork the ends. Pressing a second tube to the puncture, he squeezed her finger. Not enough blood flowed to fill another tube, even such a small one, and he reached into the drawer for a new lancet.

She snatched her hand away and stuffed it in her pocket, backing away in case he still had any ideas about using her as a guinea pig. "That's enough."

Lacroix spared her a brief look, then consulted with his researcher in low tones. They stopped and both glanced back at her, then continued their discussion. Curiosity overrode her self-preservation and she edged closer.

"How long will it take for you to get a result?" Lacroix asked.

"I don't know. A couple hours for preliminaries. Could be days for a final."

"Send word as soon as you confirm the preliminary results. I want to hear immediately."

"Okay." Dr. Chen turned to his work, ignoring them both. Lacroix glided to her side and pointed at the door.

As soon as they were in the corridor, she turned to him and demanded, "What was that all about?"

The gleam in his eyes reminded her of a starving man viewing a five-course banquet. Desperate hunger, tinged with disbelief.

"Dr. Chen is working on a cure for a degenerative blood disorder. Your blood contained one of the structures associated with the disorder. He's checking to see if you have a healthy version of one of the other structures that he can use."

"So I might be part of a cure for something?" Should she believe him? Or was this part of a complex ploy to mislead her, like letting tourists to the big city win the first game of Three Card Monte?

"It's too soon to guess. And I wouldn't want to raise anyone's hopes." He kept his voice level and calm, but she sensed the excitement in him, crackling just beneath the surface. His reaction seemed out of proportion to a simple lab experiment. What was his involvement with the Institute's research? Was his position as Director more than just a job to him? Her stomach churned. Was he looking for a cure for himself? More importantly, why did the thought of him being ill upset her so much?

He held open another door, gesturing for her to precede him. He used his left hand this time, and she caught a glint of light reflected from his wedding ring.

DESMOND HELD open the door, waiting for Ms. Morgan to recover from whatever it was that had stalled her in her tracks. Long years of controlling his emotions let him keep a calm, unruffled appearance, even though he felt like shouting and swinging the good reporter around the halls in a joyous dance. If Dr. Chen was right, Ms. Morgan's blood could hold the key to Gillian's cure.

His little girl might live. He had a chance to defeat the curse that had shadowed him for so many years.

He darted a quick glance at the woman by his side. She wore her chestnut brown hair in a sleek bob. No doubt she intended it to be professional. But her delicately boned face and wide gray eyes undercut that impression. She looked more like the traditional pictures of an elf or wood sprite. And she seemed so young, not much more than a child herself. Compared to him, she was a child. But the way she'd aroused his interest by sucking the blood from her finger had been all woman.

He forced his thoughts away from the memory. If Chen was right, he had more important uses for her blood.

"How are the research topics chosen and assigned?" Ms. Morgan asked as they continued down the hallway.

What prompted that question? He tried to scan her surface thoughts for a clue, and ran into a smooth mental wall. Intrigued, he turned to get a direct look at her.

When he'd first met her, she'd been surrounded by the same constant cloud of surface thoughts buzzing and darting around her conscious mind as most people. Although her frank appraisal of him had been flattering, propriety compelled him to strengthen his mental barriers. He'd dropped them when she suffered her panic attack, but he'd lowered them too far. She'd picked up on his mental imagery of being buried alive.

He'd kept the shields firmly in place since then, and hadn't noticed the change in her thoughts. When had they acquired such focus and strength?

"Mr. Lacroix, you didn't answer my question."

Her mental control wavered just enough to allow images of folded arms and tapping feet to swirl past. He smiled. That was it. She'd focused her mind on her story. He'd seen the same thing happen with researchers working on a particularly demanding problem, but he'd never encountered such a complete focus before.

"My apologies. My thoughts were...elsewhere." He felt her mental wall buckle slightly, lulled by his voice. "The researchers choose their own topics. Division chairs present the latest results at monthly meetings, and researchers often change topics to work in areas experiencing greater success."

The warm rush of pride filled him, as he admired his alternative to imposing suspicious research directives. By letting the researchers choose their own topics, but directing more funding toward those that addressed his and Gillian's problems, the researchers accomplished his goals with no knowledge of how the topics related. The person closest to an all-encompassing view was Dr. Chen, but as long as he remained the Institute's golden boy, with virtually unlimited funding, Chen wouldn't question anything.

All the money he'd poured into the Institute would be worth it, if Dr. Chen's tests proved positive. In two hours, they'd know if Ms. Morgan's DNA could provide the key to the healthy blood cell production that Gillian lacked.

Even viewed against the backdrop of his considerable life span, Desmond knew the next two hours would seem an eternity. For Gillian's sake, he must act quickly.

If the test was successful, Dr. Chen would need Ms. Morgan's continued help in developing a cure. Desmond could convince her to stay if he knew what she really wanted. But to do that, he'd have to get through her mental shield that muffled his ability to read her thoughts. He had to distract her, dissolve her focus. And the best way to do that was to tire her out.

He started a circuitous route through the facility. If he arranged it correctly, they could spend the next two hours walking without once retracing their steps. Meanwhile, he would dredge up every inane fact and useless piece of trivia he could remember about the Institute. By the time they finished, she'd be exhausted.

And Dr. Chen would have the preliminary results ready.

REBECCA STRUGGLED to take notes as they walked, stopping, writing, then dashing to catch up. Each time, it took longer to regain the ground she'd lost during her stop. She wished she'd eaten more than just coffee and doughnuts for breakfast. The effects of the caffeine and sugar must be wearing off.

They passed through a mixture of labs and administrative areas, with Lacroix pointing out every conference room and lecture hall. As they passed by the closed door of yet another lab, they were stopped by a gorilla of a man incongruously stuffed into a dark gray business suit.

"Mr. Lacroix, do you have a moment?"

"Of course, Evan." Lacroix glanced at Rebecca, then keyed open the lab door. "Why don't you ask the researchers about their work on T-cells? I'm sure you'll find it fascinating."

He opened the door, and she was immediately assaulted by a jazz saxophone blaring from a portable CD boom box on the counter by the door. She'd never overhear any of his conversation. No doubt that was his intent.

She stepped into organized chaos, her back against the locked door that sealed her inside. Six men and women in white lab coats hustled around the room, wheeling carts full of test tubes into and out of refrigeration units, marking results on clipboards, shouting instructions across the room at a voice-activated laptop computer, and twirling a series of dials set into a console mounted in the wall. Gradually the activity slowed, then stopped, as one by one they noticed her presence. Finally, one of the men flipped off the CD player, plunging the room into echoing silence.

"Hi. My name's Rebecca Morgan. I'm a reporter. Mr. Lacroix is giving me a tour of your institute, and suggested I ask you about your T-cell research."

Two of the researchers traded looks of disbelief, and one woman muttered, "*He* suggested you ask?"

Rebecca nodded and smiled, holding her pen poised and ready. The researchers hesitated a moment longer, then stampeded her in a herd, all clamoring to tell her the details of their work.

She scribbled barely legible notes, frantically trying to keep pace with six simultaneous explanations. Gradually, she realized they were relating the details of three years of work. She tried to interrupt the stream of information and steer their conversations into an area she could use, but they ignored any question of hers not directly related to their research.

She burned to know what they thought of the extreme security measures, the hidden facility, and what seemed to be a standing order not to discuss their work with outsiders. Other than increasing the number of nervous glances directed at the door behind her, her words had no effect.

Lacroix had granted her wish. He'd given her time alone with a roomful of his researchers. And yet, they told her nothing she wanted to know, other than confirming by their silence that Lacroix had prevented them from publishing articles or otherwise telling their peers about their work.

The loud buzz of the lock stilled all six conversations. Lacroix opened the door in complete silence.

Holding it open but not stepping inside, he smiled. "Thank you all for taking the time to speak to Ms. Morgan. I'm sure she still has plenty of questions, but we must continue our tour."

She thanked the grinning researchers, then joined Lacroix in the hall. The saxophone resumed its wailing lament, then the door sealed the corridor in silence.

Lacroix slanted her a knowing glance. "Did you learn anything you can use in your article?"

"Yes. I did." She'd learned that he was definitely hiding something. And that whatever he was hiding, that muscle-bound ape, Evan, was up to his shaggy eyebrows in it. She just needed to discover what it was.

Chapter 2

BY THE END of her tour, Rebecca had stopped writing. That had probably been Lacroix's intent, to bore her with the monotony and impress her with the Institute's unrelieved ordinariness. And unfortunately, she couldn't prove otherwise. Whatever secret he was hiding, it wasn't illegal drug manufacture, germ warfare experiments, or any other increasingly farfetched scenario she could propose.

She didn't even have anything newsworthy to report about the Institute itself. True, it was disguised from the outside. But inside, it was perfectly normal, although bigger than she'd expected. They'd gone up and down more stairs than she could count, and at some point must have passed through connecting passages between the basements of the various buildings. At least the confusing layout had prevented her from succumbing to another embarrassing panic attack, since she hadn't known when she was underground.

Finally, they returned to the marble entry foyer. Her tour was almost over, and she still didn't have a story. She'd had an unheard of opportunity, and she hadn't been a good enough journalist to find out the truth of the matter. Mentally adding up the cost of tickets from Syracuse to Phoenix, the rental car, and her hotel bills, she winced at the staggering price of her failure. The other articles she'd promised to write while she was out here might cover some of the costs, but the airline tickets were coming straight out of her pocket. She had to be able to find something she could use for a story.

When Lacroix led her to a small lounge opposite the elevator, she barely looked at her surroundings. She sat down on the couch, its blue and beige tweed rasping against her stockings. Her feet burned from so much walking, and the couch pillows looked soft and inviting. It would feel so good to lie down and sleep. Sighing, she lifted her heels ever so slightly out of her shoes.

He filled two water glasses from a pitcher on the counter. Keeping one for himself, he carried the other over to where she sat and offered it to her. She recalled a fairy tale admonition not to eat or drink anything offered by her host, but dismissed the thought as a fancy born of exhaustion. Tipping back the glass, Rebecca gulped the clear water greedily. It tasted fresh and pure, and washed away the antiseptic sting in her throat.

He poised on the edge of the chair across from her.

"Did I answer all of your questions?"

"All but one." She kept fishing, even though she no longer expected to discover anything. "Why is the security so tight?"

"The scanners aren't just for security. The keycards are used to locate the researchers within the facility, as many of them have no fixed desk or work site. Also, by restricting access to labs, we can protect against accidental contagion." He smiled. "Not, of course, that such a thing would ever happen."

"What if there was a fire? Would the scientists be trapped in their labs?" She echoed his smile back at him. "Not, of course, that such a thing would ever happen."

"No. If power is disrupted to the system, all of the locks fall to the open position."

She nodded and made a few more notes. She should get back on the road and finish the drive up to Flagstaff, but it was heaven finally to be sitting down. She blinked, trying to keep her eyes from drifting shut. As soon as her feet stopped hurting, she'd leave. She could sleep when she got to a hotel.

Someone knocked on the door, and Lacroix jumped up to answer it. She thought she saw Dr. Chen outside. The two men whispered intently for a moment, then the researcher nodded and hurried away. Lacroix closed the door and turned to her with a smile.

"That was Dr. Chen. He's gotten some very encouraging preliminary results."

"Congratulations." Was that what you said to good research results? It was a good, all purpose comment. She couldn't focus her thoughts. Her mind felt full of taffy. Or maybe caramel.

"Would you consider staying on a few days to assist him with his research? It's a chance to add a human side to your story."

She stared at his smile, a gleaming, almost predatory smile that suddenly seemed no more sincere than a politician's declarations of honesty, and snapped wide awake. He waited for her answer, his eyes glittering fever-bright with excitement. And something else. Something dark and ruthless hid in the shadows behind his smile.

In a sudden flash of clarity, she knew that if she stayed, she'd learn his secret. But she wasn't sure that she wanted to know. The price of discovery might be more than she could pay.

She forced her voice to remain light as she lied, "Thanks for the offer, but I'm on a busy schedule. I have two other interviews scheduled tomorrow."

His smile faded.

"Those interviews will have to be postponed. Dr. Chen's research is too important for you not to help him."

"What could I do? Does he need a journalist to document his results?"

"You can help him the way you did earlier today."

"As a lab rat?"

"As a valued part of a scientific research effort."

This couldn't be happening. She snatched up her notebook and stood up on shaky legs. Taking a deep breath, she announced, "I'm leaving now. And you can't stop me."

He frowned, his features darkening, and she thought her heart would burst through her chest with the adrenaline flooding her veins. Then he stepped away from the door and smiled like a perfect host. The sudden transition rooted her to the floor in fear, expecting him to transform into some terrifying creature from the horror movies as soon as she moved.

"I'm sorry. My enthusiasm got the better of me. I naturally assumed you were as interested in the Institute's work as I am. Of course you are free to go."

She stared at him, not trusting the truth of his words. Then she gave herself a brisk mental shake. Exhaustion and her failure to discover Lacroix's secret had set her on edge, and she was letting her overactive imagination get away from her.

She walked past him, through the foyer to the elevator. He followed her, not making a sound. The whir and clank of the elevator rising in response to her summons echoed in the sudden silence. With a musical chime, it ground to a halt and the doors slid open.

"Thank you for the interview, and the tour."

He clasped her hand in a firm handshake, but did not let go as he said, "It was my pleasure. And my offer still stands. Any time you're in the area, feel free to stop by and help Dr. Chen with his research."

"I'll remember that." She pulled her hand free and stepped into the elevator. The doors slid closed, shielding her from his haunting green gaze. Fanning herself with her notebook, Rebecca cursed the too hot elevator and stabbed the parking garage button.

The elevator lurched and began its downward trip, reminding her of the underground garage Lacroix had failed to mention. Now that she'd met the man, she was sure he'd omitted that detail on purpose, hoping to throw her off balance. It hadn't worked, but he hadn't needed it to. The man himself was enough to unbalance her normal good sense.

A musical chime and another lurch signaled her arrival at the parking level. The doors opened on the deserted visitors' lot, her rental car the lone sign of life. She'd drive through the employees' lot on her way out and see if there were any cars parked there. She wouldn't put it past Lacroix to bus his people in. From a walled city where they weren't allowed to talk to strangers.

She smiled at the image, but admitted that her nervousness at being underground was making her silly. It would be best just to get in the car and get out of here, into the safe sunshine of a hot Arizona afternoon.

Clutching her car keys, she stalked through the glass doors of the elevator bay to her waiting white Taurus. She fumbled with the unfamiliar lock, then wrenched open the door and threw her pad and pen onto the front seat. She jammed the keys into the ignition. Putting all of her frustrations into a savage twist, she turned the key all the way to the right.

Click.

She was already reaching for the gear shift before she realized that the engine was not purring in quiet contentment. It wasn't even coughing or sputtering. It hadn't made any noise after that one, lonely click.

Just what she needed. She couldn't even get a car to cooperate with her.

Gripping the wheel, Rebecca took a deep breath and turned the ignition back to off. She depressed the accelerator a few times, knowing some cars needed that to get the gas flowing, and turned the key again.

Click.

Nothing. But it had been working perfectly when she arrived at the Institute!

She leaned back, staring at the unfamiliar dashboard, searching for an explanation. Then she noticed the stalk on the side of the steering wheel, and the indicator pointing to the icon for headlights. She must have brushed against it when she got out of the car this morning. Of course no one had come through the lot and seen her lights on. Who knew how long she'd have to wait before someone came by to help her.

Trapped underground. Waiting and waiting for help that never came, as it grew darker and colder, and the rain made the soft sides of the cave start to crumble.

She shook off the memory. She wasn't trapped.

She climbed out of the useless car, slamming the door in disgust. Then she kicked the tire for good measure.

"Ow!" Hopping awkwardly in one dress pump, she winced and hoped she hadn't done something truly stupid like breaking her toe. She'd forgotten she was wearing interview clothes, and not her good, serviceable sneakers. Nothing was going her way today.

She limped back to the elevator, leaning heavily against the wall for the ride up. The elevator chimed as the doors slid open. Lacroix turned back from the entrance into the Institute proper, meeting her as she hobbled into the foyer. Cheeks blazing with chagrin, she tried not to look like a flamingo as she balanced on one foot.

"Did you forget something?" His eyes widened, and he hurried to her side. "What happened?"

He wrapped an arm around her shoulders and guided her to one of the tiny marble benches. His arm remained long after the need to steady her had passed, and she wondered if his concern was for her safety or a possible lawsuit against the Institute.

"My car wouldn't start," she said, reluctantly easing out of his embrace.

He lifted an eyebrow and gazed pointedly at her foot.

"So I kicked it," she admitted.

His lips twitched, not quite smiling. "I trust you showed it who was in charge."

She shrugged. "Not that it did any good. I accidentally left the lights on and drained the battery. Can I get a jump start?"

"Does your car have jumper cables?"

"No. It's a rental."

"Ah. That could be a problem. There are jumper cables in the Institute's truck, of course. But Evan took it to run an errand, and won't be back for some time."

Rebecca frowned. "Surely someone else has a set. One of the researchers?"

"Perhaps. It might be faster to simply get a new car."

"I need to call the rental company, then." She wondered if she'd have to pay extra for the second car, and if so, how much. This trip was rapidly turning into a financial disaster.

Lacroix snared her attention again. "We're a long way from

Phoenix. Even if they have offices in Prescott, it will be at least half an hour before they can get a car here. You can rest and put your foot up in the visitor's suite, and I'll make the arrangements with the rental company. Where are the keys?"

She patted the pockets of her suit coat and skirt. "I must have left them in the car."

He smiled. "Don't worry about it. They'll be safe there."

"You really don't have to go to so much trouble."

"You were here at my invitation. I feel responsible for you."

He helped her stand. After confirming she was able to walk, he preceded her to the double doors leading into the Institute. The lock buzzed, and he held the door for her.

"Maybe I should unroll a ball of string," she joked. "The one thing I learned during my tour was that all these corridors look alike."

He chuckled. "It's not too far."

They walked on in companionable silence. He turned down a narrow corridor she didn't remember, around a corner, and then the white-tiled hallways gave way to black-veined marble floors, stuccoed gray walls and recessed lighting.

She hadn't seen this in her tour. Curiosity overwhelmed the lingering throbbing in her foot. What else hadn't he shown her?

Lacroix's voice broke into her thoughts. "They may not be able to get a car up here until tomorrow. Did you bring your suitcase with you?"

A trace of her earlier fear resurrected itself. "I'm sure one of the researchers can give me a ride into town."

"Of course. Or I could drive you. But you won't be getting all the way back to Phoenix tonight. I was just concerned that you might have left all of your things back in your hotel."

"Oh." She blushed, feeling foolish. She was normally a good judge of character, but today she was jumping at shadows. Maybe residual fear from her earlier panic attacks was clouding her reason. But Lacroix seemed able to keep her off balance with nothing more than a glance or a word.

Rebecca shook her head. "My bag is in the car. I was planning to get a room up in Flagstaff tonight."

"Is that where your interviews are?"

"What?" Too late, she remembered the lie she'd told earlier. "Yes. Yes, my interviews are in Flagstaff."

He opened a door to their right with his keycard, and gestured her through. Recalling the lab she'd been trapped in during the tour, she hung back.

"I don't have one of those cards. What if I need to—"

"There are extras in the guest suite. I didn't anticipate you'd need a card or I would have brought one for you."

Not entirely convinced, but lacking a reason to resist, she walked through the door. It led into an L-shaped corridor, with a small park-like gathering of potted trees, ferns and benches at the corner. The glowing skylights above the plants reassured her, and she cheerfully followed him through the second door past the bend, into the living room of a generous suite.

White wicker furniture with ivy-print cushions clustered around a low coffee table. She sank gratefully onto the couch and kicked off her pumps, tucking her feet up under her.

"There are snacks in the cupboard and beverages in the refrigerator," Lacroix told her, pointing toward the low wall separating the living room from the kitchenette. Then he pointed toward the archway in the opposite wall. "The bath and bedroom are through there, so you can freshen up or take a nap."

"Thanks, but hopefully they'll be able to send a car right away."

She glanced around the room, but couldn't see the phone. She made a more careful perusal, finding a stained glass window, bookshelves with a TV and a VCR, a small breakfast table and two chairs. But no telephone.

"If they can't send a car until tomorrow, it would make more sense for you to stay here, rather than going south to Prescott, then turning around and heading north tomorrow. You'd only be retracing your steps."

She tried to keep her voice casual, and laced her fingers together so her hands wouldn't tremble. "I suppose you're going to suggest that as long as I'm here, I could help Dr. Chen with his research, right?"

"It would give you something to do."

"Where's the phone?"

"The guest suite doesn't have one. Unfortunately, we had a problem with visitors making long distance calls."

She stood up, shoving her feet back into her shoes. They pinched. "Then let's go where we can make the call."

He didn't move. "Why are you so set against helping Dr. Chen?"

"Why are you so determined to make me help him?"

He paused, then rose from his seat. For a moment, she thought he wasn't going to answer. Then he asked, "What would you say if I told you my daughter was dying, and we need your help to save her?"

"I'd say that seems like an unbelievable coincidence. What's your real reason? I found something, didn't I? I was getting too close, and you're afraid I'll spill the beans in my article. That's why you're making up this elaborate ruse."

He glared at her, his eyes glittering a dangerous emerald, but he didn't deny it. Ice formed around her heart as she realized the magnitude of her idiocy.

"I didn't leave my lights on, did I? You did something to my car so it wouldn't start, so I couldn't leave. That's probably what you were talking to that goon about. I'd have to be crazy to let one of your people anywhere near me with a needle. Heaven only knows what might be in it."

She remembered the lounge, and the glass of water she'd gulped so eagerly. The glass of water he'd poured for himself but hadn't touched. That's when she'd started having trouble thinking clearly. The lying cheat had drugged her!

"Are you quite finished?" His voice remained soft, but his pale hands gripped the back of the chair so tightly, his knuckles matched the white wicker.

"I haven't even started! I saw the way those researchers were scared stiff of you. You think you're so high and mighty, the ruler of your own little kingdom here. Well, it's not the middle ages. I don't care who you are, you can't keep somebody locked up against their will. Take me into Prescott now, or—"

"You're staying here. I'll just have to make sure it's not against your will."

"You probably don't even have a daughter."

Something sparked in the depths of his eyes, warning her she'd gone too far. He stepped around the chair. Rebecca dodged the other way and raced for the open door.

He reached past her and stiff-armed it shut, slamming it closed and pinning her face first to the cold steel door. Her heart beat wildly, the blood pounding in her ears.

"Let me go!" She shoved against the door. Lacroix grabbed her wrists, pulling her arms behind her back. She kicked backwards. Her injured foot betrayed her, and she pitched forward, slamming her cheek into the door. He took advantage of her unbalance and pressed up against her, using his weight to trap her against the door so that she couldn't move.

Heat radiated from the hard wall of his chest that crushed her against the door with each of his rapid breaths. As if to counter his excess heat, her pinioned hands turned cold, and her breath caught in her throat. She was no match for his size and strength. No one would hear her if she screamed. He could do anything, and she couldn't stop him.

"I do have a daughter," he whispered, his fingers tightening painfully around Rebecca's wrists. "Since her mother died, she means everything to me. But she's dying. I've thrown everything the Institute has into the search for her cure, and I'm barely able to slow the progression of her disease. Now you offer me the first ray of hope in three years."

He leaned his forehead against the door so that Rebecca looked into his glittering green eyes. "I didn't want it to be like this. I was hoping you'd volunteer. But I have no choice. My daughter's life depends on it."

She stared, captivated by the shimmering emerald reflections in his eyes, a thousand points of faerie fire that danced and leaped in strange, hypnotic patterns. She could stare into his eyes for hours.

The fear and tension melted out of her, drowned in a wave of warmth that began and ended with the man before her. Everything would be all right, if she just let him have his way.

"No," she whispered. "I don't believe you."

"Believe me. Trust me."

He eased away from her, no longer crushing her against the door, but she forgot why that was important. Her pulse sped up. It was important. She struggled to release the memory of why.

Lacroix turned her so that she faced him, tipping her head so that she looked directly into his eyes. He slid his hands down her arms to capture her hands, and she remembered his gentleness as he comforted her after her panic attack. She had nothing to fear from him. Sighing, she relaxed into the warmth.

He stepped back, pulling on her clasped hands, and she glided after him like a sleepwalker. He led her to the couch, sat her down, then took his place beside her. The whole time, she stared, transfixed, into the swirling splendor of his eyes. The secret she was searching for was hidden in those eyes. All she had to do was look. Look.

"That's right," he whispered. "You wanted to find my secret. Discover what I was hiding. I was hiding my daughter. Help her, and you'll find the secret you were looking for."

"Secret daughter."

"You do want to help her, don't you?" His voice shifted away from soothing caramel sweetness, picking up a hint of insecurity.

Rebecca blinked. How had she gotten to the couch, with her hands tucked inside Desmond's and clasped close to his heart?

"You do want to help my daughter, don't you?" he asked again.

"Of course I do," she heard herself saying. Then she added, "But I can't."

He stiffened. "Why not?"

"I can't. Got to stay independent."

A strange warmth curled through her muscles and bones, as if she'd fallen asleep in a sauna and baked all of the tension out of them. She wanted to curl up against him and sleep. But there was a reason she couldn't do that. She had to fight. Only she couldn't remember what the fight was about.

She stared at him, dazed, unsure of when he'd spread her clasped hands against his chest. His heartbeat pulsed against her palms, and the rhythm echoed through her body.

"What are you afraid of, Rebecca?" he whispered.

"Can't tell."

"Are you afraid you can't trust me?"

"Can't trust. Anyone."

"You can trust me."

He reached out, and gently stroked her cheeks, framing her face with his warm, strong hands. She sighed, closing her eyes and settling into the security of his embrace. He pulled her closer, rubbing her back with long, soothing strokes. She leaned into his touch, her pulse quickening even as time slowed.

"Do you trust me?" he whispered, his cheek pressed against hers and his voice the softest breath in her ear.

"I trust you."

"I would never hurt you. I need you. I need your help. Do you want to help me?"

"I want—I want you."

He pulled away with a choked noise, putting his hands on her shoulders and shaking her lightly until she opened her eyes.

He was all she could see. The world was only the green fire of his eyes, fire that warmed her skin where he looked at her. She felt the heat on her face, her lips. She licked her lips, and they cooled as he dropped his gaze. But then the heat was on her breasts, an aching caress of warmth that made her yearn for his touch.

The heat vanished completely when he closed his eyes. She sighed, missing the warmth of his gaze. She closed her own eyes, drifting in the memory of brilliant green flames.

"Rebecca."

She opened her eyes and found herself once again trapped in his gaze. But the dancing flames lacked heat this time, and she found she could make sense of his words.

"Rebecca, this is important. You must tell me, do you want to help? Will you willingly volunteer to help my daughter?"

"Yes."

"You will help her?"

"I will help her."

"Willingly?"

"Willingly."

Desmond smiled, the dazzling brilliance almost as bright as the green flames. His hands slid from her shoulders to her back, pulling her close for a brief hug.

"Thank you," he whispered in her ear.

She turned her face and captured his lips with her own.

REBECCA WOKE on the couch with a pounding headache. She tried to sit up, and the world spun crazily. She felt ill.

Sitting quietly until the furniture stopped bobbing and dipping around her, she tried to remember what had happened. She'd come to the room with Desmond, because her car was broken. For some reason she couldn't recall, she'd thought he couldn't be trusted. They'd argued. Fought. And then—

She gasped. No, her memories couldn't be right. Touching her fingers tentatively to her lips, she thought they might be a little swollen. But was that because she'd been kissed, or because she'd bitten her lip during their struggle?

Her breasts ached. From being caressed, or from being crushed against the door?

She'd woken up fully dressed, but that didn't mean anything. If what she remembered had truly happened, he could have dressed her before he'd gone. For the first time since she was seventeen, she wished she was a virgin. At least then there would have been undeniable evidence to prove whether or not she'd made love.

Groaning, she pillowed her face in her hands. She remembered the feel of Desmond's rock-solid chest beneath her fingers, the rapid beat of his heart against his palms. He'd pressed his cheek to hers, and breathed soft words of seduction into her ear. But after that, her memory fragmented into images that made no sense.

She'd agreed to help his research. She remembered that, although she couldn't recall what had prompted her change of heart. Perhaps he'd said something to make her think she'd found his secret and would not be allowed to reveal it? She believed he would not hurt her, but she'd already misjudged the situation once, thinking he was helping her with her car and ending up trapped instead. She couldn't risk another judgment error.

Still, volunteering to help gave her a few days to make plans. She'd be safe enough while she was giving him what he wanted. When he didn't need her any longer, she'd become a liability. She hoped if she promised to keep silent, he'd let her go. But she knew better than to count on it. If she was going to get out of here, she'd have to escape.

Glancing around the room, she studied it for possible escape routes. Soft blue and red light streamed through the window, but the intricate leading of the stained glass prevented it from being a possible exit. Even if she broke the glass, the metal web-work holding it in place would be as effective as an iron grille over the window pane.

She turned her attention to the opposite direction. The door was locked by the card scanner, but Desmond had told her the scanners unlocked in case of fire. Maybe she could start a fire beneath a sensor, and trigger a fire alarm?

No. She'd never have a chance to get away with all those people trying to leave the buildings. Plus, Desmond would guess she'd set it, and be on the lookout for her. She needed a way to release only the three scanners between here and the exit.

She'd studied engineering before switching in her Junior year to journalism, and her rusty problem analysis skills slowly ground into gear. You couldn't count on an electric signal getting through to open the doors if the building was on fire, so that meant the doors received a constant electrical signal to stay locked. Any disruption to the scanners' power supply should open the doors.

Getting out was only part of the battle. With no car, she'd need to walk, and she hadn't paid much attention to the landscape on her way in. She stood up and tried to see out the window, hoping for at least a dim view of the surrounding area. Peering through the glass, she could

just make out the outline of the fluorescent bulb on the other side.
    It wasn't a real window. She was still underground.
    She breathed deeply, struggling to keep the terror at bay.
    She had to get out of here tonight.

Chapter 3

DESMOND STAGGERED into his office, shaken and disturbed by what had happened with Rebecca. Ignoring his secretary's outraged clucks, he jerked open the mini-fridge door and pulled out a black glass bottle containing eight ounces of his medicine.

He ripped off the safety top with practiced ease. Setting the bottle to his lips, he tilted back his head and drained the thick fluid in a series of thirsty swallows.

Fresh energy flowed through him. He imagined he could feel the fluid, a kind of super sports drink, being absorbed into his veins, and converted into fresh blood by his freakish body chemistry. He could certainly feel the change as healthy cells replaced the ones destroyed in his battle with Rebecca.

He stared at the empty bottle in his hand. The fluid had been developed by the Institute researchers as a treatment for accident victims, to prevent shock by providing all of the nutrients necessary to replenish the blood supply and nourish the body's cells in an easily absorbed formula. Science and technology. Those were the keys to overcoming his curse. That's what would save Gillian.

He dropped the bottle into the recyclable bin, pulled a carton of orange juice out of the fridge, and scooped a handful of Oreos from the tin. Munching on a cookie, he finally turned his attention to his hovering secretary.

"You skipped lunch again, didn't you?" she scolded.

"I was busy."

"That's no excuse. It was that pushy reporter, wasn't it?"

"It wasn't Rebecca's fault."

"It's Rebecca now, is it?" Bernice lifted a silvered eyebrow. "Is that why you're two hours late getting back from your tour?"

He leaned conspiratorially closer. "She's the one. I know it. Dr. Chen found Gillian's antigen in her blood sample."

"That's wonderful! I take back everything I ever said about that woman. Did you convince her to come back for more tests?"

Desmond looked away. "She's in the visiting doctor's suite. She's staying with us until the full course of tests are run."

Bernice didn't say anything for a long moment, then handed him a stack of paper. "Kim dropped these off for your approval."

He didn't touch the reports. "Aren't you going to ask how I convinced her to stay?"

"I'm old enough to know you don't ask questions if you don't want to hear the answers. Evan's scheduled a ten-thirty with you tomorrow morning to go over changes to the Institute's security systems, and Philippe's asked for a half hour after that. You're free at two o'clock, but I thought you might want the time to review the reports from Kim, so I haven't scheduled him yet."

Desmond took the sheaf of paper from Bernice without looking, and stepped away from her desk. "She's a willing guest," he muttered.

"Yes, Mr. Lacroix."

He stalked into his inner office. Only the papers under his arm and food in his hands kept him from slamming the door. Bernice had no right to make him feel guilty. He hadn't coerced Rebecca. He'd only broken through her irrational fears and distrust so that she'd see the situation as it really was. The decision to help or not had always been hers to make.

His fist clenched, pulverizing the remaining Oreo into chocolate powder. Sweet cream filling squirted between his fingers. He'd never had to work so much to influence someone's thoughts. In the end, had he pushed too hard?

Sure, he'd been attracted to the determined little fighter with the gamine looks. Holding her close on the couch, he couldn't help thinking of a different kind of embrace, imagining a different kind of sharing. Her thoughts had run along the same track, starting from their mutual appraisals when they met. He remembered her husky voice whispering, "I want you," and the brief second when her soft lips had closed over his own.

He opened the juice carton and gulped the cold, crisp liquid. Those had to have been her own feelings. Stripped of her fear and distrust, she'd been free to act on emotions that normally stayed hidden. He hadn't coerced her. He hadn't replaced her thoughts with his own.

Finally noticing the cookie smeared across his palm, he grabbed a tissue from the box on his desk and wiped away the goo. Too bad he couldn't wipe away his doubts so easily.

Hours later, he still hadn't been able to shake the suspicion that perhaps Rebecca's agreement was not as willing as he'd believed. Passing through the deserted outer office, he hesitated in the doorway.

Maybe he should talk to her again.

No. He'd already worked past the time he normally returned home. He couldn't keep Gillian waiting any longer. Besides, Rebecca wasn't going anywhere.

He hurried through the dim corridors, lit only by the muted glow of after-hours safety lights. Slashing his keycard through a scanner, he passed from the lab section of the complex into the residential area. The hallway transformed into a ten-foot wide boulevard paved in green and blue terrazzo. The sky-colored ceiling receded, adding to the sense of openness, and he paused just long enough to take a deep breath.

The day's frustrations dropped away. He was almost home. He brushed through the bank of ferns screening an intersecting passageway, and opened the access door at the end of the hallway.

He sped up the stairs, two flights made of terrazzo, then another flight of wood as he ascended through the old farmhouse. One last scanner waited, opposite the blacked-out window. He triggered the lock, and stepped inside.

Gillian sat on the hardwood floor of the living room, her Little Mermaid coloring book and chunky crayons spread around her. She dropped her blue crayon with a happy squeal and launched herself across the room with the wild abandon of any three year old.

"Daddy!"

Sweeping her up in his arms, he spun her around while she giggled happily. He pressed his cheek to her thick black hair, savoring the moment, and smelled only crayons and paint. No lingering scent of vaporizer or sick room clung to her soft curls. Dropping a kiss on her forehead, he smiled down on her.

With her ravaged immune system, the slightest cold became a crisis. Every day without symptoms was a minor victory against her illness. Winning battles, but losing the war. Unless Rebecca could help her.

He forced away the fear that Rebecca would prove no more successful than previous donors, and turned to his housekeeper. Mrs. Waters commanded the room from the center of the white sofa, a pile of knitting in her lap.

"She was a perfect angel today, Mr. Lacroix," Mrs. Waters reassured him, her steel knitting needles flashing in and out of the pink worsted wool. Another sweater for Gillian, no doubt. Mrs. Waters clung to the touching belief that if Gillian could just be kept warm enough, she wouldn't fall sick again.

"I'm sorry you had to stay late."

"Your secretary called to warn me. I took dinner out of the oven and put it in the fridge so it wouldn't spoil. I can warm it up now if you like."

"You go on home. Your husband must be missing you."

"Not my Robert. He'll still be at his microscope and his test tubes." But she gathered up her yarn, ruffling Gillian's hair before she left.

Desmond put his daughter down.

"Do you know what Mrs. Waters made for dinner?"

"Sanna!" She shouted her term for lasagna and raced to the kitchen. Judging by her enthusiasm, she'd helped prepare it. She was growing into such an accomplished little lady. He only hoped she'd be given the opportunity to continue to grow.

AFTER DINNER, they played blocks, Desmond stacking the colored cubes under his daughter's strict direction. Then it was time for her bedtime story, and he lost himself in her enjoyment of the nightly ritual. Gillian drifted off just as Winnie-the-Pooh was setting out on the trail of the mysterious Heffalump, and Desmond marked the page for tomorrow. He tucked her in, brushed a kiss across her forehead and turned out the light.

For a long while, he just stood in the doorway watching her sleep. She was so small, so helpless. It was only a matter of time, unless he found an answer to the curse. Or once again, he would watch helplessly as someone he loved died.

He tried to distract himself with a book, but found himself staring at the page while letters chased each other in nonsensical patterns. The Jules Verne classic was one of his favorites, but *Vingt Mille Lieues Sous Les Mers* held no interest for him tonight.

A tap on the front door roused him from his bleak reverie. He hurried to answer, eager to put aside his depressing thoughts.

Philippe stood on the doorstep, his black leather jacket, black driving gloves, and mirrored sunglasses a stark contrast to the floral-patterned tapestry suitcase in his hand.

"Gillian's asleep," Desmond whispered. "We'll talk in my study."

He ushered his half-brother inside, taking a seat in the leather wing-back chair opposite him. Philippe tossed the suitcase onto the floor, the soft-sided luggage making only a muffled thump against the wood parquet.

"Evan reconnected the battery, and drove the reporter's car out into one of the canyons. No one can spot it from the air, but we'll be able to get it easily enough when it's time for her to leave." Philippe made a show of taking off his sunglasses, folding them and putting them away. He snuck a sidelong look at Desmond during the process. "Whenever that is."

Desmond looked away. Replacing the book he'd tried to read earlier, he studied his collection of Jules Verne first editions in the original French. Sometimes it seemed he and his half-brother spoke completely different languages, for all that they both used English now. How could he describe the dream that burned within him, when Philippe knew nothing of love? And if a spark of hope had ever shone in his heart, Philippe had doused it decades ago. He would never understand. Still, he deserved to be told something. Desmond turned back to him with a sigh.

"Dr. Chen says Rebecca might have the right blood chemistry to be a donor for Gillian. I'm keeping her here until he can determine that for sure."

"And then what? She's a threat. And every day she stays here, she's more of a danger. Get rid of her now, before it's too late."

"I didn't expect you to understand. But you can't ask me to give up without even trying."

"You have done nothing but try. And you are no closer to a cure than when she was born." Philippe spoke in a patient, reasonable voice that hovered dangerously close to condescending. "Enjoy the time you have left with her. Don't waste it on fruitless dreams."

"We'll find a cure!" Desmond got up and started pacing the room. They *were* closer to a cure. When Gillian had been born, no one even knew what was wrong with her. The hybrid disease, combining his cursed blood and her mother's hereditary leukemia, flew in the face of established medical knowledge. As an infant, her violent rejection of her first bone marrow transplant had nearly killed her. She'd stayed in the intensive care unit for over a month.

Dr. Chen linked her reaction to an unusual antigen in her blood, one shared by Desmond and Philippe. When she'd grown older, and stronger, Desmond had acted as the donor for her next transplant. She hadn't rejected his bone marrow. Instead, she'd transformed it into cancerous cells, accelerating her disease's hold. They hadn't dared to risk another operation.

But Rebecca shared the antigen. And she had a normal

metabolism. Desmond couldn't waste the opportunity.

"You risk everything for an impossibility," Philippe insisted.

"And I would risk more if I could! Gillian's life is at stake." Desmond narrowed his eyes, a horrible suspicion taking root. "Unless the risk is an excuse. You don't want her to live."

Philippe sucked in his breath. "Des—"

"I can't lose Gillian. I won't lose her."

Philippe unfolded his mirror shades and stood. Desmond made no move to stop him. The sooner Philippe was out of his home, the better. But Philippe wasn't done. "You know the terms of the curse. You love her. Therefore, she'll die."

"But she doesn't have to die now!"

"*Toujours le maudit enfant gâté!*" Philippe's eyes blazed dark fires. He clenched his fists, shattering the sunglasses. "Nothing ever changes. You want it all your way. But not this time."

Philippe threw the ruined lenses into the trash and stalked out.

Sinking into his chair, Desmond stared at the shattered plastic in the trash. He was *not* a spoiled child. Because of his curse, he would watch Gillian die. The alternative, that she would live a cursed life like his, was too horrible to contemplate. He didn't question the fact, just the timing. He wanted her to live before she died.

He ran his fingers through his hair and sighed. The stress was getting to him. Desmond was so afraid of losing his daughter, he was in danger of losing his only real friend.

It was his own fault. Philippe would never understand. How could he, when he'd been raised by a grandmother who regularly beat him for no reason, insisting, "Don't you love me, boy."

Still, Philippe did have a point. A small one. Desmond had to look past Dr. Chen's research and Gillian's potential cure. What would happen when Rebecca left? They couldn't afford for her to share the details of the work being done here. Someone might guess the truth.

His gaze crossed the suitcase, lying on its side by his desk. It was probably too late for him to talk to her tonight, but he should still deliver her suitcase. She'd want clean clothes in the morning. He'd just get someone to watch Gillian, and then he'd go over to Rebecca's suite. Maybe, if he was lucky, she'd be awake.

REBECCA'S WATCH alarm woke her from an uneasy sleep at one in the morning. She opened her eyes to the reassuring glow of the overhead light. Time to make her escape. Now, before she had a chance to think about where she was, or what she planned to do.

She crept out of bed and pulled on her clothes. After this adventure, she'd have to consign her suit to the rag bag. It hadn't been designed for middle-of-the-night escape attempts, but it would have to do, since she wasn't about to run around in a slip and bare feet.

In the darkened main room of her suite, red and blue light filtered through the room's stained glass window. Her heart beat faster. There was barely enough light to keep her from tripping over the wicker furniture as she tiptoed to the entry. Holding her breath, she pressed her ear against the door and listened. Nothing. The Institute slept.

She jammed a terry cloth towel into the crack beneath the door, so no one would see her lights on and come to investigate. Then she flipped the wall switch and bathed the room in heavenly brightness.

She paused to take a shaky breath, before she lifted the cover off of the VCR. Her makeshift tools were hidden inside: a simple screwdriver that was no more than a straight piece of metal, four thin scraps of metal wrapped with wire that could act as clamps, a long cable with bare wire showing at the ends, and a hunk of the VCR's motor to use as a hammer, doorstop or last-ditch weapon. She took out the screwdriver and wrapped the rest in a hand towel.

Now, time to open up the keycard scanner. She fitted her makeshift screwdriver into the notch on the first screw and twisted. Then listened. No alarms sounded, so she continued turning. One screw came free. The second screw came free. Wait, was that a sound?

She pressed her ear to the door, not daring to breathe. Nothing. Could she hear anything, even if there was something to hear? Dismissing the unproductive worry, she returned to work. The third and fourth screws gave easily, but the cover didn't move. Why hadn't it fallen off the wall? She had to get it off, or her plan wouldn't work.

Running her fingers around the edge of the cover plate, she squeezed the metal. A concealed latch popped free, and the plate hinged down. She twisted it and popped the other latch.

The cover was off. She set it on the floor and smiled. Step one accomplished.

She opened the towel and picked up the cable and one of the clamps. Twining the cable wire with the wire on the clamp, she secured them to each other. Then she wedged the clamp into the heart of the wires and computer chips behind the scanner. She secured another clamp to the other end of the cable. Now for the tricky part.

Holding the cable as close to the end as she could without actually touching the clamp, she stretched it toward the electrical outlet. If she was right, the plastic sheath covering the cable would protect her from shock.

The clamp connected with the electrical outlet and slid inside, then all hell broke loose. She dropped the cable and covered her head as electricity arced and crackled through the scanner, blue-green sparks leaping from contact point to contact point. A high-pitched whine filled her ears, only to be drowned out by a flurry of popping. With a final snap that spit hot shards of metal onto her arms, the cable fell free and writhed about the floor.

She grabbed it and yanked. The cable pulled from the socket and went limp in her hand. Shaking, she dropped it on the floor. That was close. Too close.

Wiping the sweat off of her forehead, she looked at the results of her efforts. The scanner had melted into slag, with bits of charred green plastic and tangled wires poking out at all angles. The stench reminded her of a car fire she'd once covered. But had her plan worked? Was the lock disabled? Only one way to find out. She twisted the doorknob and pulled.

The door swung open.

She gathered up her tools and hurried into the corridor. Recessed emergency lighting tinged the hallway yellow. There. To her left. The corridor turned, and then...yes! The door was just where she remembered it.

She hurried to the door and peered out at the main aisle through the webbed security glass. Empty. No one was running to investigate the noise or the power failure. As soon as she blew this scanner, she'd be home free. She pulled out her screwdriver and got to work. The four screws came free, and she snapped open both hidden latches. She picked up the cable and looked around for an outlet.

Nothing. No light switches, no electrical outlets, no heating grates. Just blank, smooth walls. Where was she supposed to get the electricity to short out the scanner?

She'd come too far to give up now. The scanner had wires. Some of those wires had live current running through them. If she found two that were live, and crossed them, that should short out the system. But she had no rubber gloves, no coated tools. She didn't even have that stupid plastic toothpick from her pocket knife. It was back in the rental car with anything else even remotely useful.

No point feeling sorry for herself. Thieves managed to hot-wire cars all the time without electrocuting themselves. She'd probably just get a little zap, like touching metal on a cold, dry day.

She studied the wires. They were color coded, but what did the different colors mean? She should have paid attention in her junior high shop class. Red usually meant danger. So that probably had current running through it. Green? Green meant something was safe, right? But what about white and yellow? She'd just have to pick one. Well, she'd never liked yellow.

She reached in and detached the red wire, careful to touch only the plastic coating. Now, touch the bare end to—

DESMOND SLID his keycard through the scanner, but it didn't register. He slid it through again. Still nothing. Frowning, he sliced the keycard through the scanner a third time. It didn't open, but it also didn't set off the alarm after three failures like it should. He tried the door. It wasn't locked.

He peered through the door glass into the shadowy corridor beyond. A body lay crumpled against the far wall, still and unmoving.

"No!"

Throwing down Rebecca's suitcase, he shoved open the door and charged into the hall. The smells of charged ozone and melted plastic filled the air. His heart kickstarted into a rapid beat. What had she done?

Rebecca sprawled against the wall like a carelessly discarded doll. He knelt by her side, fumbling for a pulse.

A heartbeat. And another one. Faint, but regular. She was alive.

Closing his eyes, he exhaled the breath he hadn't known he was holding. She was going to live. But was she injured? He couldn't tell. His knowledge was limited to battle field first aid and the skills needed to cope with Gillian's illness. But he didn't dare leave Rebecca's side to fetch someone who could make that diagnosis. He lifted her hand and held it, willing her to be well.

"Come on, Rebecca. You can make it. You're too damn stubborn to quit now."

Had she really been so desperate to get out that she was willing to risk her life? He remembered her reaction to being accidentally locked in the lab, but he'd thought the suite would be big enough not to trigger a claustrophobia attack. Too late, he realized her anger toward her car might have been covering her fear at being underground in the parking garage. He hadn't meant to torture her. He couldn't do anything right tonight.

He coughed, trying to clear the catch in his throat. Rebecca had to be okay. She still had to help Gillian.

He tried to brush her soft chestnut hair away from her face, but it wouldn't stay down. It clung to his hand as if it had a mind of its own. Or was full of static electricity. He glanced at the nonfunctioning keycard scanner. Dangling wires and homemade tools bore mute testament to what she had tried to do, and what had happened instead.

His grip tightened on her hand, and he bowed his head.

"Please be all right. Please don't die."

She moaned softly, and the pressure in his chest eased.

"Rebecca? Can you hear me?"

Grudging admiration for her ingenuity warred with guilt that he had driven her to such extremes. From now on, he would take better care of his reluctant guest.

Her eyelids fluttered and she moaned. She was coming around.

Rebecca blinked her eyes. She had a headache the size of the Grand Canyon, her thoughts echoing off the walls of her mind until they almost deafened her. And someone had wrapped the world in cotton gauze while she wasn't looking. Everything was blurry and out of focus.

"Rebecca?" A man's voice caressed her name, the sweet syllables melting in his mouth as if they'd been dipped in chocolate.

If she didn't already feel weak in the knees, that voice would do it to her. Actually, she felt weak everywhere. Was she sick? She didn't remember being sick. She remembered needing to do something important. What had it been?

"Rebecca, can you hear me?"

She turned her head, slowly, toward the voice. Wow! She blinked a few times, but the image before her didn't change. Dark green eyes, the color of pine needles, watched her with concern, beneath a crown of thick black hair that begged to have her fingers running through it.

And he held her hand. His touch radiated warmth, like an electric blanket on a winter morning. But why was he holding her hand? Did she know him? Were they friends? Lovers? She glanced at his hand. A wedding ring. She looked at her own hand. No. He was married, but not to her. What a shame.

"How are you feeling?" His green eyes shone intently in his pale face. She'd frightened him, and wished she knew why.

"I'm okay. What happened?"

He smiled, like the sun coming out on a cloudy day. Her stomach flip-flopped, as if the flock of butterflies inhabiting it had all suddenly stopped and changed direction. His smile hinted at wonders she desperately longed to know.

Maybe she was having an affair with him. Was she the sort of person who had affairs with married men?

She frowned. She knew what affairs were. Shouldn't she know if she was having one?

"You got a little bit of a shock," he told her, reaching out to tuck a strand of hair behind her ear. "You may be confused for a while. Can you stand up? Does anything feel broken or sprained?"

She struggled to her feet, then swayed as the world dipped and pitched around her. His arm wrapped around her, strong and secure. She leaned against him, absorbing his strength and warmth.

"Are you ready to move?" His breath stirred her hair. She felt his words reverberating in his chest, through their connection and into her very bones. They even seemed to echo inside her head.

"I don't ever want to move."

He chuckled, the deep sound reminding her of rich, dark chocolate. She wanted to turn around and press close against him, let his warmth drive into her and burn her uncertainties away. She couldn't feel this connected to someone unless they'd been intimately related in the past, could she? Oh, why didn't she know?

"We're going to be standing in the hall all night, then. I can't carry both you and your luggage."

The heavy fire door was crushing an ugly rose-tapestry suitcase against the door frame. She remembered buying the case for 60% off at a remainders sale, but not why it was here. "Are we in a hotel?"

But why were the lights such a dim yellow? Power failure? She shivered. Losing the lights would be disastrous, although she couldn't remember why.

"Shh. It's all right." The man's arm tightened around her shoulder, warming her, and he rubbed her upper arm in a reassuring caress. She tilted her head and smiled at him. He'd protect her. Whoever he was.

They started walking down the hall, one small step at a time. What was his name? She could feel it floating near the edge of her memory, but it skittered away whenever she reached for it. D-something. David? No. Derek? No. Devon? Close. Very close. It was...Desmond! His name was Desmond! Desmond Lacroix. He was the director of....

She stopped. He'd kidnapped her. How could she have forgotten? She'd been trying to escape, and must have short circuited herself instead of the scanner.

He halted beside her, concern darkening his features. Then his face became an emotionless mask and he lifted his arm from her shoulder. "Your memory's returned."

"Yes." She tried to put all of her hate and loathing in the word. It must have worked, because he took a step back.

"Rebecca, I'm sorry. But you said you were claustrophobic. That's why I gave you one of the biggest suites. I didn't realize you would get so upset merely at being underground."

Memories overwhelmed her. She was trapped underground, unable to escape. What happened to the light? She needed light.

She struggled to breathe. The liquid darkness swept over her, drowning her. She was going to die, alone in the dark. Far off in the distance, she heard a voice, but couldn't make out the words.

Warm hands framed her face, and she concentrated on them instead of the darkness. Strong fingers spread across her cheek bones. Firm palms cradled her chin.

"Rebecca. Listen to me. I'm taking you above ground."

Above ground. Outside. She took a deep breath. The darkness clouding her vision receded, and she focused on Desmond's handsome face inches away from her own.

"Where?" she croaked.

"There's an empty bedroom on the top floor of one of the buildings. It's a perfect solution."

A perfect solution, all right. She could climb down from a second story window, no problem. It was too good to be true.

"What's the catch?"

"The room belonged to my late wife. It's right next to mine."

Chapter 4

SILENTLY, DESMOND lifted Rebecca's suitcase and led her into the main hallway. He didn't have to giver her Olivia's room. There was a couch in the false office used for deliveries. He could make that into a bed for her, and ask Evan to stand guard to make sure she didn't try any unsupervised exploration.

But that wouldn't be fair. Not to Evan, and not to Rebecca. Desmond had put this fiasco in motion so it was up to him to clean up the rubble. And keep Rebecca from creating any more.

He stalked through the main corridor toward the first of the turns leading to the residential section. Her heels clattered on the floor behind him as she struggled to match his pace, and he slowed his steps until the rhythm of her walk steadied.

Leading the bizarre parade of two through the deserted hallways, he took a moment to reflect on his actions. He'd mishandled her, making things worse than they'd had to be. He should have explained Gillian's condition to Rebecca when Dr. Chen first hinted at a match, or as soon as the doctor returned with confirmation, not waited until Rebecca tried to leave. But he'd started hiding personal information about himself so long ago, the habit was deeply entrenched.

Perhaps he could have offered to make her a guest in his home originally, but he'd feared what she might learn. What she might still learn. Wrong decision or not, he'd committed himself to this line of action. He had to see it through.

He realized the clatter of her footsteps had stopped, and turned to see what was wrong. Rebecca stood in the center of the wide blue hallway, her lungs filling with deep, slow breaths. A beatific smile lit her features, and she practically glowed with a contentment that radiated from her in waves. A rush of desire slammed into him with such force, he took a step back.

Her relaxed, almost somnolent expression, following her tightly-wound tension of the last few minutes, reminded him of the release of making love. He felt a sudden longing to be responsible for her glazed, happy look.

"We're almost there."

Abruptly, her eyes turned cold. Tightening her lips, she swept her gaze across him as though he didn't exist. Then she marched past with her chin in the air.

Her rejection hit him like a slap on the face. He obviously hadn't learned his lesson from her earlier dismissal. At least this time she hadn't lashed out with hatred and revulsion. He stretched his pace to catch up to her. It would be a relief to put an end to this interminable day.

They entered the miniature park that marked the intersection of hallways, with its red tipped palms and bushy ferns surrounding an antique bench of wood slats and wrought iron. He reached out and touched her arm.

"Turn here."

She hesitated only a moment before spotting the path between the ferns. Her steps sped up as she spied the red emergency escape door at the end of the corridor, and Desmond had to hurry to block her hand from the push-bar.

"You'll have sirens going off all over."

She lowered her hand, but as soon as he tripped the lock with his keycard, she pushed open the door, shoving past him into the stairwell and sprinting up the stairs. He didn't want to frighten her, but he couldn't let her get away. Burdened by her suitcase, he ran up the stairs after her.

They pounded up the two flights of terrazzo stairs. By the time they emerged into the narrow hallway of the farmhouse, he was just behind her. She ran down the hall to the left, ignoring the wooden staircase continuing up on her right. The spill of moonlight through the plate glass windows sprinkled her with silver sparks, but he could not slow to appreciate the sight. The red metal door at the end of the hall gave directly onto the desert. He could only hope that the orange plastic safety strip, designed to snap under continuous pressure, would delay her the tenth of a second he needed to catch up. Chasing her around the Institute was bad enough. He didn't want to be running all over the desert after her.

She slammed into the push-bar. The safety strip stretched then popped open, but the door did not. Lunging past her, he grabbed the bar and held the door shut.

"No!"

She pounded her fists against the unyielding door, sending aftershocks rippling up his arm to echo her frustrations beating against his mind. Then she pressed her forehead against the door and took a long, shuddering breath. He thought he heard her sniff.

"Rebecca?" he asked gently. When she didn't respond, he wrapped his hand around her left fist and pulled it away from the door.

She spun around and punched his jaw. The sudden explosion of anger drove him back a step, but he tightened his hold on her other hand.

He dropped the suitcase, leaving one hand free to block whatever she might try next. They stared at each other in taut silence.

"Let me go, damn you." Rebecca whispered.

He shook his head. "Not until the tests are done."

Bernice's doubt haunted him again. He hadn't forced Rebecca to help, hadn't forced her to give her blood or her bone marrow for Gillian's cure. No. He hadn't broken his vow, because she had agreed willingly.

He straightened his shoulders and fixed her with a cold stare. "You gave your word."

She studied the floor at his feet, idly shaking out the hand she'd hit him with. When she looked up, her eyes and voice were soft and uncertain.

"I promised to help your daughter," she whispered. "But you were using some kind of influence over me when I did."

He breathed deeply, struggling to control the images assailing him. A dark-haired, pinched looking woman. A black marble wall filled with neatly lettered names. The emotional importance of Rebecca's scattered surface thoughts punched through his light shielding.

Before he could strengthen his guard, stroboscopic memories of their argument in the guest suite spun past him. In her memory, Desmond was larger, darker, and more ominously looming than in reality. Even before she'd realized she was underground, he'd terrified the poor woman. An image of a dark cave, familiar from her earlier panic attacks, engulfed her other thoughts.

Desmond snapped up his shields, breaking their contact. Then, hoping he appeared friendly and non-threatening, he said gently, "Dr. Chen will only need your help for three days. After that, you'll be free to go, with my thanks."

She tilted her head and studied him. "Three days? That's what I agreed to?"

"Yes."

"But I've already been here for one. So I'll only be here for two more days." Her bold gray gaze challenged him to deny her, to admit he was lying or changing the rules.

He waited until she looked him square in the eyes, then pronounced each word with crystal clear precision. "Three days of helping Dr. Chen. You haven't begun to help him yet."

"Why does he even need my help? Can't I just donate enough blood for him to do the tests?"

"You already promised you would help him."

Either his expression or his tone convinced her not to argue any further. Instead, she leaned down and picked up the suitcase.

"Three days," she agreed. "Then I'm out of here."

Desmond turned, leading the way back down the hall, past a door she'd overlooked in her rush for freedom. If she ran now, she'd be out the door before he could catch her.

Shaking her head, she trudged after him. She'd be running across the desert in dress pumps, carrying a suitcase. How long would it take for him to catch her? No, let him think she'd resigned herself to being his "guest." If he was telling the truth, she'd be leaving in three days. And if he wasn't, he wouldn't be expecting her to try to escape again.

They climbed a wooden staircase at the end of the hall. The second floor hallway echoed the first floor, even to the placement of a keycard-locked door opposite plate glass windows. Rebecca glanced out at the black desert and scattering of stars in the sky. She couldn't even see the road. She'd made the right decision, not to run.

Desmond touched her arm, pulling her attention from the view. "My daughter is asleep. Please be quiet."

"You mean no one is watching her? You left her alone?"

He shrugged. "I didn't expect to be gone for an hour. And she's not unattended. My housekeeper is with her."

"I'll be quiet." Just because she was angry at Desmond, that was no reason to take it out on his daughter, especially if the girl was as sick as he claimed.

He unlocked the door with his keycard and guided Rebecca into a large living room, dimly visible by the moonlight streaming through the doorway. He touched a dimmer switch beside the door, bringing up the track lighting that encircled the room. Light reflected off the bright white ceiling to bathe the room in a soft glow, drawing her attention to the supple white leather couch reigning over the gleaming wooden floor, and the middle-aged woman dozing on it.

The woman snapped awake as the light struck her face.

"Mr. Lacroix, you were gone so long—" She spotted Rebecca, and her expression turned icy. "Who's this?"

"Rebecca, this is Mrs. Waters. Mrs. Waters, meet Rebecca Morgan." Desmond whispered. "More thorough introductions can wait until the morning."

"Of course," Mrs. Waters answered, gathering her things. "We don't want to disturb Gillian."

While the two of them talked, Rebecca studied the room. A smaller love seat and glass topped coffee table completed the minimal furnishings. Three doors, normal doors without those stupid keycard scanners, lined each of the walls on her left and right. Another door in the far wall mirrored the position of the front door. Every detail precise, coordinated and controlled, typical of the man beside her.

After Mrs. Waters left, he led Rebecca across the living room and through the far left-hand door into a bedroom. The simple Shaker-style furniture in an apple-green finish seemed strangely innocuous. She'd expected the bedroom of a dead woman to be furnished in heavy, dark wood, like the setting of a gothic thriller. This reminder of normalcy heartened her.

She tossed the suitcase onto the bed, where it settled into the thick, ivy-patterned comforter with a soft thwump.

"The bathroom's there." He pointed to the door she'd thought was a closet. "The front door's alarmed, so don't try sneaking out. I don't want you disturbing my daughter."

He started to leave, then turned back. "Oh, and I suggest you leave the light on. The windows are electronically polarized, and activated by external light. When you wake up, they'll be completely black."

He closed the door before she could ask him why. Conditioned by recent events, she immediately ran over and made sure she could open the door. She opened and closed it three times before she trusted it to stay unlocked.

She set the suitcase on top of the dresser, unzipped it, and dug through her clothes until she found her cosmetic case. Her camera was still inside. He hadn't searched the contents of her luggage at all. Rebecca let out a deep breath.

Three days. She didn't like it. She'd still rather leave right away. But now that she was above ground and the end was in sight, she'd be able to survive. She had three days to find out exactly what was going on around here. The Institute conducted real research. Desmond had convinced her of that. But his methods and his motives remained obscure. And suspect.

Desmond's effect on her went beyond the normal reaction to a heart-stoppingly handsome man. There was something darker, more sinister. How had he manipulated her original agreement? She'd uncover his secret. Even if she never used the information, she had to know. For her own safety.

She picked up her night shirt and walked into the green-tiled bathroom, careful to find the light switch before closing the door. She intended to search everywhere for clues.

A second door opposite the one she'd just come through called for immediate attention. If the room beyond was unoccupied, she could examine it now. She pressed her ear to the wooden door. No sounds reverberated from the other side.

Ignoring the bathroom for the moment, she eased open the door. Another bedroom. This one done in black and dark green Art Deco style furniture. A shiver rolled down her spine.

Desmond's room, the one he'd said was next to the room she'd be staying in. She pictured him in that big bed, covered only by the satin comforter the same glossy black as his hair and cushioned by a pillow the same brilliant green as his eyes. Maybe she should have run after all.

Rebecca retreated back into the bathroom and closed the door. His bedroom would be the best source of clues about Desmond, but she didn't want to risk being discovered while she searched. Especially not at night. Bedrooms became more than just another room at night, with starlight glittering on the black satin. She remembered the feel of his arm around her when she'd woken from her shock. Warm. Possessive.

It must be the aftereffects of shock and the adrenaline of her escape wearing off that made her tremble.

She ran cold water into the sink and splashed her face until she felt normal. Then she examined the bathroom. It was fitted out with a pale green fiberglass shower/tub enclosure. The lower walls and floor were tiled in the same pale green, with a row of darker green tiles at waist height. The upper walls were a pattern of alternating dark and light tiles. Was green Desmond's favorite color? Or had it been his wife's?

A man's electric razor sat on the dark green vanity counter, along with a bottle of after-shave. She hesitated, her fingers on the cold glass of the medicine cabinet. If she could possibly learn anything, she had to look. She opened the medicine cabinet.

It was empty, except for a rose-patterned plastic cup upended on the bottom shelf. Obeying her instincts, she took it down, and a brown plastic prescription bottle fell out. She picked it up. The bottle was empty. Why would someone keep an empty medicine bottle?

The prescription was for Dr. Olivia Lacroix. Rebecca blinked. A doctor. Desmond had been married to a doctor. She read the rest of the prescription, making a mental note of the drug's name to look up later. Dated three years ago, the medicine could be taken up to eight times a day "as needed for pain." Eight times? She placed the bottle and cup back where she'd found them, and closed the cabinet.

In a daze, she changed into her night shirt and went back to her room. She tossed her ruined suit onto the simple wooden chair beside the window. No wonder Desmond was so determined not to see his daughter go through the same suffering. Was it the same sort of insidious disease that had taken Rebecca's father? She'd been told he lingered for months in the hospital, not dead but not truly alive. When the monitor finally flatlined, it had been a relief to all concerned. Except Rebecca. He hadn't lingered quite long enough for her to find him.

She forced her attention to the present, and searched her bedroom for clues. The dresser drawers and closet had been emptied. Even the night stand drawer was bare. She slid the drawer closed, and heard the faint crinkle of paper.

She pulled the drawer out, lifting it off its track, then reached inside the cabinet and felt around the dry wood. Her fingers brushed across a piece of paper crushed against the back, and she pried it loose. Smoothing the piece of flowered stationery against her leg, she noticed the many cross-outs and revisions. Olivia must have been drafting a letter, and had put it away in the night stand. She'd never gone back for it.

Feeling a bit like a voyeur, Rebecca read the text. Or tried to. Olivia wrote as incomprehensibly as most doctors.

My darling,

You probably think I'm a fool, blinded by love. At first I was. Not anymore. But how could I speak of what was kept silent for so long? Now that it's too late—

Olivia had scratched out four attempts to finish the sentence. Rebecca couldn't decipher any of them, and her tired mind spun fancies as romantic as the Victorian roses on Olivia's stationery. It sounded like an apology of some sort. But for what?

Rebecca sighed. Desmond no longer seemed quite so sinister. Only sad and rather tragic. She forced her sympathy aside. Things happened in everyone's lives. That didn't give them the right to interfere in other people's lives. Past injuries were no justification for present transgressions.

She looked out the plate glass window. It couldn't be opened. A false sash was glued to the outside, so it appeared to be a normal window. But the illusion failed on this side. The inch thick glass was already murky and difficult to see through. The sky was graying in the east, stars fading as dawn approached. The sun wouldn't rise for a few more hours, but the night was over.

She crawled under the crisp cotton sheets printed with sprigs of ivy. The pillows smelled of rain fresh fabric softener. It was a reassuringly normal smell, and she felt the tension draining out of her. But she left the light on.

REBECCA YAWNED and stretched. She'd been so tired, and Desmond had insisted on waking her every hour. He must have finally decided she didn't have a concussion and let her sleep.

She fumbled for her watch. Ten o'clock. She tossed off her covers and padded across to the window. The glass had turned completely opaque. Not the slightest glimmer of light leaked through. She didn't want to admit it, but she was glad Desmond had warned her.

She dressed and opened the bedroom door. A soft glow filtered off the bright white ceiling of the living room, and she realized the room had been designed without windows. The distinctive buzz-click of the keycard lock drew her attention to the front door. She hurried toward it.

"Des?" a man's voice called. A brown-haired man in a black leather jacket pushed open the door and stepped inside.

"Hello," she began. "I'm—"

"What are *you* doing here?" Eyes narrowed, he advanced on her. "Using your feminine charms to get what you want?"

He lunged forward with the speed of a striking snake, and grabbed a fist full of her shirt. The fabric tore, and two buttons bounced loudly on the hardwood floor. She jerked out of his grasp and backed away, keeping a careful watch on him. The man was crazed. She wasn't letting him close enough to touch her again, but she didn't want sudden movements to provoke him.

"Rebecca, Philippe, I see you've met." Desmond's voice came

from behind her, and she spun to face him, anticipating another attack. "I was about to go down and see you."

"I thought you'd have come to your senses by now," Philippe said. "Didn't you listen to anything I said?"

"Did you listen to me?"

"I heard you say you'd do anything. I didn't think you were that desperate."

Desmond glanced her way. His eyes narrowed as she gathered the fabric of her gaping shirt together. No other gesture or expression betrayed his feelings, but the emerald fury blazing in his eyes was so fierce, Rebecca took an instinctive step back.

He turned from her and locked his attention on Philippe, his voice soft with unspoken menace. "Is that your opinion of me? After all these years?"

"You were upset." Philippe spread his hands. His lips twitched in a nervous smile as he backed toward the door. Desmond glided forward, each precisely placed step moving him relentlessly closer to Philippe. The madman was backing away now, but if Desmond cornered him, he might put up a fight. She sensed that neither man would pull his punches, if they ever came to blows, and she didn't want to be an innocent bystander caught in their crossfire. For once, a sense of self preservation overrode her curiosity, and she started edging toward her room.

"Last night I was upset. But now?" Desmond's hand curled into a fist. "You thought I broke my vow."

"No. Of course not." Philippe's lips quivered, shaking his smile. "She's a reporter."

"And thus without morals or rights to be used as I see fit, without regard to her consent?"

Rebecca froze, chilled by Desmond's words. They were too close to her own fears for her to leave without hearing the rest of this argument.

"A woman's body is a useful tool, one she might be willing to use to learn your secrets." Philippe scowled at her, his gaze pure venom. She'd just made a very powerful enemy.

"You overstep your bounds, brother."

Brother! As the two men glared at each other, Rebecca tried to spot a familial resemblance between them. They were the same height and basic build, although Desmond's frame was solidly muscled, while Philippe was too thin. Instead of Desmond's striking combination of black hair and pale skin, Philippe's brown hair and darker skin made him appear muddy. But Philippe's brown eyes shone just as vividly as Desmond's green ones, and they both projected the same air of controlled force. In Philippe's case, however, the control had definitely slipped.

The tension between the two silent, staring men was so intense, Rebecca's stomach clenched in sympathetic anxiety. A child's cry broke the tableau.

"Daddy!"

Desmond jerked like a sleepwalker coming awake.

"Philippe, you're no longer welcome here. Get out."

"Daddy!"

Desmond hurried to his daughter, leaving Rebecca alone with Philippe. She edged toward the nominal safety of her room. Philippe glared at her, his lips curling back in a snarl.

"This is all your fault."

"What? I'm not—" Wait. Weren't you supposed to agree with crazy people? It might at least keep him quiet until she reached her room. "Yes. It's entirely my fault. I'm sorry."

"Sorry? No, you're not. Not yet. But you will be," he threatened. Black hatred coiled in the depths of his eyes, trying to draw her into his madness.

She turned and ran the last few feet to her room. Once inside, she slammed the door shut, and shoved the chair under the door knob. Hunched in the far corner of the bed, she clutched a pillow to her chest and watched the door.

Oh, God, she wanted out of this nut house. Yesterday. She wouldn't say a word about any of it to anyone.

The front door slammed, and she slumped down. Then her muscles started to shake. First hypnotized. Then electrocuted. Now attacked by a madman. What next?

In the living room, Desmond soothed his daughter. Although Rebecca couldn't hear his words, the reassuring timbre of his voice carried clearly. She relaxed and let the calming tone carry away her fears, hungry for the same reassurance. He would protect her and keep her safe. No one would hurt her while he was here. She had nothing to fear.

She put on a new shirt, unblocked her door, and went out looking for answers.

Desmond sat on the couch, cradling his daughter on his lap. Her head rested on his shoulder, her midnight black curls mingling with his. The noise must have woken her from her nap, as she was dressed in a red and yellow play suit and bunny slippers. One small fist rubbed at her eyes, and she yawned and snuggled closer to her father. Her bunny-clad feet kicked at nothing, and she sighed back into sleep.

Rebecca studied the girl. Gillian. The reason she'd been imprisoned. Even the softness of sleep couldn't hide the faint blue shadowing under the child's eyes, or conceal the pinched look of her face. Rebecca didn't know much about children, but she knew they weren't supposed to fall asleep so easily in the middle of the morning.

Desmond looked up and met Rebecca's gaze. A wistful half-smile played upon his lips.

"She's already forgotten she was frightened." He stroked his daughter's hair, careful not to wake her. "Life's a lot easier to deal with when you're only three."

Rebecca didn't want to intrude on the private scene, but she had to know. "What's going on here?"

"I apologize. Philippe didn't expect to find you here, and jumped to the wrong conclusion."

"He thought you...and I...?" She looked away, feeling the heat flush her face. She'd pictured the same thing herself, last night, when Desmond's warm hands woke her from a sensual dream. But she'd dismissed the thought as the product of too little sleep and unusual circumstances.

She gathered her wits.

"That still doesn't explain why he tried to tear my shirt off. Or why he threatened me."

"He threatened you?" Desmond's emerald eyes riveted her gaze. She could lose herself in their depths.

"He blamed me. For what, I don't know, but I didn't want to provoke him, so I just agreed and said I was sorry. He said I wasn't sorry yet, but I would be." She frowned and shook her head, unable to express the scene still so vivid in her memory. "It wasn't his words, so much as his expression. He looked like he wanted to kill me."

"Don't worry. Philippe's harmless. He would never hurt you. He just needs some time to cool off."

"Oh." Despite her doubts, Desmond's words reassured her. She smiled. He'd spoken in the same soft tone he'd used to comfort Gillian, and it obviously worked just as well on her. She wouldn't mind curling up against his other shoulder. Of the two brothers, Desmond was clearly the more dangerous. But not to her. Never to her.

"Dr. Chen is expecting you around noon. Would you like coffee or breakfast before you go?"

"I was hoping I could stay up here." How else would she get a chance to search Desmond's room? And she really didn't want to return to the lab. She tried to look pathetic and play on his sympathies. "I don't want to go back underground."

"You won't be alone. Either Evan or Dr. Chen will be keeping you company the whole time. And the labs are very well lit. Besides, the tests will be done much more quickly with your help."

The threat was subtle, but Philippe's actions had sensitized her. Desmond might not let her go if she didn't cooperate. She didn't have a choice.

"All right, I'll go. But I'd better have some coffee, first, or I'll be less than useless to him."

Desmond put Gillian back in bed, and fetched Rebecca an earthenware mug of coffee from the kitchen. It was black and barely warm, but she drank it greedily. She'd just finished when someone knocked on the front door.

Desmond unlocked the door, his keycard provoking a buzz-click from the scanner. She hated that noise. It grated on her nerves like the constant chiming of an elevator that stopped on every floor when she was riding all the way to the top, reminding her that other people walked freely in and out while she was trapped.

The shaggy-browed brute she suspected of tampering with her car stood outside.

"Evan, escort Ms. Morgan to Dr. Chen's lab. He's expecting her," Desmond said, his voice returning to the cold formality of last night. It was almost as if he didn't want the guard to know he'd been nice to her.

"Yes, sir."

Desmond prodded her out the door, leaving her stranded in the hall with Evan.

"Let's go," Evan said.

"Yeah. Sure." She glared back at the door. Every time she'd just about decided that Desmond might not be so bad after all, he started ordering her around. He could have asked politely. He didn't have to threaten her, then hurry to get rid of her before she changed her mind.

She didn't move fast enough for Evan. He grabbed her arm and pulled her after him.

"Hey, let go! I'm coming."

He looked at her, then dropped her arm.

"Come on, then."

He set off down the stairs and into the warren of corridors they'd traversed last night, leaving her to follow. If she didn't match his pace, he'd probably drag her.

Evan stopped before one of the featureless white doors.

"This is Dr. Chen's lab. I'll come back for you this evening." He slid his keycard through the scanner. The scanner buzzed and the door clicked open. She stepped into a different lab from the one she'd been in yesterday.

"You came! I was afraid you'd changed your mind." Dr. Chen rushed over to greet her, his voice raised over the constant hum of fans.

He was the first person in this madhouse who seemed happy to see her, and she warmed to him despite her resentment. It wasn't his fault his boss was an autocratic jerk.

"I'm here. But what can I do?"

"I need a lab assistant to do all the tests as fast as Mr. Lacroix wants them, but all the assistants are already assigned to projects. I could preempt one, but then I'd have to explain why my research was more important. In detail."

He shook his head, obviously distressed at the thought of disclosing enough information for other researchers to capitalize on his work. It made sense that he got along well with Desmond. They were both paranoid about secrecy.

Dr. Chen held out a package from a vending machine, interrupting her thoughts. "Twinkie?"

"Uh, no thanks." His trash basket overflowed with empty Twinkie wrappers that fluttered in the constant breeze of the fans. No wonder he was so jumpy. He must be on a perpetual sugar high.

"Take one. Keep your blood sugar up. You'll need the energy."

She sighed. "Can't you use the blood samples you took yesterday?"

"No, no. They're busy replicating, okay?" He gestured at rows of petri dishes sitting inside a Plexiglas box, filled with yellow goo that gleamed beneath a heat lamp. "It'll be another day before there's enough to test. No, I need your help here."

She looked at the Plexiglas enclosed desk top he pointed at. A series of test tubes, their insides coated with a clear substance, stood beside a brightly colored machine reminiscent of a carnival thrill ride.

"What goes in those?"

"I need another blood sample, okay? I have something else I need to test. As long as you're here." He pulled on a pair of surgical gloves.

"But I don't want to—"

"Just a little. You'll hardly feel it. Okay?"

He advanced on her with a needle.

She swallowed and nodded. Needles weren't so bad. And if she didn't do it, she wouldn't get out.

He sat her in a chair and drew a vial of blood from her arm. It stung a bit, but didn't hurt. She pressed the cotton pad he gave her to her arm, and watched with interest as he carried the vial to the sealed area, opened an access hatch, and popped the vial inside the sterile area.

Peeling off his gloves, he sat down. He pushed his hands through a pair of gloves attached to openings in the Plexiglas, and poured the contents of the vial into one of the pretreated test tubes. Rebecca stood up and came over, observing over his shoulder. The process intrigued her.

He added a clear liquid to the tube and capped it, then dropped it into the machine. He switched the machine on, and it twisted and whirled the hapless vial. Just looking at it spinning about made her queasy. Dr. Chen grinned.

"Okay! It's going good now!"

"What are you doing?"

"Breaking up the blood." He turned off the machine and peered at the vial, adjusted something and turned it on again. It spun faster. "I'm only interested in the white blood cells. The T-cells, leukocytes and neukocytes."

Rebecca watched Dr. Chen, glad of something to help her avoid looking at the whirling blood.

Keeping her gaze fixed on him, she said, "T-cells are part of the immune system. I remember that from a story I did on AIDS. And leukocytes are involved in Leukemia, although I forget if it's too many or not enough of them. But what are neukocytes?"

Dr. Chen stiffened, then turned away so that she couldn't see his face.

"If you're going to help me, you need to put on some gloves. There's extras in the top drawer."

Chapter 5

BY THE END of the afternoon, Rebecca had her story. Using a combination of fawning interest and indirect questioning, she'd weaseled a wealth of information out of the brilliant but naive Dr. Chen. She'd get an official confirmation, or official "no comment," before she submitted it, but she had all the facts she needed.

Chen and his colleagues had discovered a new kind of white blood cell that revolutionized the way the body's immune system worked. A better understanding of the mechanics of this cell might be the breakthrough needed in the fight against AIDS and previously incurable cancers.

This scoop would be her ticket to the big time. She couldn't wait to write it up.

Evan returned for Rebecca at six o'clock, and she rushed him out of the lab before Dr. Chen had a chance to let slip how much he'd told her. Fortunately, Evan was his usual brusque and untalkative self as he led her back to Desmond's apartment. She didn't want to be distracted before she could write everything down.

Evan knocked on Desmond's door, interrupting a medley of shouts and laughter inside. Desmond answered the door after a minute, his daughter giggling and kicking as he held her upside down in one arm.

Gillian wriggled loose, and he grabbed her before she could fall. She laughed as he set her down.

"Do it again, Daddy. Do it again."

"Not now, sweetheart. Play time is over. We've got company."

Gillian stopped fidgeting and peeked around her father's leg at them. Rebecca didn't know whether or not to be insulted when Gillian ignored her and Evan, and lifted her arms to Desmond.

"Up, Daddy. I want up."

He picked her up and tried to introduce her to Rebecca, but she was more interested in flipping his collar up and down.

"Gillian, this is...Gillian? Are you listening?...This is Rebecca. She'll be staying with us...Gillian? Oh, never mind." He turned to them and smiled. "Dinner will be ready in about fifteen minutes. Rebecca, why don't you wash up? And I'll see you the same time tomorrow, Evan."

Evan nodded and closed the door as Rebecca stepped inside.

"Dinner?" she asked. "You cook?"

"Hardly," he said with a laugh. She followed him into a kitchen decorated entirely in brick, natural oak and gleaming copper. The homey atmosphere coaxed a smile from her, until Desmond set Gillian on the counter in front of a blacked-out window. Then Rebecca recalled the lengths to which Desmond had already gone for his daughter's sake. He wanted her here because he thought she could save Gillian. He'd be furious if he found out Rebecca planned to expose their research.

His muttered, "Damn!" gave her a guilty start, as she thought for a moment she'd somehow given herself away. But his attention was focused on Gillian. Then he turned to Rebecca.

"I should have asked Evan to stay," he said, shaking his head. "I don't know what I was thinking of. Can you give me a hand? It's time for her shot."

Gillian started squirming and trying to get free. "No, Daddy! No shot! No!"

He let out his breath in an exasperated sigh. "Can you hold her?"

Not quite sure what else to do, Rebecca stepped up to the wriggling girl and placed her hands above Desmond's. The brief contact touched off a tingling charge up her arms, then she had to focus all of her attention on Gillian.

"No! No shot! I had Daddy medicine today! I don't need a shot! No-o-o!" Gillian flailed her heels and fists. When that didn't work, she tried to bite Rebecca.

"Gillian! No! Little girls *do not bite people*." Desmond grabbed his daughter and pulled her off the counter. Gripping her tightly, he turned to Rebecca. "I'd better hold her. Can you get the medicine from the refrigerator? It's in the cold cut drawer."

Trying to ignore Gillian's screaming, Rebecca opened the refrigerator. Tiny glass bottles filled two-thirds of the drawer, lined up in neat rows like little soldiers. She took out one of the little bottles. The glass chilled her fingers.

Suddenly her story became more than just a collection of facts. It was the story of one little girl's fight against a killer she couldn't hope to understand, a disease so new it didn't even have a name yet.

Shaken by the revelation, Rebecca turned back and placed the medicine on the counter. Desmond had somehow managed to get a needle ready while wrestling with his daughter. He nodded to Rebecca.

"Will you take her again?"

Rebecca grabbed hold of the squirming child, too numb to care about the kick to her thigh. Operating on sheer instinct, Rebecca managed to tuck all of Gillian's arms and legs close to her body and pin her there. Gillian wriggled, and screamed louder.

"No! I hate you! You want to hurt me! My Mommy would never hurt me! I want my Mommy!"

Desmond's hands were steady as he pierced the bottle's rubber seal and filled the needle with fluid. He cleared the air out of the needle, spurting drops of medicine across the counter, and turned back to Gillian. Feeling illogically guilty for Gillian's suffering herself, Rebecca was amazed that he could remain so impassive. And then she saw his eyes.

He'd heard every word his daughter said. Every accusation, every complaint. His face could have been carved from marble, it was so still, but his eyes shone brightly with unshed tears.

He took Gillian's arm and buried the tip of the needle in it. She shrieked, and started to cry. He held her arm steady, depressing the plunger with constant pressure. When the needle was empty, he pulled it free and tossed it into a red plastic canister on the counter, where it crunched against other needles.

Lifting his daughter from Rebecca's arms, he cuddled her close, crooning soft, soothing endearments into her hair while her sobbing subsided. She sniffed and hiccuped, then looked up at him, tears staining her face.

"*Hurt*, Daddy."

He closed his eyes and whispered, "I know. I know."

Not wanting to intrude on them any further, Rebecca tiptoed quietly out of the kitchen and back into the living room.

The big white couch looked inviting, and she sat down with a sigh. She hadn't expected that. Sure, Desmond had said Gillian was sick, but aside from being too thin, she looked like such a happy, healthy little kid. All that medicine. She must need shots once or twice a day, at least.

Then she remembered Gillian's mention of "Daddy medicine." Gillian must have inherited at least part of her condition from Desmond. Were some of those bottles for him? Was he so skillful at injecting medicine because he had to administer it to himself?

She hadn't realized the importance of Dr. Chen's words this afternoon, but their meaning was all too clear now. He'd only been working on his current project for three years—since Gillian was born. Before that, he'd been working on a similar, but different, project. Many of the other researchers had also switched focus at that time.

Desmond had taken them off finding solutions for his illness, and set them to solving his daughter's.

Rebecca stared at the wall. She'd spent her whole adult life believing that people always put themselves first. But Desmond was risking everything for his daughter.

Pain sliced through Rebecca's chest, and she struggled to breathe. Since she'd learned of her mother's betrayal, she hadn't trusted anyone. She hadn't believed she could. Now here was proof positive that Desmond Lacroix was a man who would put his own life on the line for someone he loved.

She hadn't realized how much she needed to believe people like that still existed. More importantly, she discovered that she wanted to *be* a person like that. She didn't want to be like her mother, destroying someone else's chance for happiness because of petty selfishness.

Desmond came out of the kitchen, his daughter asleep against his shoulder, and walked over to the couch.

"She cried herself to sleep," he said softly. "She doesn't have the stamina for a prolonged fight."

Rebecca looked into his eyes, waiting until he realized she had an important pronouncement to make.

"I'll help you. However long it takes."

It was the first time she'd ever seen a smile spread all the way to his eyes. "Thank you," he said, and put his free hand on her shoulder.

Golden warmth ran through her, spreading out in waves from his touch. She tilted her head to look at him. His eyes shone a deep green, warm and welcoming. Did he feel the sparks between them, too? If he wasn't holding his daughter, would he kiss her?

He opened his mouth to say something more, and the kitchen timer pinged. He smiled again, the wry smile more familiar to her.

"Dinner's ready."

She followed him back into the kitchen. No signs remained of the recent struggle. He woke Gillian up and strapped her into a booster seat, then pulled out a chair for Rebecca.

Gillian tugged lethargically at her napkin, pulling it out from under her rubberized silverware to cover her plate. Ignoring his daughter's silent protest, Desmond removed a casserole dish from the oven. He set it on the table and lifted the cover, releasing a cloud of steam that was fragrant with the scent of beef and onions. Rebecca's stomach growled.

"That smells terrific. I thought you said you didn't cook."

"I don't," he answered, dishing out servings for the two adults. "But Mrs. Waters is a wonderful cook."

Rebecca nodded, lifting a forkful of the ground beef, onion and rice mixture to her mouth. The meat was a little rarer than she liked, but still delicious.

Gillian watched them eat for a minute before sweeping her napkin off of her plate, and demanding to be served. Desmond put a small helping on her plate and she attacked it with her blunt-ended fork, using her left hand, the arm that hadn't gotten the shot.

What she lacked in skill, she made up for with enthusiasm. About half of her food ended up smeared on her face or clothing, with another quarter decorating the kitchen table. Very little food seemed to actually make it into her mouth. Even so, she was finished and playing with her silverware before either adult was done.

"She doesn't eat much, does she?" Rebecca said.

Desmond stiffened. "No. I don't think any child does, at that age."

She hadn't meant the comment as evidence of Gillian's illness, but that's obviously how he'd taken it. Trying to clarify what she'd meant would only sound awkward.

She couldn't help staring as he took a third helping for himself. Where did he put it? The turtlenecks and clinging silk shirts he favored would have ruthlessly exposed the least ounce of body fat, had he possessed any. Which he didn't.

"Something wrong?" he asked.

"No." She swallowed and studied the table, mortified to be caught staring. "I was just wondering how you stayed so thin."

"I have a very high metabolism."

"Oh." Should she say more? Or was that a part of his illness? He didn't seem to feel any need to elaborate. If she continued with this topic, she'd end up offending him. Normally, she wouldn't care what he thought of her, not if she could get information for her story. But her feelings of being connected to him, united in pursuit of a common goal, were too new and precious to risk trampling. Better just to drop it.

"Uh, you want any help with these dishes?"

"There's no need," he answered automatically, then reconsidered. "If you could rinse them and stack them in the sink, I can start cleaning up Gillian."

"I'm not dirty, Daddy," Gillian protested, showing him the hand she'd managed to keep clean. "See?"

Rebecca had to hide her smile behind her napkin.

"You did a wonderful job of staying clean, sweeting," he told Gillian, with a perfectly straight face. "But I think you should have a bath anyway."

"I don't want a bath. I don't need one, Daddy, 'cause—"

"Bathtime Pooh will be very lonely without you."

Gillian considered this new information, her little face screwed up in concentration. Then her eyes lit up. "I'll give Pooh a bath. I don't need one."

Desmond coughed, not looking at Rebecca. Gillian just grinned, confident that her solution made perfect sense.

"All right," he agreed. "You can give Pooh his bath. But I think it would work best if you were in the tub with him."

"Okay, Daddy."

He pulled her out of her booster seat, careful of the food smeared across her shirt, and carried her out of the kitchen. Their departure left Rebecca strangely sad, and she sighed as she started gathering up the dishes.

She'd devoted all her time and energy to her career, first putting herself through school, then working two jobs while she established a reputation as a dependable freelance journalist. Every liar, cheat and crook she'd exposed along the way had strengthened her conviction that people couldn't be trusted. Now she realized she may have made a mistake by focusing on the seamier aspects of society. What else might she have been wrong about?

Her few relationships with men had been brief, fed from the scant time and energy left over from her work. Assuming that any relationship was bound to fail, she'd ended them before she could be betrayed. How different might her life have been if she'd trusted one of those men enough to stay with him? Might she be married by now, with her own little girl?

She rinsed the last dish and stacked it on top of the others, pleased that her hand didn't shake. She didn't have time for a husband, much less for a child. No point regretting her decisions now.

She looked back at the table. The dishes were taken care of. What about the leftovers? Should she leave them out? No. They might spoil. She'd cover them back up and put the casserole dish in the refrigerator.

Moving a carton of milk aside to make room, she discovered a collection of black glass bottles. Their arrangement echoed the precise rows of Gillian's medicine bottles, and she turned one to read its label. These belonged to Desmond.

She stuffed the casserole dish onto the shelf and wandered into the living room. How sick was he? He looked healthy enough, except for being so pale. But then, except for being so thin, so did Gillian.

Laughter and splashing sounded from across the living room. Rebecca turned away. Now was the perfect time to sit down and write up her story. Yet she couldn't bring herself to do it. Instead, she sat down on the couch and leafed through a discarded coloring book, in a vain effort to distract herself.

The pages depicted classic fairy tales, with smiling princesses standing before beautiful castles. The sting of imminent tears pricked her eyes, and Rebecca set the book aside with a sigh. When she was a child, she'd dreamed of finding her Prince Charming. The image of her prince changed with her moods, but when he rode up to greet her, dressed in his royal finery, he invariably resembled the photographs of her father in his uniform. Her mother's stories had filled Rebecca's head with visions of her father as a proud, brave hero, who had given his life for the country he believed in. But that man had been as much an illusion as her daydream prince.

The gurgle of the tub brought her back to the present. When it stopped, she could hear Desmond's voice rising and falling in smooth, melodic phrases. She couldn't catch the words, but knew from the tone that he had to be reading Gillian a bedtime story. The ebb and flow of sound soothed Rebecca as well, lulling her into a drowsy stupor.

She jumped when Desmond dropped next to her on the couch in a sprawl, his arms outstretched across its back. She hadn't seen him come in.

Moving to the side, she instinctively put space between them. Then, realizing what a foolish picture she must make hunched over the arm of the couch, she leaned back, trying to act casual. As if she couldn't feel the heat of his arm behind her shoulders. As if the hairs on the back of her neck weren't standing on end, drawn to him like iron filings to a magnet. Yes, that was a good analogy. He radiated invisible lines of force, too. And she felt herself aligning with them, as if she had no control over herself.

She needed to distract him, distract herself. Her fingers brushed across the discarded coloring book, and she held it out to Desmond.

"I was admiring your daughter's work." She forced a lighthearted smile. "Although I didn't realize princesses had green faces."

"I'm happy she finally mastered staying on the paper. Realistic colors come later, when she's older. Don't you remember that from your own youth? Or were you the youngest?"

"I was an only child." She turned aside, discouraging any comments.

Her mother had denied her the chance to have siblings. True, she had half-brothers and -sisters. But they didn't count. She'd never known about them while she was growing up.

They'd grown up with the father she'd thought was dead. She clenched her jaw, fighting against the bitter anger she still felt toward her mother.

He brushed his fingertips across her shoulder. "I didn't mean to offend you."

He must think she was angry at him. She forced her rigid muscles to relax, and leaned her head back against his arm. She closed her eyes and took a deep breath, then counted to ten and let it out.

"You didn't. You just reminded me of something."

He curled his arm around her shoulders, offering silent sympathy. She soaked up his warmth and vibrancy, feeling the life beginning to flow back into her.

"You're doing so much for me, and for Gillian." He hesitated, his uncertainty only making him more appealing.

"You seem so sad," he continued. "Is there anything I can do to help?"

"No." She shook her head and looked away. Her eyes felt funny again, and she didn't want him to think she was crying. "It's nothing. Old news, over a long time ago."

He reached out, cupping her chin in his hand, and turned her to face him. She still refused to look at him. He held her jaw until she met his gaze.

"It may be over, but you're not over it. Perhaps talking about it will help."

She'd never told the whole story to anyone before. Why would she, when they'd only use it against her? But Desmond was different. She felt that she could confide in him. The unfamiliar trust surprised her.

"I never knew my father," she began. "When I was a little girl, I'd spend hours in front of his picture. I made my mother tell me the stories about him over and over again, until I thought I knew every minute of their two years together."

He placed his hand over her chilled fingers, fisted in her lap, and gave them a reassuring squeeze. She searched his eyes, but saw no hint of censure, only encouragement.

"Everything would have been fine if it hadn't been for the Vietnam War Memorial," she continued. "When I told my mother we should go see it, she became distraught. She forbade me to go anywhere near it."

"But you went?"

"I went." Rebecca smiled wryly, "I always was very determined."

"I'd noticed." He returned her smile, but also tightened his grip on her hand.

"I emptied out my savings account and bought a bus ticket from upstate New York all the way to Washington. The line for the memorial was very long, full of people bringing gifts and mementos for the loved ones they'd never had a chance to say good-bye to. Somehow, I felt connected to all of them, bound by a common purpose. We all wanted to see the wall and touch the one special name chiseled into the stone, as if that could make the deaths real. As if that could bring them home."

She bit her lip, determined not to cry. The day was engraved upon her memory, as if it had been only yesterday. The elderly man in front of her, leaning on a cane and smelling of camphor, who clutched a pair of shoes to his chest. The weeping woman behind her, who held a bouquet of carnations and babbled on about how they were her son's favorite flower. And between them, the girl whose innocent love was about to be destroyed by the cold, hard truth.

Desmond pulled her close, cradling her in the warmth of his embrace. His arms held her safe, protecting her from her memories, until she could continue her story. She listened to the steady thud of his heart beneath her head, felt the rise and fall of his chest with each slow inhale and exhale of breath. Gradually her pulse slowed to match his, and her breathing steadied. But she didn't move, unwilling to look at his face as she finished her tale.

"When my turn came, I stepped up to the directory of names, my heart pounding and my mouth dry. I knew the date I wanted, and ran my finger down the list, looking for Private Charles Morgan. He wasn't listed."

"Not listed?"

"No. I flipped backward and forward in the book, thinking that maybe my mother had gotten the date wrong. He wasn't listed anywhere. He wasn't listed, because he hadn't died." She took a deep breath, and finished her explanation in a rush of words. "That's why my mother hadn't wanted me to see the wall. Because I'd find out how the story really went. Charles Morgan hadn't been a young hero, killed before he could return to his young wife and infant daughter. He'd been a frightened teenager, who'd returned from the most harrowing experience of his life only to be confronted by his girlfriend and a baby she insisted was his. He couldn't deal with either one."

Desmond's arms tightened around her, and he rocked her gently, murmuring soothing words into her hair. He stroked his hands down her back with slow, rhythmic warmth.

She sniffed. "I promised myself I wasn't going to cry."

"Go ahead and cry. For your father, and for you."

She looked up, surprised at the husky note in his voice. His eyes seemed unusually bright, as well, so she blinked to clear her tear-smudged vision. His gaze met hers, and she forgot to breathe.

His eyes gleamed with the brilliant green of sun-dappled leaves, as he lowered his gaze to her mouth. She knew he was about to kiss her, and that she could stop him with a word. But she didn't want to. She'd never felt so close to another human being, and couldn't bear the thought of pushing him away. It would be like pushing away her own heart.

He bent closer and touched his lips to hers. As if he'd closed a circuit, an electric thrill coursed through her at the contact. Her eyelids fluttered closed, and she gave herself up to the sensation. He slid his kiss to the corner of her mouth, then whispered against her lips.

"Did you ever see him?"

She wanted to stay floating in the soft fog Desmond's kiss inspired, insulated from her past. But his words called her back. The story seemed somehow distant, though, as if she was listening to herself tell it, rather than telling it herself. That made it easier.

"No. I spent years trying to find him, and eventually tracked him down. He'd gotten married, and had three sons and two daughters. I met his wife when I went to see him, determined to find out why he'd abandoned me. She's the one who told me he was dead. For real, this time. A victim of Agent Orange, a few months before I got there."

"After all those years, to miss him by a few months must have been terrible."

"Not as terrible as what she said next. You see, she knew who I was. My father had told her about me." Rebecca shivered, seeing again the pity in the woman's eyes. And the fear when she glanced toward the yard where her own children played.

Again, Desmond's touch drew Rebecca back to the present. She turned to him, blindly seeking comfort to ease the freshly opened wound. "After he'd recovered from his experiences in the war, my father came back and tried to patch things up with my mother. She turned him away. My father wanted me, and she told me he was dead!"

Rebecca hid her face in Desmond's shoulder, shaking as the long-denied emotions rocked through her. Desmond stroked her back, her shoulders, her hair, soothing her pain until he made her shiver with a different kind of need. Turning her face, she captured his lips in a kiss.

She didn't need him to distract her anymore. She'd faced her memories. But she wanted a new memory, a better memory, of love and caring, to replace the old memory of betrayal and neglect. And Desmond cared more than anyone else ever had.

He stilled, as if sensing the change in her, then wound one hand in her hair and pressed her even closer. She opened her lips beneath a fiery onslaught that seemed to draw the very air out of her lungs. She couldn't breathe. She couldn't think. She could only feel.

Feel, as his tongue traced the edge of her lips. Feel, as his mouth slid across her jaw, and down the sensitive column of her neck. She twisted her head to the side, encouraging his exploration. His tongue rasped across her tender skin, and he pressed a kiss to the sensitive pulse point.

His hand in her hair tightened, pulling her head back and lifting her throat to his kiss. Her breathing quickened, rapid butterfly breaths. She wanted this. She wanted him. Here. On the couch. On the floor. Anywhere. As long as it was now.

Desmond tore himself away from her and Rebecca moaned, low in her throat. He struggled to control his breathing, waging a harder battle to control his hunger. He'd only meant to comfort her, not to become carried away like this.

As soon as her first powerful memories had struck him, he'd raised his mental shields. Strong thoughts carried clearly, even if the other person wasn't telepathic, and he had no wish to pry. But such strong shielding took a lot of energy to maintain, and he'd lowered the shields at the end of their conversation, wrongly assuming that her calm appearance indicated a calm mind. Rebecca's last thoughts had been vividly erotic.

She reached for him now, eyes closed, tuned in to her own world.

He caught her hand and guided it away from him, back to her. Not that he didn't want to make love to her. He ached with wanting her. But not now. Not like this, in blind response to the emotions called up by her memories.

When they made love, it would be because they'd chosen to. Because they were ready. That day would come. He was sure of it. And when it did, they'd not only share the pleasures of their bodies. They'd share the passion of their blood.

The drink his researchers had invented freed him from ghoulishly haunting hospitals and other sites of death, as he'd once done to satisfy the needs his curse created. Yet there had been times when living bodies had sustained him, had offered more than mere sustenance.

His gaze dropped to Rebecca's arched throat, slick with a layer of sweat. He imagined her beneath him, her pulse racing, the thick, sweet taste of her blood mingling with the salty taste of her sweat. He swallowed, eyes closed, picturing the ecstasy of their joining.

She whimpered softly and he opened his eyes to look at her. She leaned back into the couch, her neck stretched provocatively. Her pulse hammered faster than before, her shallow breath coming in quick pants. He'd caught her up in his fantasy somehow. Maybe not the details, but the general slant of his thoughts certainly seemed to have gotten through. But how? He'd been guarding his thoughts from transmission.

The explanation struck him with the force of a lightning bolt. She'd picked up on his thoughts the same way she'd countered his earlier attempts to mentally control her. By using her own mental powers. She shared more than just a blood type with Gillian. She shared the telepathic gift as well.

Obviously, she didn't know how to use it. She probably didn't even recognize the ability. To most people, she'd just seem to be remarkably intuitive and unusually persuasive.

Look what she'd done with only her raw telepathic ability. With training, she might have skills equal to his. He'd need to find out just how strong she really was, but he already knew the most important thing.

This changed everything.

Chapter 6

DESMOND PREFERRED to spend his mornings with Gillian, whenever possible. But today he needed to see Philippe. Their disagreement had lasted long enough. After 150 years, a few ill-chosen words spoken in the heat of anger shouldn't drive them apart.

He'd already dressed and fed his daughter, and put her to bed for her morning nap. She wouldn't miss him if he left while she slept. At least, that had been his reasoning when he called Mrs. Waters and asked her to come over early. She arrived just after Gillian drifted to sleep.

"Thank you, Mrs. Waters. She should sleep for another hour or so."

"I'll be quiet."

"Oh, and my guest will be staying in all day. She's still in bed, since she didn't sleep well." Rebecca had suffered a string of nightmares. The first time, her frightened telepathic cries had woken Gillian. After that, he'd kept a light connection to Rebecca's mental state. Not a deep enough connection to eavesdrop on her actual thoughts, it sufficed to let him sense her rising panic as she slipped into a nightmare. Each time, he sent a quick burst of mental energy back along the pathway and woke her up.

Neither of them had gotten much sleep. He didn't need much, but she'd been exhausted. Just as the rising sun put an end to the night, she'd slipped into a deep, dreamless sleep from which she had yet to awake.

Mrs. Waters glanced at Olivia's old room, then slid her gaze across to Desmond's door.

"Will she be wanting a breakfast?"

"She only had coffee, yesterday. I imagine that's all she'll want today." He glanced at his watch. Philippe would be leaving for his office soon. "I hope having her here doesn't inconvenience you."

"Not a bit. After all, she's your guest."

"She is." He caught the emphasis Mrs. Waters gave the word *guest*, but didn't have time to waste arguing over Rebecca's exact status. "If she's bored, she might like to read one of the books in my study."

"I'll tell her, Mr. Lacroix."

Leaving the household in the capable hands of Mrs. Waters, he went downstairs and knocked on Philippe's door. No answer. He'd missed him. He'd planned to meet privately, but now he'd have to catch Philippe at his office and hope no one else was around.

Since time wasn't an issue any more, he could check on Dr. Chen's progress first. Chen's lab was between here and Philippe's office in the administration building, and the brief detour would give Desmond the additional ammunition he needed in his battle with Philippe. He headed toward the main area of the complex.

Reaching Dr. Chen's lab, he triggered the scanner with his keycard. The scientist looked up as he entered.

"Mr. Lacroix. I didn't expect you so early."

"How are the tests coming?"

"Well, most of them are finished. We can discuss the results now if you want."

"That would be fine." Desmond pulled over a chair and sat down. He shouldn't anticipate Dr. Chen's response, but after discovering Rebecca's mental powers last night, he knew the results had to be positive.

"Okay. You know all about what sort of transplant your daughter needs?"

"Yes." She needed a bone marrow transplant, and bone marrow donors were rarely found outside of the immediate family. He'd been prepared for disappointment. Until last night.

"I checked the compatibility of Ms. Morgan for a potential donor. Gillian's system would not reject a transplant from her."

"Excellent!" He'd been right about Rebecca. Once Gillian's body absorbed the functioning cells, her immune system would revert to a healthy state. His little girl would live. "When can we start?"

"It's not that simple."

"Nothing ever is with you scientists. Now what?" He didn't want to hear any of the laborious details Dr. Chen would use to try and impress him. He wanted to run home and tell Gillian they'd found her cure. She wouldn't have to suffer through any more shots. She'd have the strength to run and play like other children.

"Accepting the donor's blood marrow is not enough. She'll still produce the bad cells. Unless those cells are recognized by her immune system, they will gradually overpower the viable ones, and go back to destroying her healthy cells."

Desmond squeezed his eyes shut and bit down on his lip, hoping the external pain would blind him to his emotional pain. He'd been so sure Rebecca held the answer. Even now, he couldn't bear to give up. There must be some way to salvage this, some way to save Gillian.

"Isn't there anything you can do? Make Rebecca's cells capable of identifying Gillian's illness?"

"Not directly. But I thought she might have that reaction, so I tried combining Ms. Morgan's gene sample with other samples we'd tried in the past. A combination of Ms. Morgan's genetic matter with yours is capable of identifying and neutralizing cells transformed by your daughter's illness. It might be possible to introduce that combination into the deepest layer of Ms. Morgan's DNA, so that her bone marrow generates the new type of cells."

"Combine my DNA with Rebecca's, then give her a transplant so that she can give Gillian a transplant?" It sounded plausible. What was Dr. Chen waiting for?

Desmond leaped up and grabbed the doctor's shoulder. "Then do it!" he ordered.

Dr. Chen paled and fell back against his desk. Damn! Desmond let go of the scientist. He'd forgotten his strength, and squeezed too tightly. Stupid, stupid. Hopefully Chen would think it was an extreme overreaction, but a human one. Desmond couldn't take much more of this, having his hopes raised and then dashed. Like a piece of wire that had been bent and straightened one too many times, another reversal would make him snap.

Dr. Chen lifted his good arm and felt the injured shoulder. He must have been more surprised than hurt, because his color was already returning. He straightened his jacket.

"Well, you see, Mr. Lacroix, we can't. Not today. We don't have the technology. I'm sorry. But new discoveries are being made every day. With the resources of this Institute—"

"No. There's a way to cure her. I know there is."

Desmond paced the lab, stepping around the scientist. There had to be a way.

"Well, there is one possibility," Dr. Chen offered hesitantly.

Desmond rounded on him and demanded, "What?"

"To insert new genetic codes into an existing system is still beyond our technology. But manipulating genes in a forming system has already been done with great success."

"Damn it, speak English!"

"Okay. Any offspring of you and Ms. Morgan—"

"Absolutely not!" Desmond clenched his fists and fought to control his temper. Dr. Chen didn't realize the magnitude of what he was suggesting.

"We'd make sure the right genetic codes were present. If we did it here in the lab—"

"I said no. It's out of the question." He leaned against the counter. There were some things he couldn't do, not even for Gillian. Persuading Rebecca to donate cell samples and creating a child specifically to use as a donor were two entirely different propositions. He'd orchestrated events to obtain Rebecca's assistance, but only after she'd given her consent. She'd freely offered her help. He hadn't violated his oath. If he followed Dr. Chen's suggestion, he'd be doing something much worse.

No. The thought sickened him. Yet the seductive reasoning of the scientist pulled at his beliefs. Whatever the nature and rationale of the child's conception, surely he'd love it as much as he loved Gillian. Brothers and sisters frequently acted as donors for siblings that needed them. The child would no doubt want to act as a donor for Gillian. He'd be acting on his or her wishes.

Rationalizations and excuses. He'd sworn to never take anything from a person that wasn't freely given. He had to find another way.

"Doctor," Desmond turned and asked, startling Dr. Chen. "You said Gillian wouldn't reject a transplant from Rebecca."

"Yes. But I explained, it won't cure her."

"I understand. But will it give her more time?"

Dr. Chen stopped and stared into the distance. Desmond tried to remain patient as the minutes stretched out, with no sign of movement. Finally, Dr. Chen's eyes cleared and he nodded.

"I can't guarantee anything, okay? It depends on the rate of reproduction, amount of absorption, and a bunch of other things. But, yes, she should get at least two more years from the procedure. Maybe even as many as five or six."

Desmond whispered a heartfelt thanks to any god that was listening. "I'll make sure Rebecca understands what is needed from her, but I don't expect any problems. Schedule the operation for tomorrow."

Desmond turned away and left the baffled scientist. He'd raise Dr. Chen's research grant. Maybe find him a new assistant. With enough money, they'd be sure to find a permanent solution to Gillian's illness. All they'd needed was enough time to work. Rebecca could buy them that time. He owed her more than he could ever repay.

His mind already sorting through everything that needed to be done, Desmond walked toward Philippe's office. He had to have Philippe's help. Patching things up between them was more important than ever. At a time like this, he needed his family.

DESMOND TAPPED on Philippe's open door and looked inside the office. Philippe hunched over a pile of paperwork.

"Just a minute," he called without looking up.

"Take your time."

Philippe snapped upright, dropping his pen. "Des!"

Desmond strolled into the office. Hooking a chair with one foot, he dragged it over to Philippe's desk and sat down. He wanted to blurt out his good news right away. But first, he had to make things right between them. Not quite sure how to start, he glanced around the office for inspiration. "How long have we been friends?"

"Since 1873, when I showed up at your plantation to kill our father." Philippe straightened the pile of papers before him.

Desmond remembered the moment well. "You were too late. He was dead. They were all dead. All except me. And you."

"The curse."

"You know more about voodoo than I do."

Philippe shrugged. "I was my grandmother's errand boy. It was her curse. She mentioned it from time to time."

"Her curse made us what we are. But does it keep us that way?"

"It would if she still lived. With her death..."

The triumphant smile that flitted across Philippe's face sent chills down Desmond's spine. He hurriedly changed the subject.

"Rebecca's been confirmed as a donor for Gillian."

Philippe blinked. "That's a surprise. I'm happy for you, Des. And for Gillian. I hope the transplant operation goes well."

From his tone of voice, Desmond knew Philippe didn't expect it to be a success.

"Dr. Chen said it won't cure her, but it might give Gillian a few more years."

"You think the curse can be delayed?"

"I think we can fight it with modern science."

"Of course we can fight." Philippe shrugged. "But we will lose in the end."

"Not this time." Desmond would do anything to keep the curse from claiming another victim. Then he remembered Dr. Chen's suggestion. Almost anything.

Philippe chuckled. "You look quite fierce."

"Dr. Chen had a crazy idea, straight out of *Frankenstein*, about creating life in the lab."

"From what?"

"Donor cells from me and Rebecca. I told him to go to hell."

"Good for you." Philippe flashed a devilish grin. "With a woman as good looking as her, I'd prefer the old fashioned method of creating life, too."

"Philippe!" Desmond didn't know whether to be outraged or amused. Philippe's humor usually had that affect on him. But at least they were friends again.

REBECCA WOKE up with a splitting headache. Strange dreams had tormented her all night. In some, an evil presence pursued her, drinking in her fear. And in others, she chased down innocent victims herself, delighting in their terror. She wasn't sure which dreams frightened her more.

The smell of toast drifted past her, making her stomach rumble. She was starving. What time was it? These blacked-out windows made it impossible to gauge time.

She found her watch on the nightstand. Eleven-thirty. She must smell lunch, then, not breakfast.

Taking a few minutes to wash and get dressed, she made sure she was presentable. She didn't want Desmond to see her all disheveled from sleep. Desmond. She smiled, remembering last night.

He'd aroused her in a way no other man had ever done, touched some level of her heart that had never been touched before. She wasn't sure what he'd done when he caressed her, but it had unleashed feelings unlike any she'd ever known.

Her cheeks heated as she recalled her reaction to his kiss. She'd stayed dazed, her nerves humming with energy, until he'd suggested they retire to their separate rooms. Listening to him get ready for bed had nearly driven her mad. She'd imagined him undressing, his clothes sliding off his smooth, muscled body.

She splashed cold water on her face. That had been quite the kiss if the memory still affected her this morning.

Ready to face him, she stopped with one hand on the door. What if the kiss had been nothing special to him? What if her reaction had been nothing more than a result of her keyed up nerves?

She had to find out for sure. Even if her reaction had been a fluke, or he didn't feel anything special, she'd still help Gillian. Rebecca wasn't the sort who went back on her promises. At least, not if the promises hadn't been extorted from her.

But she needed to know where she stood with Desmond. Was he interested in her for her own sake, or just because of what she could do for his daughter? Better ask now, before she started thinking silly thoughts. Sometimes the truth hurt, but she preferred knowing it anyway. She opened the door and followed the smell of toast into the kitchen.

The housekeeper she'd met the other night stood by the stove, grilling a sandwich. Gillian sat at the table, drinking a glass of milk.

"Good morning," Rebecca said. "How are you this morning, Gillian?"

Gillian frowned, and slurped her milk.

"Good morning, Ms. Morgan," the housekeeper said. "I suppose you'd like some lunch? Or breakfast?"

"Yes, thank you. Whichever one you're making now is fine."

Rebecca walked over to the stove. Mrs. Waters watched the sandwich as she answered, "I'm making grilled cheese. You may have this one if you like."

"I can make my own—"

"Nonsense. I'll do it. If you want to help, get a glass of milk or juice out of the refrigerator."

Rebecca opened the refrigerator door, and tried to ignore the medicine bottles. She didn't want to think about Desmond being ill. A half-full can of tomato juice appealed to her, and she poured it into a glass.

Gillian shook her head as Rebecca sat down at the table.

"No medicine at lunch," she scolded. Rebecca looked to Mrs. Waters for help.

"She thinks the tomato juice is Mr. Lacroix's medicine."

"Oh." Rebecca looked at her glass. It didn't look anything like medicine to her, but Gillian was only three. Didn't kids mistake aspirin for candy at that age? "Is it okay if I drink it?"

"You've poured it. It'd be a shame to waste it." Mrs. Waters said. Then her voice warmed a good twenty degrees as she told Gillian, "That's not medicine, sweetheart. That's tomato juice." Gillian ignored her.

Rebecca sipped her juice. Mrs. Waters didn't like her. That much was obvious. But why? She'd never get any useful information from the woman at this rate.

"We didn't really have a chance to say much when we were introduced. But I'll be staying here for a few days."

"Yes, Ma'am. Mr. Lacroix's told me everything I need to know about you." From the frost in her voice, Mrs. Waters hadn't liked what she'd heard. She flipped the sandwich out of the frying pan onto a plate, slashed it into quarters and set the plate in front of Gillian. "Here you go, sweetie."

Mrs. Waters threw bread and cheese into the frying pan. "Yours'll be done soon."

"That's fine."

Mrs. Waters didn't say another word until the sandwich finished cooking. Then she merely tossed the plate in front of Rebecca with a muttered, "Here."

Rebecca took a bite. The gooey cheese and crisp bread mingled with the tomato juice, and reminded her of pizza. The housekeeper might not be much of a conversationalist, but she was a great cook.

"Mr. Lacroix suggested you'd be happier in the study, while he was at work," Mrs. Waters announced Desmond's wishes with all the weight of a royal proclamation.

"All right." She was, after all, a guest. But she'd had just about enough of this frigid politeness. Time to find out what was going on. "I'll be there or in my room."

"Mr. Lacroix thought you'd like to look at his books. You should stay in the study, rather than go back into Mrs. Lacroix's room."

Rebecca heard the subtle emphasis on the word *Mrs.* Why did everyone assume she was sleeping with Desmond?

Rebecca's cheeks heated. The thought had crossed her mind a few times during the long night, too. But that didn't mean she'd done anything about it.

"So, what else has Mr. Lacroix told you about me?"

"Nothing, really, except that you're his houseguest."

People used the word "houseguest" about as often as the phrase "just good friends." And usually to mean the same thing.

"Well, I'm a little more than that. I'm here because I'm helping Dr. Chen with his research."

"Helping? How?"

Rebecca thought she detected a hint of a thaw in the woman's voice, and followed up her advantage. "He discovered I share a blood type with Gillian, as well as certain rare antigens. I'll provide samples for research, and hopefully, a treatment."

Rebecca darted a glance at Gillian, unsure how much the little girl would understand. Adults didn't normally discuss these sorts of things in front of children.

She needn't have worried. Gillian stared down at her sandwich, her forehead wrinkled in concentration, oblivious to Rebecca and anything she might be saying.

Mrs. Waters had paid attention, though. She turned to Rebecca, favoring her with a big smile. "Really? You're going to help our little angel?"

"I hope so."

The housekeeper brought Rebecca a second sandwich. When she finished that, Mrs. Waters offered her milk, more juice, apples, oranges, and homemade brownies.

"No, please, Mrs. Waters. I'm full. Thank you. It was delicious. But I really can't eat another thing." The housekeeper hesitated, holding the tin of brownies. Rebecca stood up before more food could be thrust at her. "I think I'll go take a look at those books now. Where's the study?"

"If you're sure." Mrs. Waters put two brownies on a plate for the silent Gillian. "It's on the other side of Mr. Lacroix's room."

Rebecca escaped the kitchen, and the smothering attentions of Ms. Waters. On her right, three doors lined the living room wall. The first led to her room, and the second to Desmond's room, with no door from here to the connecting bath. The study was behind door number three.

She opened the door, and inhaled the dusty smell of old books mingled with the scent of leather furniture. She sneezed.

"Bless you," Mrs. Waters called from the kitchen. Rebecca shut herself in the study, away from any more help. Or food.

Bookshelves lined the walls, crowded with hardcover books until they looked ready to collapse. In one corner of the room, two leather chairs shared an end table and a reading lamp, while in the opposite corner an antique desk held an out-of-place looking computer. A telephone sat on the end table.

She rushed over and picked up the receiver. A dial tone buzzed loud and strong in her ear. She started to dial the editor who'd requested the travel stories she'd officially come to Arizona for. 1 - 3 - 1 - 5 The phone clicked, and rang through to an extension.

She hung up before anyone could answer. Of course. The phones must be connected on an internal network for the whole facility. She probably needed to dial 9 to get an outside line.

Getting dial tone again, she pressed 9. The tone shifted to a lower-pitched buzz. She dialed the editor's area code and phone number. It rang once, twice, three times, four times, and then his answering machine picked up.

"Hi, it's Rebecca Morgan," she told it. "I'm out here in Arizona, got a little side tracked. Don't try calling my hotel. I won't be there. I'm staying at the Prescott Institute. I'll give you the number next time I call, or you can ask information if you need to get in touch with me. The research for your stories is done, and I'll have the first one to you by the end of next week."

She hung up the phone. At least he wouldn't worry now. If this assignment was anything like the previous times she'd worked for him, the editor had already tried to call her once with a brilliant take for her story that couldn't wait until she got back.

She smiled and shook her head. Her attitude had certainly done a one-eighty since her attempt—was it only two nights ago?—to escape. Now she trusted Desmond completely. She paused, wondering if he trusted her. Or even if he should.

Forcing her attention to the room around her, she noticed the walls filled with book shelves. Desmond's books, a mixture of French and English, and even a few that looked like Latin, lured her to explore. She wondered if he'd ever opened some of the weighty treatises on land management and Victorian social reform, or if they'd been purchased wholesale at an auction to fill the shelves. She found a surprising number of first editions from the last century, including works by H. G. Wells and a collection of the novels of Jules Verne in the original French.

Reluctantly, she turned away. She'd come into the study for a reason. She'd promised her editor that article on day hikes around Phoenix when she got back. Opening the desk drawers, she found paper and a pen and sat down to write.

Chapter 7

REBECCA SPENT the rest of the afternoon organizing her notes and drafting a rough copy of her promised travel article. She'd hoped to use the computer occupying one corner of Desmond's desk, but it wouldn't work without the right password. Considering his mania for security, the lock on his computer had disappointed but not surprised her.

She finished transcribing the last of her notes onto squares of paper and spread the papers across the desk, shuffling them into the order she planned to use them. This was the part of writing an article she loved the most, starting with simple facts and building her story from the ground up. As each layer was complete, she tested it, probing for weaknesses. Only when she knew it could stand on its own did she begin building the layer that rested on top of it.

She was deep in her work when the study door opened, sending a gust of air across the desk. She instinctively shielded her work with her body, pinning the papers to the leather desk blotter.

The back of her neck tingled with awareness, but she refused to turn around. Desmond was the only one who would enter without knocking, and she wasn't in any hurry to face him. The memory of last night's kiss invaded her thoughts, speeding her heart with a mix of anticipation and fear. She didn't know what expression she hoped to see on his face. Desire? Regret? Neither?

Giving herself time to get her thoughts under control, she gradually unfurled off the papers, gathering them up in order. When she'd picked up the last paper, she had no more excuses not to turn around. She looked up, to see Desmond framed by the doorway.

"You've been busy," he said, nodding at the papers clutched in her hand. Was that a hint of censure in his voice? She double-checked the desk top, making sure she'd removed all traces of her activity.

"Mrs. Waters said I could use your study."

"Of course. You're my guest." Waving away her concern, he sauntered over to the desk and leaned against the edge. His hip rested inches away from her.

Her every sense registered his presence, from the hint of his spicy-sweet cologne brushing the air to the wash of heat radiating from him.

Might he be equally aware of her? He'd seemed interested last night. But when he hadn't followed up on their kiss, she'd thought his attention was more likely because of what she could do for his daughter, than because he found Rebecca appealing. Had she been wrong?

"Did you get the results from Dr. Chen?" Rebecca forced her gaze up to his face.

"Yes." His broad smile told her everything she needed to know, about the results and about her appeal. "He's confirmed your suitability as a donor."

She shivered, as the reality of what she'd promised cast a sudden shadow over her. Desmond and his daughter would both be depending on her. What if she failed them?

Desmond leaned over and took Rebecca's hands between his, sharing his warmth. His touch sent threads of fire through her fingers, up her arms, and into her heart until her blood seemed to smolder. She stared at their clasped hands.

"Are you all right?"

"Yeah. It's just—" She couldn't tell him how his touch affected her. "I hadn't really believed it would be a match."

"Are you having second thoughts?"

He let go and backed away. Her hands seemed twice as cold without his warmth.

She searched his face for a hint about why he'd moved away from her, but his normally expressive features displayed nothing. Even his eyes gave nothing away, dulling to a flat bottle-green. Yes, she was having second thoughts. Anyone would. That didn't mean she was backing out.

If he'd just give her a clue as to how important her possible second thoughts were to him, she'd know how to frame her answer. But maybe he had. Maybe his complete lack of display proved he feared that she would change her mind completely. And that he'd respect her wishes and let her go rather than trying to coerce her into staying if she no longer wanted to help. The thought of finally being the one in control of her situation gave her an unsought rush of power, tied to a responsibility she didn't want to bear alone.

"It would help if you told me what's expected from a donor. I mean, I know Gillian needs blood cells, but how's it all happen?"

A relieved smile transformed his face, and he extended one hand in chivalrous escort. She took the time to stack her pile of notes in the middle of the desk where they wouldn't fall, then let him lead her to the pair of leather chairs. He settled her comfortably in one, then he sat in the other and leaned forward, elbows on his knees.

"Gillian needs a bone marrow donor, so she can create her own blood cells. The doctor will withdraw the bone marrow cells from the donor, and inject them into Gillian's blood stream, where they'll eventually be absorbed."

"So it's like the blood samples Dr. Chen's already done, only more so?" She relaxed. That wouldn't be so bad.

"Except the bone marrow isn't taken from the blood stream. It's drawn from the middle of the long bones in the leg."

"The middle of the bone?" Her voice squeaked. She couldn't help it. The cells they wanted were still inside her bones.

"Rebecca? You're very pale. Would you like a drink?"

"Drink? No." She didn't need false courage. She needed the real kind, and found it sorely lacking. "How do they get at the middle of a bone?"

"It won't hurt. They give you a local anesthesia, and the procedure will be over in a matter of minutes."

"I asked how they get at the middle of the bone."

Desmond tilted his head and eyed her with suspicion. "Are you sure you want the details? You already look faint. Isn't it enough to know it won't hurt?"

"No. It's not enough. I can deal with the truth, however awful it is. Don't you see? It's not knowing that scares me, because I can imagine things that are a million times worse."

He nodded. "It's a simple operation. The doctor makes a small incision, chips the bone, and withdraws some of the cells. As soon as the anesthetic wears off, the donor walks away. That's it."

She stared at the wall of books, her thoughts churning. Local anesthesia. No hospitalization. How much could it hurt? Chipping bone. Incisions. It could hurt a lot.

"Rebecca?" Desmond tapped her lightly on the arm, pulling her back to the present.

"She'll die without my help, won't she?"

Desmond sat up straight, his face once again an unreadable mask. "Yes."

"Then I guess I really have no choice. After all, it's not like giving up a kidney or something. Bone marrow grows back. It does grow back, doesn't it?" She shot him a worried glance, and he nodded. She sighed. "Okay, then. I'll do it. But let's get it over with quickly."

"Thank you. I'll schedule it for tomorrow." He smiled, impulsively catching up her hand and pressing a kiss to it. A spark seemed to jump between them, tingling all the way up her arm. She looked down just as he looked up, their gazes meeting and locking in a moment that seemed to transcend time.

She'd never really noticed how green his eyes were. Not just sea green, or moss green, or neon green, but all of those and more. A rainbow in every shade of green shimmered in his eyes, each color in turn emphasized as the deep black iris expanded. Desmond continued to stare at her, as if he'd never seen her eyes, either. She couldn't imagine why. They were a plain, ordinary gray. Nothing to excite such lengthy perusal.

A wave of self-consciousness assailed her, and she blinked. So did he. Then he let his hand drift down, away from hers. Still moving at half speed, he stood up and stepped away.

He started to leave the room, but turned around when he reached the door.

"If you'd changed your mind and didn't want to help her anymore, I wouldn't have forced you to, you know."

"I know." She frowned. What an odd thing to say. She understood now that his impulsive kidnapping of her had been an act of desperation, and he'd only wanted time to convince her to help his daughter. But all along, he'd insisted on gaining her willing cooperation.

"In light of Philippe's comments this morning, I just wanted to make sure. Even though I'm concerned about Gillian, I still know the difference between right and wrong."

He didn't wait for an answer, turning and leaving the room as soon as he finished. Which was a good thing, because she had no idea what to say to a statement like that. Unbidden, the line from Shakespeare sprang into her head. *Methinks thou dost protest too much.* She wouldn't have dreamed of questioning Desmond's moral integrity. Until now.

MRS. WATERS had made one of Gillian's favorite meals, chunks of chicken in a thick sauce of tomato paste and sour cream, accompanied by dumplings of all shapes and sizes. Intent on finding all of the treasures hidden on her plate, Gillian ignored the adults.

Desmond smiled, watching his daughter's enthusiastic attempts to spear a particularly slippery dumpling, then turned his attention to

Rebecca. Hoping to keep the conversation light, he asked her, "What were you working at so industriously when I came into the study?"

"My story." She blushed, and hastened to add, "I'd promised an article about Phoenix as a tourist destination to one of the editors I work with."

"As opposed to your story about the Institute?"

"Mm-hm." She avoided answering by shoveling forkfuls of chicken and dumplings into her mouth.

"I won't ask about it, if you prefer." His mild words startled her, and for a moment he was afraid she would choke. Even Gillian stopped playing with her food to watch Rebecca cough, turn red, and then gulp half her glass of water, which started her coughing again.

When she recovered, she smiled weakly. "I guess I expected you to be more protective of the Institute's secrets."

He shrugged. "I did invite you."

At the time, he'd been concerned about how much she knew, and wanted an excuse to meet in person with her so he could use his skills to learn the truth. He'd quickly discovered she had suspicions, but no facts. His efforts during her tour had dissuaded her from her suspicions. Yet her reaction proved she did not trust him.

He couldn't blame her. After all, he didn't trust her. For a moment, in the study, he'd hated the secret he was keeping from her. He still did. Against all reason, he wanted to prove she was trustworthy. That he could confide in her, and leave no secrets between them.

Smiling, he began his delicate cross-examination. "What are some of the other places you've written tourist articles about?"

"I really haven't traveled that much. The library, internet, and occasional phone call usually suffice."

"But isn't free travel one of the main benefits of being a travel writer?"

"It is. But I'm not. I write features ... except I write other things to pay the rent."

"Such as?"

"Well, I did a series of science articles for the Sunday supplement of a newspaper."

His blood chilled. Did she have the background knowledge to piece together what was going on at the Institute? Perhaps he should have let her stay in the apartment. Dr. Chen would have needed only one more day to complete the experiments on his own.

"Really? What sort of science articles?"

"This and that." She lowered her gaze and pushed her food around her plate. "It's not that interesting."

His mind heard what she did not say out loud. She'd profiled doctors involved in AIDS research, cancer research, and revolutionary heart bypass surgery. She suspected the nature of the Institute's research. And she hid her suspicions from him.

"What interesting things have you written about, then?" He forced himself to keep the conversation light. "Six-legged calves and dog-headed boys?"

Gillian looked up from the dumpling bridge she was constructing. "A boy with a doggie head?"

"No. No dog-headed boys."

Gillian persisted. "Any dogs?"

"No dogs for you," Desmond interrupted, recognizing his daughter's intent. "Not until you're well."

"Lots of dogs. Big dogs and little dogs and brown dogs and black dogs and—"

"When you're well."

She sighed, and stabbed another dumpling with her fork.

"I did do a story on a carnival, once," Rebecca volunteered.

That was promising. He remembered carnivals. Siamese twins, bearded ladies, and all manner of human oddities. If she accepted them—

"It was all about how the owners were taking advantage of the people attending. The county sheriff closed the carnival down after my story ran."

Desmond winced. No sympathy there.

"But didn't that put the carnival people out of work?"

"They could get other jobs. Honest jobs."

"Even the freaks?"

Rebecca frowned. "If you mean the side show acts, most of them were hucksters, no more unusual than you or me. The few that did have unique conditions would have been better served getting decent medical help than prolonging their suffering as a means of employment."

He winced again. No, he couldn't trust Rebecca with the truth. She'd spent too much time trying to overcome the differences in her background and upbringing to understand some differences could not be overcome.

Gillian saved him from continuing the awkward conversation, by announcing, "All done, Daddy."

He pushed his chair away from the table. "If you'll excuse me, I'll get her washed and put to bed."

"I'll do the dishes."

Scooping up his daughter, Desmond beat a hasty retreat.

When he came out of Gillian's room after reading her a story, he found Rebecca waiting for him in the living room. She sat on the couch, head bowed and hands clasped between her knees. Praying for salvation? He didn't know if she hoped for a repeat of last night, or feared what might happen between them. And he didn't dare lower his mental shields enough to find out. Especially since he'd yet to make up his own mind.

He cleared his throat to give her warning, then joined her on the couch.

"So," he said, forcing a carefree note of bonhomie into his voice. "How does being a freelance journalist differ from working for a newspaper or magazine?"

"Gillian's asleep," she said, still staring at her hands. "You don't have to pretend to be interested anymore."

Her opinion of him stung. "I wasn't pretending."

"I saw your expression. You looked like you were visiting a dentist, and he found a cavity. Don't worry. I'll spare you the drilling."

"Rebecca—"

"I thought you liked me." She lifted her head and looked at him, her wide gray eyes reminiscent of a small woodland animal watching an eighteen wheeler bearing down on it and unable to do anything to get out of the way. "After last night, I thought.... But being a reporter is more than just what I do. It's who I am. And if you hate reporters—"

"Rebecca, please. You're getting yourself all worked up over nothing." He forced a hearty smile, and covered her fisted hands with a gentle caress. He wanted to pull her into his arms and sear her with kisses, proving just how much he *liked* her. But he couldn't. He refused to turn her into emotional roadkill by promising something he couldn't deliver. Whatever the nature of the relationship between them was, he couldn't risk letting it develop any further. Not until he was sure of her.

"I don't hate reporters," he continued. "And I don't hate you. It's just that working here in the Institute, I'm used to a very high level of security. Some of your comments were...alarming."

Her face could have belonged to one of Philippe's wooden carvings for all the expression she showed. He let down his mental shields bit by bit, unfolding the layers like tissue paper until they were virtually nonexistent, but not a trace of her thoughts reached him. Her mind was sealed behind a wall as impenetrable as the look in her eyes.

"Why would you say that? Unless you have something to hide? I already know all about Dr. Chen's discoveries, and the new kind of white blood cell."

Damn! For a shy introvert with all the social skills of an orangutan, the doctor had engaged in a surprising amount of chitchat. Desmond flashed on the scene used in so many old war movies. A beleaguered captain stood on his bridge, water streaming around him, red lights strobing and an angry klaxon wailing, as he shouted, "Damage control!" She'd torpedoed him well below the water line. And he didn't know how many shots she had left.

"What made you decide to become a journalist?" he asked. His counterattack cracked her mental wall enough for him to glimpse an abstract melange of construction equipment and building plans. Before he could probe further, she recovered her composure and sealed the flaw.

"The Great American Dream is just that, a dream. No one really has it. I spotlight the illusion, and show it for the sawdust and paint it is. Too many things are covered up or swept under the rug, under the pretext that it's better if people don't know about them. I think it's better if people know what's really out there."

"Rhetoric." He might not understand her mental images, but one thing was clear. They were thoughts of building, of the joy of creating. They didn't match her cynical words.

"What?"

"That might be the party line you think all good journalists are supposed to spout, but it's not true. Not for you. At least, that's not all there is to the truth."

She frowned, her forehead creasing as she studied him. "You're right. I do enjoy the writing, for the writing's sake. I like taking a jumble of incoherent facts and making an easily understood story out of them. But no one's ever seen past the stock answer before. They hear what they expect to hear and move on. What makes you so different?"

He sighed theatrically. "Now I'm the subject of your investigation. Can't you ever just have a conversation?"

"Not when the person I'm conversing with is trying to hide something." She leaned forward, a new spark in her eyes.

"Must you know everything? Don't you realize there are reasons for keeping secrets?"

"Of course there are."

He started to relax.

"And most of them are bad," she finished.

"Even when you're protecting someone? Keeping a secret when you know they couldn't handle the truth?"

"That's exactly the sort of self-aggrandizing hypocrisy I mean!" She slapped the arm of the couch in disgust. "How can anyone ever make that judgment for another person? You don't know what someone can or can't handle until they've tried."

He thought he discovered a chink in her armor.

"What if telling someone the truth would cause a lifetime of misery? Would you still want them to know?"

Crimson shame flooded her cheeks.

"Oh, God," she whispered. She squirmed on the couch. "Gillian. I'm sorry. I didn't mean...That is...There are always special cases. Of course you would only tell her what she was old enough to understand."

He hadn't been thinking of Gillian, but of the way things had turned out for Philippe and his wife. Still, as long as the misconception stopped Rebecca's attack, Desmond wouldn't quibble with it.

"You can never know the truth about the future," she said, trying to escape from the corner she'd painted herself into. "By truth, I meant things that have already happened. Things you can prove. But a best guess about the future doesn't necessarily come true. A doctor's prognosis is not a guaranteed outcome."

He sat up straighter, finally seeing a way to keep his secret from her without guilt.

"Then you'd pardon someone for withholding information, if it was only an opinion?"

His gaze bored into her, riveting her with the bright green of his eyes. She swallowed with a suddenly dry throat, no longer certain what they were discussing. As happened in so many of her conversations with him, she sensed that Desmond was layering another meaning on top of his words. She couldn't possibly answer him correctly, because she didn't understand the question behind his question.

Searching his eyes for an answer, she lost herself in their brilliance. So bright. Like green fire, hungering to consume her. And she didn't care. She leaned closer, welcoming the heat. She wanted to be consumed, burned to a cinder in the flames of his embrace.

The thought shocked her to her senses, and she pulled away. Retreating to the far end of the couch, she risked a quick glance back at him. He hadn't moved.

He'd asked her a question, although she didn't remember what it was.

"What's your view?" she stalled.

"On truth and opinions? My opinion is you ought to be in bed. You need to be well rested for tomorrow's procedure."

She heard echoes of her own frustration in his voice. But she didn't want to go to sleep. To sleep, perchance to dream. She'd rather stay up all night than face those nightmares again. Stay up with Desmond.

Her thoughts headed back into treacherous territory, as she imagined sliding closer to him on the couch. She could almost feel the heat of his body pressed against hers as he leaned over and claimed her lips in a sizzling kiss.

She doused the fires of her imagination. She'd go to bed. Alone. Just like always, nothing unusual. She'd put on her nightshirt, brush her teeth and climb into bed.

But to put on her nightshirt, she'd have to undress. She pictured Desmond unbuttoning her shirt and sliding it over her shoulders, leaning forward to—No. Never mind the nightshirt. She forced herself to think about brushing her teeth, a terribly ordinary and unerotic action. She could almost taste the minty foam as she imagined the toothbrush scrubbing up, down, up, down. Her mind leapt to a vision of the two of them entwined in his sheets, moving in the same driving rhythm.

She wrenched her thoughts back to the present, guilt scalding her cheeks, and snuck another glance at him. Had he guessed the direction of her thoughts?

The lamp light reflected from his eyes, making green flames dance within them. He'd just licked his lips, and they glistened, moist and kissable. She hungered for their touch against hers.

"Yes, I should be in bed," she blurted. "I mean, I should be asleep. Asleep in my bed. That's what I meant. Good night."

She stood and hurried from the room. If he hadn't guessed what she'd been fantasizing about, her last little speech would have given it away. She might be too embarrassed to go to the hospital with him tomorrow.

The hospital. The obvious explanation for her unusual reactions calmed her. She was frightened. Her strong attraction to him was a result of fear heightening her senses. Everything would be clearer in the morning. Once the procedure was finished and her fears dispelled, he'd stop affecting her so strongly. The morning seemed a long time away, however. It would be a very long night.

Desmond watched her flee the room. Now maybe his equilibrium would return. Her reaction to his comment had sent him reeling. She'd broadcast her interest and availability as clearly as if she'd shouted through a megaphone.

Suddenly, all he could think about was tearing her clothes off, and seeing her bathed by the light of the moon. He pictured carrying her into his bedroom and falling with her into the mound of blankets and silken sheets. He wanted to bury himself inside her, to lose himself completely in her. The only problem was, he didn't know who'd imagined that first, him or Rebecca.

He'd never come so close to completely abandoning his identity before, and it frightened him. He kept a tight control over his thoughts and feelings, ever vigilant for the sort of destructive, self-indulgent behavior that led to his father's suicide. If his father hadn't used his wealth and position to all but rape Philippe's mother, there never would have been a curse.

That was one of the reasons Desmond had sworn to never use his mental powers to satisfy his needs without a person's willing consent. He'd meant his cursed needs. But his need for Rebecca was all human, all male. If he made love to her, he knew she would be willing. It would be what they both wanted. But it wouldn't be right.

If he could only put a name to what he was feeling, he wouldn't be so concerned. It wasn't desire, although he certainly desired Rebecca. No, after 150 years he'd become familiar with all the nuances of desire, both human and cursed. This was something more.

It wasn't love. He loved Gillian, had loved his wife, even loved his half-brother, Philippe. Each love was different, and what he felt for Rebecca was like none of them.

No, what he felt for her was something completely new. A hunger to merge his thoughts with hers, to absorb her feelings into him, to see through her eyes and taste with her lips. He didn't understand it. But he had to have her. And with every taste, with every glimpse, his need grew stronger.

He could stretch her visit out a few more days, claiming that she wouldn't be fit for travel. He'd use those days to convince her that she couldn't live without him. Because he was afraid in that time, he'd find out he couldn't live without her.

THE NEXT MORNING as Gillian attacked her cereal, he slipped off to Rebecca's room to wake her.

The sight of Rebecca, her long limbs tangled in the sheets, rekindled all the desires he'd banked the night before. He wanted to fall upon her and lose himself in her wonders. He ached to join himself to her, to empty himself into her and to fill himself from her. The new sensations tore at him, and he clutched the door frame until splinters pierced his fingers.

She woke with a gasp, and rearranged the sheets to conceal herself from his gaze.

"What are you doing here?" she asked.

"I came to wake you. We'll be leaving shortly."

"Thank you."

He turned away, leaving tiny drops of blood on the door frame. Of course, she spotted the stains.

"What happened? Are you hurt?"

"I'm fine. A splinter, that's all."

"Are you sure? Splinters don't usually bleed like that."

She thrust her sheets aside and padded over to examine his hand. Her night shirt left her legs bare, something her sudden concern for him kept her from noticing. But he was painfully aware of her semi-dressed state. He let her draw him closer to the light, savoring the touch of her soft fingers against his, and the delicate brush of her cotton covered breast against his upper arm.

She gasped, and he saw his injury as she must. Thick blood oozed from the puncture wounds, already swelling and puffing where the splinters of wood remained. He'd heal as soon as the splinters were removed, but she had no way of knowing that.

"We need to clean those cuts, and pull the splinters out. You don't have any hydrogen peroxide in your bathroom, but warm water should work. I'm more concerned about how we'll pull the splinters. Do you have any tweezers?"

"No, but I won't need any." He dropped his other arm around her waist and gave her a light squeeze, the briefest of caresses, before he broke away. Regrettably, he couldn't linger with her. She needed to get ready.

His touch reminded her of her undressed state, and she hopped back, trying to stretch the nightshirt to cover more of her legs. Taking pity on her, he turned aside. She relaxed, unable to tell he could still see her out of the corner of his eye.

"I'll use the other bathroom," he told her. "You'll need this one. We're leaving for the hospital in twenty minutes. You'll finally get your chance to see the research application wing of the Institute."

"Twenty minutes?" She whirled and ran into the bathroom, slamming the door shut behind her.

Alone in the other bathroom, he held his hand over the child-height sink. Thick blood oozed from the wounds, running down his fingers to drip into the sink. Slowly, the blood forced the splinters from his flesh. Thinner blood gushed out, cleaning the wounds, then slowed to a trickle. He leaned down to rinse off his hand and splash the blood off the porcelain. By the time he put down the towel, his puncture wounds were only slightly reddened blemishes. In half an hour, they'd fade completely.

He stepped out of the bathroom, then stopped. Rebecca would notice the sudden change. And she'd demand an explanation.

He kept a box of adhesive bandages decorated with cheerful teddy bears in Gillian's medicine cabinet. They were silly things for a grown man to use, especially since he didn't need them, but it would forestall any questions.

He rejoined Gillian in the kitchen. She noticed his new plumage at once. A montage of memories slipped through his thin mental shielding, images of Gillian with a skinned knee, cut finger, skinned elbow and other minor cuts and abrasions common to young children. Each time, he or Mrs. Waters had been instantly at her side to kiss her "ouchie" and make it better, as well as applying bandages and disinfectant.

"Did you get an ouchie, Daddy?"

"Yes. I cut myself on a splinter."

"Let me kiss it and make it better." She sat up straight and tall, and held out her hand with the regal grace of a princess.

Smiling, he placed his injured hand in hers. She bent over his hand and made loud kissing noises over the bandages, performing the magic ritual previously reserved for adults. The opportunity thrilled her.

"All better," she announced.

"Thank you, sweetheart. It feels better already." He ruffled her soft mop of curls. "We're going to make you better, too."

Today she'd get her last shot. The doctor would inject the bone marrow cells from Rebecca into Gillian, along with enough of her normal medicine to keep her immune system functioning until the healthy cells started producing. With luck, Desmond would never have to subject his daughter to the torment of shots again.

But first he had to get her ready to go to the hospital. He picked up her empty cereal bowl and put it in the sink. Then he collected her silverware, and dropped that in. Finally, he lifted her out of her booster seat.

"Don't put me in the sink!"

He laughed. "I won't."

He set her on the counter and soaked a cloth in warm water. Soggy remnants of breakfast decorated her face and hands. Hands?

"Gillian, were you eating your cereal with your fingers?"

"Uh-huh." She grinned and mimed how it was done. "Big flakes!"

They both turned when Rebecca spoke from the doorway.

"Is breakfast over with, or can I have some?"

"The doctor doesn't want you to have any coffee. Because of the anesthesia," he told her.

"No coffee?" Her plaintive tone stopped just short of whining. Rebecca was obviously not a morning person. He tried to keep a straight face as she continued grumbling. "Who scheduled this thing so early in the morning, anyway? The doctor can't possibly be wide enough awake to operate."

"You won't see the doctor right away. There's a good deal of preparation to be done before the procedure."

"At least the doctor will be awake by the time he gets to me. I'll be zonked long before I get any anesthesia, though. Are you sure I can't have any coffee?"

"Positive."

Gillian echoed his sentiments, pointing toward the garbage, where he'd thrown the grounds. "All gone."

"We may as well head for the hospital, then. No reason to hang around here." Rebecca turned and left the kitchen.

Desmond picked up Gillian and carried her out, shielding his concerns from her while keeping a comforting mental touch.

"Don't pick me up, Daddy. I wanna walk."

"It's too far for you to walk, Gillian. I have to carry you."

"No. I wanna walk. I'm not a baby." She looked at Rebecca, and Gillian's face crumpled in the precursor to a fit of tears. She'd proved she wasn't a baby by kissing his hand and making it better.

He calmed her with a quick image of her marching self-importantly by his side. He'd let her walk, if it meant that much to her.

"All right." He set her down on the floor and took her hand. "You can walk. But as soon as you start getting tired, I'm carrying you."

"Okay." Her smile radiated pride.

He opened the front door and ushered the ladies through. Then they walked at a child's pace through the corridors of the Institute toward the hospital wing. Midway through the second miniature park, Gillian admitted she needed help. He carried her the rest of the way.

When they arrived, they were greeted by Doctors Chen and Laurence. Dr. Chen nodded a welcome, while Dr. Laurence introduced himself to Rebecca.

"Hi, there. I'm Dr. Michael Laurence. You're going to be my patient today. How are you feeling?"

"As well as can be expected without my coffee."

Desmond and Dr. Laurence laughed. Rebecca frowned, and muttered something under her breath about not being awake enough to laugh.

A nurse walked in with an armful of colorful child's toys, and set them on the carpeted floor of the waiting room. Gillian spied the distractions, and squirmed to be let down. When Desmond stood her on the floor, she hurried off to the pile of toys at the fast walk that was her top speed. He watched her go, making sure she got to her destination safely, before turning his attention back to Dr. Laurence.

"Before the nurse preps you, Ms. Morgan, I wanted to make sure you didn't have any last minute questions. As soon as you're ready, I'll give you your first anesthetic shot."

"Let's just get this over with."

Dr. Laurence motioned for the nurse to lead Rebecca away. She glanced over her shoulder at Desmond.

"I thought you were coming with me."

"You want me to?" He forced his face to remain impassive, even though he felt a grin struggling to break free.

"Of course I do," she snapped. "What's the point of being brave if there's no one there to see it? You're my witness."

"I'd be honored." Despite her explanations and rationalizations, he was certain she felt the same connection between them as he did, and wanted his presence to comfort and strengthen her. But he wouldn't burden her with that particular truth just yet. After all, it was only his opinion.

The door burst open and Philippe rushed in, out of breath.

"Am I late?"

"No," Desmond told him. "In fact, you're just in time. I need you to watch Gillian while I go with Rebecca."

"Sure." He headed for where Gillian sat, surrounded by blocks. "How ya doing, squirt?"

Gillian laughed and waved her arms. "Unca Philippe!"

Desmond's chest tightened as Philippe leaned down to give her a hug and kiss. Seeing them together, Desmond didn't doubt Philippe's love for her. Perhaps much of his attitude was fear that his curse had strengthened the effects of Desmond's, that he was somehow responsible for the speed and strength of her illness.

Desmond shook his head, forcibly dispelling the negative images. Rebecca's sacrifice would do what no medicines could. Not slow the disease, not even stop it, but for a while completely reverse its insidious effects. He pushed aside the irrational fear that the transplant wouldn't happen, that Rebecca would back out at the last minute, and walked over to his daughter for a hug and kiss of his own.

"See you in a little while, sweetheart." Desmond turned to Rebecca. "I'm all yours."

"That's a bit excessive. I don't think I'll need all of you." Her return smile shook a little, and she reached for his hand. "But I wouldn't mind something to hold on to."

His hand held tight in her grip, Desmond followed Rebecca to the prep room.

Chapter 8

"OKAY," REBECCA called through the door. "You can come back in."

Desmond reentered the small examining room. She perched on the edge of the paper covered table, and tucked the blue cotton hospital gown more closely around her legs. Her fear swirled about her, assaulting him with random visions of doctors, nurses, needles and late-night horror movies.

He strengthened his mental barriers automatically, shutting out her fears. But she still suffered from them. Her face paled as she clenched and unclenched her hands and fidgeted from side to side on the table, tearing the fragile paper. He couldn't help her if he didn't know what was bothering her, so he lowered his shields again until her fears just brushed the edges of his thoughts.

Normally, he'd try to calm her with mental suggestions. But the thought that she might change her mind and back out at the last second terrified him, and he didn't dare risk transmitting that suggestion to her along with the helpful thoughts he meant to send. So he relied on the old-fashioned method of distracting her.

"That's a new look for you," he joked, waving a hand at the gown. "I think you might be starting a new fashion."

She rewarded him with a nervous laugh. "The color's okay, but the fit leaves something to be desired."

"It's a standard size—one size doesn't fit anybody." He smiled, and admitted to himself that the fit left him desiring a lot of things. No matter how she hitched the gown, it either slid down, exposing the soft white skin of her shoulder, or slid forward, revealing the creamy fullness of her breasts barely contained in her wisp of a bra.

"Why are they taking so long?" She kicked her legs, fluttering the hem of her gown.

Desmond forced himself to look away from the tantalizing glimpses of her thighs, staring instead at an inane photograph of daffodils on the far wall. Picking up on images of bumbling doctors dropping instruments and nurses preparing the wrong equipment, he hurried to reassure her that everything was running according to schedule.

"It hasn't even been five minutes since you finished the questionnaire and the nurse took your blood pressure."

"Well, that's too damn long! It's your hospital. Can't you demand better service?"

He spun around. How had she learned that he owned the Institute? He scanned her face for a clue to her words, unable to pin down her chaotic thoughts. Rebecca looked impatient and cranky, not pleased as she should have been at having pried loose a secret. Perhaps she didn't realize the importance of what she'd said.

"My hospital? I may be the Institute's Director—"

"So direct somebody!"

He grinned with relief. She'd been speaking figuratively, not literally.

"And here I always thought the story of monsters transformed into people by a morning cup of coffee was a myth," he teased her.

She glared back at him. "Missing my morning coffee is *not* funny. When you were describing this procedure, you didn't mention that they'd be torturing me first. And wipe that stupid grin off your face!"

He made an effort to comply with her demands, but couldn't keep the grin from tugging at the corners of his mouth. She just looked so adorably indignant, like a kitten who'd been playing with a water balloon and couldn't understand why it had gotten soaked.

The door opened, admitting the nurse.

"If you'll follow me, please."

"It's about time," Rebecca grumbled, and hopped off the table. But she clasped Desmond's hand briefly as she passed. He gave her hand a reassuring squeeze and followed her to the larger examining room prepared for her procedure. As they entered the room, the sting of fresh antiseptic burned his throat. She turned aside, surreptitiously rubbing at her eyes.

The nurse hovered by the padded operating table, while Dr. Laurence waited by a rolling tray full of needles in a range of sizes. Concerned about Rebecca's reaction to the sight of so many needles, considering her earlier fears, Desmond stepped between her and the tray, blocking her view.

Rebecca pushed aside the nurse's outstretched hand and climbed up onto the table without assistance, then positioned herself face down on the table exactly as she was told. Once in place, however, she refused to lie still. She kept twisting around to readjust the back of her gown. Dr. Laurence noticed the problem, and stepped forward to intervene.

"Ms. Morgan, you have to lie down or we can't do this."

"But the gown doesn't stay closed."

"I assure you, Nurse Peters and I have seen plenty of gaping gowns in our time. Don't let it bother you."

"It's not you I'm worried about."

Three pairs of eyes trained their gazes on Desmond.

"I can leave—"

"No!" Rebecca grabbed for his hand. "Don't leave. Just don't look."

"All right. I won't." He stepped around to the front of the table, and looked at the nurse. "Can I sit over here?"

Nurse Peters traded glances with Dr. Laurence. At his nod, she fetched Desmond a molded plastic chair. He sat down, his face on a level with Rebecca's, and looked into her wide gray eyes. Normally the silver-gray of moonlight on white roses, panic had darkened them to the color of weathered driftwood.

Holding her hand, he focused on calm and soothing thoughts, hoping she would absorb his mood. Her eyes gentled, no longer wide with fear, and lightened to their normal color. He felt her thoughts begin to line up in an orderly progression, before they slipped behind her own mental wall.

"Satisfied?" he asked.

She nodded, and released the gown.

"All right, Ms. Morgan," the doctor said. "Time to get started. I'm going to give you the first shot of anesthesia now. You'll feel a little pin prick, but that's all."

Rebecca twisted her head to see what was happening behind her, but the nurse stopped her with a light touch.

"It's better if you don't turn and look."

Rebecca nodded, and focused her gaze on Desmond. When the doctor jabbed her hip with the first needle, her breath hissed out and she closed her eyes. But she quickly opened them and smiled grimly.

"That wasn't so bad."

Desmond smiled back, encouraging her, even though he wanted to leap up and throttle the doctor for hurting her. And it wasn't only because the sharp pain had knifed through his shields before he could block it.

In the face of her stoicism, any words of encouragement he could offer would be trivial. But maybe that was what she needed, trivial conversation to distract her from what the doctor was doing.

"Have you been to see the Painted Desert yet? The scenery is really quite remarkable."

She frowned, her forehead furrowing in confusion. Then her expression cleared and a radiant smile broke through, like the full moon coming out from behind a cloud. "No, not yet. I was planning to drive through it on my way up to Flagstaff, after I left here. I heard there's some sort of cathedral cut into the stone that's supposed to be very impressive."

They discussed banalities of travel and tourism, and she told him about the article she was writing. Through it all, he held her hand, giving her his physical support as he tried to keep his expression smiling and relaxed. He couldn't let her see any of his apprehension at the larger and larger needles being used by the doctor. Finally, Dr. Laurence picked up something that looked more like an awl than a needle, and interrupted their conversation.

"I'm about to go into the bone. You're going to feel a bit of pain, but it will be over quickly."

"How quick—Oh!" She clenched her hand, bruising Desmond's fingers, and the color drained from her face. She let out her breath in a sudden puff, her fingers tightening. Desmond's body would repair any damage she might inadvertently do, but in the meantime, it still hurt.

"Rebecca?" he whispered. He didn't want to disturb the doctor during the most delicate part of the operation. "Could you ease up a little on the grip?"

The color came back to her face, and she let go of his hand with a self-conscious laugh. "If that's a bit of pain, I don't want to know what you think a lot of pain is, doc."

"Well, it's all over now," Dr. Laurence reassured her, tying off the last of the bandage. "But I'd like to keep you here for observation. When the anesthetic wears off, we might need to give you something more for the pain."

"Keep me here? That's not part of the program. I'm supposed to be able to go home." She turned to Desmond, her expression just short of pouting. "You promised."

"It sounds like you'll just be here for a few more hours, until the anesthesia wears off. Right, Doctor?"

Desmond looked up at the doctor, certain his concern must show. She wasn't supposed to need observation. Not only that, but the

Institute stocked only two pain killers stronger than aspirin—codeine and morphine. If Dr. Laurence thought Rebecca might need some, he must expect her to be in considerable pain. What had gone wrong?

The doctor frowned and shook his head, unwilling to discuss whatever it was in front of Rebecca. Desmond barely controlled his impatience as they loaded a grumbling Rebecca into a wheelchair and rolled her down to the infrequently used rooms containing hospital beds. But he restrained himself, for her sake.

She settled into bed easily enough, and motioned Desmond to her side. "I didn't expect to be staying here for any length of time, or I'd have brought my work. Could you bring it back for me?"

And to think, people accused him of being a workaholic.

"Shouldn't you be resting, or recuperating?"

Rebecca dismissed those options with a snort. "I'd really rather not spend the next few hours staring at the ceiling, thank you. Although I would appreciate my morning coffee."

"I'll get your papers when I take Gillian home. In the meantime, Nurse Peters should be able to arrange for some coffee."

He flagged the nurse over. Leaving her to argue with Rebecca about the advisability of coffee so soon after her operation, he stepped outside to talk to Dr. Laurence.

"All right. What's the problem?" Desperate for answers, Desmond lowered his mental shields, hoping he could pick up some information that way.

"There's nothing to worry about, Mr. Lacroix," the doctor said, his arrogance lasting only until he saw Desmond's expression. Then he stepped back, sweat beading his forehead. *It's not my fault. He's going to blame me. He's going to cut my funding. It's not my fault....*

Slamming down his mental barriers, Desmond absorbed the moment of silence before he gave voice to the doctor's last thoughts. "I know something went wrong, but I won't blame you unless it was your fault. So tell me what really happened."

The doctor's eyes widened, and he stammered, "I d-did everything correctly. It wasn't a mistake on my part."

"If you did everything correctly, you have nothing to worry about. Now tell me what went wrong."

"Oh." The doctor passed a shaky hand through his hair. "I had trouble opening the bone to withdraw the marrow. It took three tries." Setting his jaw, he added, "I did say you should fly out to one of the cancer treatment centers that specializes in these transplants, instead of trying to do it here. They'd have had the equipment to deal with a contingency like that."

"She'll be all right, though, won't she?" Desmond fought back the urge to shake the answer loose. That would only scramble Dr. Laurence's thoughts worse than they were already.

"Yes. She'll probably hurt like hell, but other than that, the operation was a complete success. As far as complications go, it was a minor one. But painful. That's why I'm recommending keeping her on codeine until the worst of it is over."

"Do it then." Desmond used his command voice, refusing to let the doctor sidestep his next question. "Is there any possibility Gillian might have a similar complication?"

"No. Hers is a completely different procedure. It'll be just another shot."

"You're positive?"

Dr. Laurence shifted his weight from foot to foot, refusing to look Desmond in the eyes.

"Doctor," Desmond snapped, his voice jerking the man to full attention. "Is my daughter in danger?"

"There is always a possibility, with any kind of transplant, that the host body will reject the graft. We've taken every precaution, and type-matched Ms. Morgan's cells with your daughter's to minimize the risk. She's in more danger if she doesn't have the transplant."

Desmond nodded, letting the doctor relax. Finally, an answer he could use. He looked in the direction of the waiting area, where Philippe sat with Gillian. Did she understand anything of what was about to happen? Was she scared? He needed to be there with her, to comfort her. But he owed it to Rebecca to be with her, too. Torn, he took a single step toward the waiting room, then stopped.

"Go get the codeine," he told the doctor. "I'll tell Rebecca you'll be bringing it."

He'd tell Rebecca her medicine was coming, and make sure the nurse had brought her coffee. Then he'd go back to Gillian.

REBECCA STRUGGLED back to consciousness. Bits of dreams clung to her perceptions, but she shook them off. She lay on a firm mattress, with crisp new sheets below and above her. A thin foam pillow barely cushioned her head.

She opened her eyes, blinking to clear her vision. White walls, white sheets. The hospital. The operation must be over. But it was supposed to be outpatient surgery. Why was she in a hospital bed? And why did she feel so out of it?

"Rebecca?" Desmond's voice. To her left.

She turned her head, slowly. He sat by the side of her bed, looking out of place in an ugly plastic chair. She'd never seen him use anything but the best. He should be seated in one of those leather armchairs from his study. They suited him. Not ugly plastic. Then again, those plastic chairs didn't really suit anyone. Hospitals only used them to encourage visitors to leave quickly. She hoped he wouldn't leave quickly. She liked looking at him.

"How are you feeling?" His voice rumbled, reverberating in his chest. If she placed her hand against his chest, would she hear his voice through her hand? She remembered something about shock waves, and how they traveled through air and earth at different speeds. Would his voice through her hand match the voice she heard? Or would it be like a badly dubbed Japanese movie?

She smiled, and reached out a hand toward him. Or tried to, anyway. Her hand didn't seem to be obeying the orders of her brain. It flopped a little, but didn't come close to the graceful arc she'd envisioned. She tried again.

He slid his chair closer and enfolded her hand in his own. The warmth of his palms spread up her arm, and she curled her fingers around his.

"Doctor Laurence said you might be disoriented for a little while. And you may feel weak. But the operation was a success."

A success? Then why did she hurt so much? He must mean it was a success for Gillian. Gillian. Why wasn't Desmond at his daughter's bedside?

"Gillian," she croaked. Her mouth felt like it was lined in cotton, and her throat felt cracked and dry. Never mind the question. "Water."

Desmond let go of her hand to pour her a cup of water from the ewer on the bedstand. Perching on the edge of her bed, he put an arm around her shoulders and lifted her to a sitting position. With his arm a warm weight around her shoulders, he picked up the cup and guided it to her lips.

She reached up and rested her hands against his. Her muscles obeyed her directions now. But she didn't take the cup from him, she merely pressed his hand to tip it. The cool water poured into her parched throat, and she gulped it greedily. He tried to lower his hand, but she held tight, refusing to let him go.

When she'd drained the cup, she kept her hands around his. He radiated gentle warmth, soaking into her hands, her arms. Her shoulders and neck warmed beneath his touch. She wanted to absorb all of his heat, and melt her pain away.

He lifted the cup from her lips, and this time she let her hands drop away. But when he turned to place the cup on the bedstand, she stopped him before he could slip his arm from around her shoulders.

"No. Don't go just yet."

"Very well. But let me find a more comfortable way to sit." He swung his legs up onto the bed, leaned back against the headboard, and curled his arm more securely around her shoulders. She rested her head against this new and preferred pillow.

"Now, will you tell me what's going on? Why am I in the hospital?"

"You came in for the operation to donate bone marrow for Gillian."

"I know all that." She dismissed his answer with a wave. "I remember arguing with Nurse Peters over my coffee, and asking you to get my notes. Did you get them?"

"Yes. They're on the table. And then?"

"Thank you. Anyway, then Doctor Laurence said he was giving me a little something for the pain. Next thing I know, I'm out cold."

"It seems the good doctor erred on the side of comfort, and overmedicated you. You slept all afternoon and straight through the night."

"Huh. I don't think he's a very good doctor, then."

He refused to comment, instead changing the subject.

"You asked about Gillian," he reminded her. "Her part of the procedure was much easier, a simple injection. Once they were sure she wasn't going to react to it, they sent her home."

"How come you aren't home with her?" She liked having Desmond warm and close beside her, but under the circumstances, he probably shouldn't be here. She inhaled the earthy tang of his cologne, and studied the hint of shadow along his jaw. No, he definitely shouldn't be here. She hoped he wouldn't leave.

He chuckled, a rich rumble that tickled her ear and vibrated through her from their connection.

"Mrs. Waters decided to celebrate by baking chocolate chip cookies with Gillian. They haven't forgotten the disaster I created the last time I tried to help bake, and banished me as far from the cookies as they could." He turned to her, his lips inches from her face. She wished he'd close the distance between them, and claim her mouth with his own. The memory of their explosive earlier kiss filled her thoughts, blocking out everything else.

Desmond's voice recalled her to the present. "I can never thank you enough for what you've done."

Reliving that kiss would be thanks enough. She lifted her gaze from his lips, to find him staring into her eyes. As if he'd read her thoughts, he dropped his gaze to her lips. If she didn't stop him, he would kiss her. Her world seemed to pause, and everything hung in the balance.

Nothing could come of deepening their relationship. He wouldn't leave his Institute. And she had her career. They'd probably never even see each other again. But as she'd told him, no one could ever really know the future. And as long as there was a possibility for a future between them, her choice was clear. She parted her lips in invitation.

He leaned over her, his hand at her waist, and bent his head. When he touched his lips to hers, an electric thrill coursed through her.

She leaned into him and returned his kisses, flames licking her senses. He tasted of shadow and mystery, a tantalizing familiarity she almost recognized. She opened her mouth, hungry for a deeper kiss, but he pulled away.

Passion flushed his face, making his eyes seem almost to glow. When he spoke, his voice had a husky sound that sent shivers of desire chasing across her skin.

"I want you, too. You're making it hard to think of anything else. But this isn't the time—"

"The nurse?"

"Won't be back for hours."

"Doctors? Other patients?"

"Deserted. Not even monitors."

"So...?"

She pulled his head down for another kiss, cutting off his answer. Twining her fingers in his thick curls, she pressed her lips against his, hard. Harder. She wanted no boundaries. She wanted to breathe his breath and fuse their spirits. She wanted to be one with him.

A faint tremor shook him, and he almost pulled away. Instead, he surrendered to her kiss. He slid his lips to the corner of her mouth, pressing a light kiss there, then started a nibbling, kissing exploration along her jaw. She closed her eyes and smiled, reveling in the sensations he sparked. It felt like a parade of butterflies brushing against her skin. Warm, moist butterflies, with lascivious intent.

He guided her back down onto the bed, so she rested on her uninjured hip. She snuggled closer, wrapping her arms around him. When he found the opening of her hospital gown and slid one hand beneath the flimsy cotton, she moaned with pleasure. His touch felt so right.

She tugged at his shirt, hungering to touch him the way he was touching her. He rubbed her back and shoulders with warm strokes, pressing the tender tips of her breasts against his firm chest. She sighed and gave up her efforts at loosening his shirt, instead focusing on the hot rush of pleasure flowing from his hand.

With his other hand, he brushed the hair from her eyes, sweeping around her brow and cheekbones in a soft caress that made her feel as pampered and adored as a Siamese. She nestled her face into his hand, pressing kisses against his palm and the pulse point of his wrist. He caught his breath sharply, then let it out on a shaky moan.

"Rebecca," he whispered, his ragged breath hot and moist against her skin. "I don't want to hurt you."

She laughed, deep in her throat. As if the pain mattered. All she cared about now was getting closer to him. She wanted to feel his bare skin against hers, hot and slick with passion. She wanted to feel his strength as he plunged into her. And she wanted to blur the edges of their identities, so that for a brief moment, they would become one.

She arched against him, pressing her hips against the swelling evidence of his desire, and breathed into his ear, "Nothing could hurt me now."

With a harsh sound, equal parts moan and growl, he claimed her ear, nipping and sucking the lobe. She felt him struggle to pull aside the sheet pinned between them. He could've removed it easily if they weren't pressed so tightly against each other, but neither of them would back away.

Her hands ached to feel the silky heat of his skin beneath them, and she yanked his shirt free from his pants. Sliding her hands up beneath the fabric, she caressed the length of his back, each stroke pressing them closer together. He arched his head back with a cry of delight, and she followed up her advantage by pressing kisses on the exposed skin of his neck. She tasted his spicy-sweet cologne, and the salty moisture of his aroused sweat. But mostly, she tasted the musky, rich flavor of him.

She swept her tongue across his neck, following a bead of sweat, then pressed a hungry kiss to the spot just below the pulse point where it lingered.

He trembled beside her, his breathing coming in short gasps. She heard fabric tear—the sheet? Her hospital gown? His clothes? She didn't care. Neither did he.

He pulled off his shirt, ripping it in his haste. Her flimsy gown shredded beneath his hands. They pressed together, skin to skin, rapidly beating heart to rapidly beating heart. It still wasn't enough. He kicked off his shoes, and she helped push his pants away.

He rolled over, lifting her above him, and settled her against the strength of his arousal. He captured her lips in a savage kiss, all heat and explosive desire, and she opened her mouth, drawing him in, welcoming their union.

His tongue plunged into her open mouth, tasting her, caressing her. She pulled, demanding more. She dug her fingers into his back, fusing herself to him. He answered her demands, wrapping his arms around her in a tight embrace and thrusting his tongue deeper.

More. She needed more. She needed him.

Anticipating her request, he slid his hands down to her hips. The tips of his fingers brushed the edge of her bandage, and he paused, twisting his head aside. His hesitancy struck her like an arctic wind, and she shivered with need. Bracing her weight on her hands, she lifted her hips and pressed herself against the heat of his arousal, rubbing against him when he still lingered.

"You're sure?" He had barely enough breath to talk, his words little louder than a thought.

She moved against him, letting her actions speak for her, but he refused to go on until she answered him in words. "I'm sure. You won't hurt me."

He thrust into her, pulling her down in a shattering explosion of heat and light. She wouldn't let him take the time to go gently, grinding against him and clutching him deep within her. Darkness filled her vision, but she didn't care, straining toward a blinding light.

He glided his lips over her neck, nipping and sucking in the same pounding rhythm. He touched the pulse at the side of her neck and she moaned in ecstasy. It was if her soul were leaving her heart and being drawn directly to his lips. She'd never experienced anything like it.

Tremors shook her body, and with heart and soul, she reached for him. Sensations flooded her. His hard strength filled her, and she pulsed and clenched over his arousal. She felt his lips, moist on her neck, and also her sweet warmth against his tongue.

She arched, every muscle straining for release. He thrust one last time, lifting her with the force of his stroke, and hot fire filled her. Like a wildfire burning out of control, a rush of thoughts and feelings swept over her, consuming her in a blaze of passion. She spun into space, whole galaxies whirling past her in a crazy dance. And amid all the light and movement, one sun burned brighter than all the rest. Desmond. With him as her lodestar, she found her way home.

"REBECCA?" DESMOND'S out-of-focus face peered down at her. He brushed his hand across her cheeks and forehead in a lingering caress. She blinked rapidly to clear her vision, and focused on his face.

Desmond breathed a fervent, "Thank the gods." Then he gently kissed the corners of her eyes. "You gave me one hell of a scare. I didn't know what I'd done to you."

He didn't know what he'd done? A sleepy smile pulled at the corners of her lips. If he didn't know, she couldn't tell him. She had no words to describe the wave of emotion that swept through her at their union. She'd never experienced anything like it before, and still felt shaken by its power.

"Thank you," she whispered. He had to know what she meant. He couldn't have rocked her to her very foundation without feeling something, too.

"Marry me," he answered. His eyes glowed with an echo of the light that had blinded her, and moisture glimmered in their corners. He'd been as affected by their lovemaking as she had.

"I'll take that as a compliment."

"I mean it." He cupped her chin in his hand and looked deeply into her eyes. "Marry me."

His sincerity stunned her. People just didn't propose marriage to relative strangers, no matter how incredible they were together. If she'd succumbed to momentary insanity by making love with him, what sort of madness prompted his suggestion? She had to reintroduce a dose of reality to this conversation.

"We hardly know each other."

"I know you more deeply than I've ever known anyone. And you know me more than you'll admit." His velvet voice caressed each word, blanketing the statement in sexual innuendo. Rebecca tore her gaze from the hypnotic intensity of his eyes. Desmond Lacroix might be many things, but she'd never yet known him to be obvious. His words couched a deeper, hidden meaning. She was sure of it. But the way her wits had been scattered by their lovemaking, she couldn't puzzle it out.

"What are you talking about?"

"I'm talking about this." He bent his head and kissed her, a slow, lingering kiss that roused the banked embers of her passion. Scant minutes after the most profound lovemaking she'd ever experienced, she ached for his completion again. But she refused to be distracted.

"I know *that*. But what else were you talking about?"

"Rebecca." He pushed himself away, to gaze sternly at her. "There is a time and a place to be a reporter. This isn't it."

"But I—"

He silenced her with a kiss. By the time he lifted his lips from hers, she'd become lightheaded. But she persevered.

"What I—"

He dropped another kiss onto her open lips. "No." A kiss. "More." A deeper kiss. "Questions." A kiss that seemed to reach into her very soul.

Closing her eyes and sighing, she abandoned her questioning. She couldn't recall what was so important, anyway. Nothing mattered except Desmond, and what was happening between them right now.

He rearranged the blanket and pillows so that she nestled in a cloud of softness that supported her but still left her open for his advances. Leaning over her, he kissed and caressed her face, her breasts, her neck, her shoulders, until she thought she'd go mad from wanting him. His nearness tantalized her, but every time she reached for him, he shifted out of her way and continued his patient exploration. Giving up, she relaxed and let him have his way.

Chapter 9

DESMOND WATCHED Rebecca's eyes flutter closed, a gentle half-smile sweetening her expression. The first time they'd made love, she'd surprised him by reaching out to him with her fledgling telepathic gifts. He'd felt the connection too late to prevent his own surge of power from sweeping through her. The backlash could have killed her, unaccustomed to psychic powers as she was. This time, he intended to give her pleasure without the danger.

He glided a caress down her arm, following it with feather light kisses. He lingered over the sensitive skin of her inner elbow, his tongue flicking out in a Morse Code message of submission and arousal. All the time, he listened to the constant whirl of her surface thoughts, punctuated by soft whimpers and moans.

When she balanced on the edge of agony and ecstasy, he broke off to trail kisses down to her hand. He nuzzled her palm, and took each finger into his mouth to suck lightly before moving on. He sensed her pleasure, but there were other things she'd enjoy more.

He lavished attention on her breasts, kneading them gently, then covering them with kisses. She whimpered, low in her throat, and he felt himself swelling in sympathetic arousal. Thoughts and images cascaded through his mind, but they were not his.

Trembling, he struggled for control. He finally managed to separate her thoughts from his, while still leaving his mind completely open to her. He'd never lowered his defenses so thoroughly before, but that was the only possible way he could detect a gathering of her telepathic power before she used it.

He swept his tongue over her already sensitized nipple, shivering as her pleasure flowed over him. She arched her back and buried her hands in his hair, drawing him closer. The turbulent wash of images strengthened, drawing his mind closer to hers as well.

They were too close. He pulled free of her mental hold, then reached up and untangled her physical clinch. He guided her hands back down to the bed.

"Lie back. Relax."

For once she didn't argue with him, simply relaxing and trusting him to give her pleasure. He did. With his mental defenses down, he felt the building waves of desire as he caressed her stomach, pressed gentle kisses across her hips, and parted her legs. When he brushed his fingertips lightly across her, her pleasure and need rocketed to new heights.

He lifted his head, his breathing ragged, and admired her taut body, glazed with a sheen of sweat. Her fists clenched the pillow beneath her hips, and her head lashed from side to side in time to her soft moans. A wild hunger filled him, but he fought to master it. He couldn't give in to the hunger. Not yet.

His arousal pressed against her, and her need sliced through him. Abandoning her passive role, she grabbed his buttocks and pulled him forward as she arched beneath him. He slid inside her, feeling himself fill her. They cried out together. It was everything, but it wasn't enough.

She moaned, moving beneath him.

"Sh. You'll hurt yourself."

"But I want you."

"Then you shall have me. But gently."

He flexed his hips, moving within her, and she gasped his name. Her nails dug into his back as she urged him onward, but he refused to be rushed.

Beads of sweat ran down from his forehead, stinging his eyes. He blinked, unwilling to close his eyes and shut out the sight of her, flushed with passion.

"Please, Desmond. Now."

He slid most of the way out of her. She whimpered, and pierced his back with her nails, driving him forward to fill her again. They sighed as one.

He withdrew, the momentary separation a painful ache until he thrust into her again. The heated slide of flesh inside flesh threatened to send him over the edge, torturing him with her mounting passion as well as his own. But her newly awakened mental powers stayed unused.

His next stroke plunged deeper, the one after that deeper still. She writhed and moaned beneath him, an aching void ready for his fulfillment, her mind a whirling maelstrom of power. He thrust again, touching the heart of her. He recognized the first feather touch of a telepathic connection in his mind, then all hell broke loose.

She spasmed, shaking with the intensity of the pleasure that ripped through her. His body arched, finding its own pleasure, but his mind was lost in the waves of ecstasy flowing over him. They climaxed again, their shared passion tearing them apart and putting them together again in a blinding flash of light.

He collapsed on top of her, straining to breathe. Multicolored spots whirled in front of his eyes, and she clutched him in a bear hug. Aftershocks rocked through him, or her, or them. He couldn't tell where she ended and he began. It wasn't possible to be so close to another person, but he was, and he never wanted it to end.

"Oh, God," he panted. "Rebecca. Marry me."

"Yes."

He couldn't live without her. She couldn't live without him. They were soul mates, completion.

He pressed a kiss to her lips, hard enough to draw blood. But she didn't mind. A gentle kiss couldn't do justice to the awesome power of their union.

When he pulled away, they were both breathless. He shifted his weight off of her, curling up against her side, and pulled the sheet back over them. Without their passion to support it, her telepathic link faded, leaving him aching for that unity of spirit. But she had the gifts. All she needed was the training.

He dusted caresses over her shoulder and arm, unwilling to relinquish their bond. She sighed, then ruined the effect by yawning.

He smiled at her, filled with a joyous light that demanded an outlet. Bending his head, he kissed her nose. "Somehow, I don't think this is what the doctors meant when they said you should stay in bed and rest."

"I won't tell them if you won't." She snuggled closer and buried her face in the hollow of his neck. He breathed deep, reveling in the warm feel of her tucked against him, and stirred against her.

He rubbed her back, long soft strokes that soothed and relaxed her.

"Try to get some rest. Or I won't be able to visit you again."

His threat worked. She closed her eyes, and drifted into slumber a few minutes later.

He watched her sleep, smiling at her complete trust. She knew nothing of telepathy, or mental powers, and had no idea what they'd just done. If he tried to explain, she'd think he was lying, or insane.

The explanations could wait. So far, she'd only used her burgeoning telepathic powers during the pinnacle of sexual experience. He needn't worry about her accidentally touching other people's minds.

He dropped a light kiss on her temple, and felt a flutter in his own mind. He stopped. Closing his eyes, he turned his attention inward, to the telepathic union they'd shared. She'd left the mental connection wide open.

Curious, he followed the connection into her dreams. She was replaying their recent lovemaking. He smiled as he retreated, withdrawing his consciousness back into his own mind.

As soon as his thoughts were wholly his own, he began to worry. Without shielding in place, she could unknowingly broadcast her thoughts. Worse yet, she could be prone to mistaking others' thoughts as her own. He would protect her when they were together, but he needed to start training her as soon as possible.

He closed his eyes, dreaming of Rebecca as a trained telepath, and the ecstasy they could share. Now he recognized the feeling her kisses inspired, the feeling he hadn't been able to name before. It had been the merest hint of this profound union. While they made love, he'd actually lost his mind for a moment. She surrounded him, filled him. He was nothing without her.

He had to have her by his side always. It wasn't love. It was more primal than that. He needed her. She was his other half. And he would never let her leave him.

DESMOND WOKE to Nurse Peters's startled gasp. She stood in the doorway, her mouth rounded in a comical "O" of disbelief.

He couldn't stop an idiotic grin from covering his face. "You may be the first to congratulate us. We're to be married."

She blinked, assimilating that fact, then smiled broadly at the pair in the bed. "Congratulations. But Ms. Morgan needs her rest."

"Of course." Desmond turned to Rebecca, or where she'd been until the nurse arrived. A huddle of blankets confronted him. His bride-to-be was shy.

"Rebecca. Darling. If Nurse Peters was going to censure anyone, it would be me. So poke your head out and accept her congratulations."

Rebecca mumbled ascent and pushed aside the sheet, revealing her crimson face.

"Thank you," she said softly. But her internal monologue carried clearly to him. *How could I be so swept away by passion that I'd agree to something so stupid? This is all a terrible mistake.*

The shock snapped his mental shields up, cutting off Rebecca's unwanted revelations. Second thoughts? They were perfect for each other. She had to see that.

A chill premonition doused the lingering warmth of his happiness. She'd already proved how far she was willing to go in order to escape from situations she found untenable. If she felt that way about their engagement, she might take desperate steps to correct the situation. He couldn't risk losing her.

"Mr. Lacroix?" Nurse Peters asked. "Is something wrong?"

"I just realized that I'll be separated from my fiancee when I go home to look after Gillian. Is there any reason why she can't be released now? I promise I'll look after her very well."

"We have to talk," Rebecca whispered.

"I'll check with the doctor," the nurse answered, gifting them with a knowing grin, "but I'm sure there won't be any problem. In fact, I'll go get him now, and be back in a few minutes."

She hurried from the room, rattling the door knob after she left to make sure the door closed securely.

"I believe that's my cue to get dressed," Desmond said, slipping out from beneath the covers without touching Rebecca. He gathered up his clothing, putting it on as he found it. Although his shirt had lost two buttons during their frenzied disrobing, he'd lost his soul during the aftermath, the first time they'd made love. That loss couldn't be put right with a tailor's needle.

Rebecca didn't say a word during his search, didn't even look at him. She disappeared under the covers, resurfacing with the hospital gown crumpled in her hand.

"I can't wear this. It's torn."

"Nurse Peters hung your clothes in the closet. I'll get them for you."

"Just the shirt should be fine."

He opened the closet door and pulled out her shirt, the soft cotton reminding him of the way her hospital gown felt as it parted beneath his hands. He could convince her of their rightness for each other if he made love to her again. But there had to be a way to convince her when she wasn't half mad with pleasure, some argument that her rational reporter's brain would accept.

"Here you go." When he handed her the shirt, his fingers brushed hers in a soft caress. She snatched her hand away as if he'd burned her.

"Thank you." She waited, glaring at him. "Well? Aren't you going to turn around?"

"Rebecca, I just kissed every inch of you. There is no reason on earth for you to be bothered by my seeing you."

"You took advantage of me." Her soft voice chilled him, a finger of doubt insinuating itself deep into his heart. Then his anger flared up to burn away his fears.

"And how did I do that? I told you I wanted to wait, for fear of hurting you. You're the one who insisted."

"That wasn't me. It was the drugs."

"Liar. You wanted us to make love as much as I did. If you're upset now, it's because you wanted sex with no strings attached."

He stepped closer to her bed, hands clenched and telepathic powers gathered in readiness for a battle on both fronts. Anger stained her cheeks brilliant scarlet, and the sheet fell forgotten around her waist.

"Why, you—" She raised her arm, her hand open to slap him. She surged forward, then fell back with a cry, her eyes screwed tight against the pain.

"Rebecca!" His anger disappeared, drowned in a sea of cold fear. If she'd injured herself because of him....

"I'm fine," she whispered through clenched teeth.

"I'm sorry. Whatever you want is acceptable to me."

"About time."

"Just promise me you won't do anything rash."

"Oh, you mean like agreeing to marry someone I barely know? Okay. I won't."

"No. I meant things that would hurt you." He meant physical pain. But where did one kind of pain leave off and another begin? He didn't want to hurt her in any way. After what they'd just experienced, he knew separation would hurt her. But he couldn't make that decision for her. He couldn't play it safe and back away from the point, either, or she'd never trust him again. He had to go for it, and believe in the strength of their connection.

He took a deep breath. "If that's what you decide you want, I'll accept your wishes."

"You will?" She opened her eyes and looked at him. Pain and confusion clouded her eyes, and he longed to take her in his arms and console her. But he couldn't.

"I will. If what you really, truly want is to be left alone here, I'll tell the doctor that when he comes in. And then I'll go away and leave you alone."

She frowned. "I don't want to be alone. It's just...Everything's moving so fast."

"I don't want you to be alone, either." He took a chance and sat down on the side of her bed. She didn't tell him to get off. "Why don't we get to know each other, more slowly this time?"

"Yes." She nodded, a faint smile breaking through her restraint. "I'd like that. You can come here—"

"Here?" He may have promised to honor her decision, but he'd do his best to maneuver her into his way of thinking while she was still making up her mind. "I thought you'd want to get above ground as soon as you could."

"We're underground?" Her frightened gaze darted from side to side, as if she expected the earth to knock through the walls at any moment. He nodded. He hated himself for raising the specter of her fear to torment her, but he refused to be separated from her simply because she wanted to assert her independence. His need for her overcame such trivial concerns.

She picked up her shirt, and he helped her struggle into it. When she'd fastened it, she lay down and stared at the ceiling.

"In that case, I'd like to leave as soon as the doctor says I may," she said.

"If that's what you want, that's what we'll do."

The silence between them hadn't quite reached the point of being painful, when Doctor Laurence knocked and entered the room. He hesitated when he spotted Desmond's protective position by Rebecca's side. When Desmond did not comment on Rebecca's long sleep, or accuse him of any medical mistakes, the doctor advanced and picked up Rebecca's hand to take her pulse.

"How are you feeling?"

"Fine. When I don't move too quickly."

"Any throbbing, pulsing or burning sensations?"

Rebecca flushed, and shook her head, "No. Just a sharp twinge if I sit up or turn to the side."

Doctor Laurence nodded, and turned to include Desmond in his answer. "That's normal. Move slowly, and try to avoid bending too far. Especially, avoid any twisting motion. You need to immobilize those muscles over your hip as much as possible."

"For how long?" Desmond asked.

"You can add movement gradually, a little more each day. If it hurts, stop. Within a week or so, you should be able to resume your regular routine."

"So there's no reason I can't leave the hospital?"

"Leave?"

"She means leave the hospital room," Desmond clarified. "I thought she'd be more comfortable upstairs."

"Of course. As long as she stays quiet and someone looks in on her every so often, there's no problem." He turned to face Rebecca. "I'll give you some tablets, in case the pain gets to be too much for you."

Doctor Laurence fetched the wheelchair they'd used to transport Rebecca to the hospital room, while Desmond helped her finish dressing. The wheelchair arrived just as he finished, and Desmond carefully transferred her from the bed to the chair. Doctor Laurence fussed and frittered over Rebecca, until she slapped her hand against the armrest on the wheelchair and snarled, "Enough already! In case you didn't realize it, this is *not* a comfortable position. Get the hell out of my way so I can lie down someplace!"

The doctor leaped aside, leaving the door clear for Desmond to push Rebecca out in a grand exit. He rolled her through the Institute's wide corridors, blessing his foresight in having Evan clear the route. They saw no one.

He parked her wheelchair in the miniature park nearest the stairs to his apartment.

"Why are we stopping?" she asked.

"My apartment is not handicapped accessible."

"But you promised." Her plaintive tone wasn't quite a whine.

"I know. And you'll be able to stay there. It just means I'll have to carry you upstairs." He wished he could dwell on the erotic possibilities of having her captive in his arms. But the possibilities for jostling or bumping her and aggravating her injury loomed too darkly.

"Carry me? Up all those stairs?"

"Yes," he said, wounded pride making him brusque. Did she think he was a weakling, incapable of carrying her?

He reached into his pocket and yanked out his keycard. "Here. I'll have my hands full, so you'll have to open the doors. Just run the card through, top to bottom, with the magnetic strip on the left. Think you can do that?"

He handed her the card, distracting her for the crucial moment while he lifted her into his arms and shifted her hip muscles. She continued to turn the card over in her fingers, examining it, as he carried her to the door.

"Any time now," he reminded her. "You aren't exactly a bag of feathers, you know."

She held the keycard just above the scanner. "If you're trying to say I'm too heavy for you, maybe you should put me down and ask for Evan's help. I'm sure he wouldn't have a problem."

"That's not what I meant at all. I doubt you're more than a hundred pounds, sopping wet." He'd forgotten how touchy women could be about their weight. Especially since Olivia had needed to be reassured she wasn't too thin.

His arms tightened around Rebecca. He wasn't going to lose her, too. He couldn't.

REBECCA TRIED to ignore the feel of Desmond's arms around her, behind her back and beneath her legs. She tried to pretend the arm she'd wrapped around his shoulders encircled nothing more exciting than a fence post. But no post ever felt so warm and alive, or sent electric charges through her at their contact. Even something as inconsequential as his hair, brushing back and forth across the skin of her arm as he turned his head, tickled her with ripples of desire.

His heart beat steadily beneath her. Each strong thump vibrated her skin, echoing along her ribs where they rested against his chest. No, her weight didn't inconvenience him in the least. She was having more trouble breathing normally than he was.

They came out onto the landing in front of his door, and Rebecca placed the keycard into the scanner. But she couldn't bring herself to trigger the door. When the door opened, Desmond would carry her inside. He'd carry her across the threshold. Even though he'd promised to go along with her wishes and forget she'd agreed to marry him, the action seemed too symbolic.

Had he really said he'd forget about the marriage proposal? She replayed their conversation in her head. No. He'd agreed to respect her decision, then steered the conversation until her decision had been whether or not she wanted him to leave the hospital room. She'd naturally assumed he'd carry over respect for her decision to include the whole situation, but experience was making her cautious where Desmond was concerned. He probably still meant to hold her to her acceptance.

She pulled the keycard away from the scanner.

"Put me down. I want to walk in."

"What?"

"You heard me. I want to walk."

"Rebecca." She recognized that tone. Her demand had caught him by surprise, but now he was going to try and reason with her. Well, she had her reasons, and she was going to walk. "You heard the doctor. You're supposed to rest."

"He said rest as much as possible. That's different. If you want, you can carry me again once we're inside. But I want to enter the apartment under my own power."

He studied her face, then asked softly, "This is important to you, isn't it?"

"Yes."

"All right, then. But as soon as you're through that door, you stop and let me carry you again. Agreed?"

"Agreed." She didn't want to walk the rest of the way. Her painkillers must be wearing off, because getting dressed had been painful enough. Walking would be agony. But she could manage a few steps. That's all she'd need.

Desmond set her down, careful not to jostle her or move too quickly. Then he plucked the keycard out of her fingers, and triggered the door.

"I'll go in first, in case—"

"Daddy!" Gillian yelled as soon as Desmond pushed open the door, running across the living room. When she saw Rebecca she stopped, her eyes going wide, and ducked behind the couch. She poked her face around the arm of the couch and stared at Rebecca. "Is she gonna die, Daddy?"

"No, honey." Desmond shot a worried look at Rebecca, as if his daughter might have picked up on something he'd missed. Then he hurried over to comfort Gillian, kneeling beside her. "She's just hurt. She had to have a shot."

Gillian nodded with a wisdom beyond her years. "Shots hurt."

"But after yesterday's shot, you won't need any more for a long, long time."

Gillian smiled. Rebecca took advantage of the distraction to make her way inside the apartment. She felt like a sailor who hadn't quite gotten his land legs back, and the fewer people who watched her shuffling walk, the better.

Desmond whispered something, and Gillian turned and ran back into the kitchen. Desmond smiled as the swinging door wafted the scent of chocolate chip cookies into the living room. He opened Rebecca's bedroom door and turned on the light before returning to her.

He scooped her off her feet smoothly, cradling her against his chest as he carried her to the bedroom. His action called to mind a variety of her fantasies, and she slanted a glance up at him. He grinned.

"This isn't the bedroom I'd like to be carrying you to. And I can think of much more pleasant activities to do in bed than rest." His grin faded, and his voice became earnest. "But you need to get well. That's the important thing. Can you grab the covers?"

She looked down. He held her over the bed, but if he put her down, she'd be on top of the covers. She reached out and flicked them aside, revealing clean sheets in a new striped pattern. Desmond lowered her into the bed without so much as a twinge of pain, and pulled the sheet and blanket over her.

"Do you want more pillows, so you can sit up a little?"

"No. I'm tired." The operation, followed by their enthusiastic lovemaking, had worn her out. By the time she managed to get ready for bed, she'd be exhausted. "Just hand me my nightshirt. I left it hanging in the closet."

He opened the closet, revealing only empty space.

"It's not there." He looked around, and pointed to the suitcase leaning against wall. "You must have packed it with the rest of your things."

She hadn't. And she'd left the suitcase in the closet, too. Mrs. Waters must have done it. The woman couldn't wait to be rid of her.

"Could you get it out, then?"

He ruffled through her clothing until he found the nightshirt. "Here it is."

She almost asked how he knew which T-shirt it was, until she remembered he'd come in to wake her up. Was it only yesterday morning? It seemed so long ago.

"Thank you."

"Rest well." He stroked a light caress along her jaw, trailing it down along her arm. Then he walked out and shut the door behind him.

She stared at the ceiling, her skin tingling where he'd touched her. How had she gotten herself into this predicament? And how on earth was she going to get herself back out?

She liked Desmond. She really did. Oh, he could be infuriatingly self-confident and arrogant. But he was also the sweetest, most considerate man she'd ever known. Except she didn't know him. Not really. And that was the problem.

Rebecca sighed, and wished she could turn over and plump up the pillow. Lying in bed was going to get old quickly. Her cheeks heated as she remembered Desmond's comments, and their earlier lovemaking. There was no denying her attraction for him, or his for her. They made sparks like flint and steel whenever they touched. But that was no basis for an enduring relationship.

Her mother had proved how foolish pinning your hopes to a dream could be. She'd had two years to get to know Rebecca's father, and still hadn't known him well enough to predict he'd desert her.

Rebecca recalled how devastated she'd felt, when she'd finally discovered the absent father she'd idolized all those years was nothing more than a figment of her mother's imagination. She could forgive her father for leaving, and her mother for inventing a new reality to replace the one that had treated her so poorly. But that didn't mean Rebecca wanted to go through that nightmare of heartbreak again. Not when she could avoid it by thinking with her head instead of her emotions.

Satisfied, she started to undo her shirt. *Desmond's not like that. He'd sacrifice anything for his family.* She stopped with the shirt half unbuttoned. Where had that thought come from? It had just appeared in her head, without warning, fully formed. Like her hunches when she was working on a story.

Rebecca closed her eyes and concentrated. Her hunches were usually the product of her subconscious, sifting through clues and facts to produce theories. If she followed the threads of her thoughts, she could usually piece together enough supporting evidence to warrant trusting her hunch. So what had triggered this hunch?

Gillian, obviously. Desmond's devotion to his daughter needed no clarification. But that wasn't enough. How had she made the leap from *daughter* to *family*, and from *devotion* to *sacrifice*? Something more. Something she was missing.

Had Desmond mentioned any family? No, it was something else. She remembered Dr. Chen's mention of the changed research. That must have been what triggered her hunch.

But now that she considered it, she wondered what research they had been doing originally. What disease did Desmond suffer from? And most importantly, how did he come to be the director of a secret research facility that specialized in that condition?

Chapter 10

PHILIPPE WAITED until Desmond closed the study door before asking, "How's Gillian?"

"She's doing well. I'm watching for signs that her health is improving, even though I know it's too early for the transplant to have taken effect." Anxious father that he was, he'd even imagined evidence. But he knew better than to tell Philippe that. He leaned against the edge of his desk, and tried to look casual. "The transplant itself went smoothly. For Gillian, at least."

"I heard." Philippe settled into one of the leather chairs and crossed his leg comfortably. "How's Rebecca doing?"

"As well as can be expected, given the circumstances."

"Which means?"

Desmond chuckled. "It means she's as obstinate and strong-willed as ever, and likely to drive herself and everyone around her insane if she has to remain in bed for too long. Other than that, she's recovering nicely."

"If she'll be bedridden for at least a few more days, why do you want Evan and me to fetch her car tonight?"

"I don't just want the car retrieved. Bring it to the airport and leave the keys in the all-night drop box."

"Take the car to the airport?" Philippe uncrossed his legs and leaned forward. "Why not just bring it here?"

Desmond frowned. Philippe didn't question his judgment this much on other matters. But when it concerned Rebecca, Philippe doubted Desmond's every decision.

When Desmond didn't answer, Philippe prodded, "Won't it be easier to let her return it when she gets her flight out? It will only be a few more days."

"No, it won't. She's decided to stay."

"She's staying." Philippe shook his head, as if his ears were playing tricks on him. "Even though all she's wanted to do the whole time she's been here was get out? She's changed her mind?"

"Apparently." Rebecca had fallen asleep by the time he'd brought her dinner in, so they hadn't been able to discuss every detail. She hadn't explicitly said she planned to stay, but how could they get to know each other better if she left? "I asked her to marry me, and she said yes."

"You *what?*" Philippe leapt out of his chair. "That's crazy! I know you're grateful to her for helping Gillian, but isn't marriage a bit extreme?"

"That's not it at all."

Philippe gripped Desmond by the shoulders, and stared into his face. "You're not taking Dr. Chen's suggestion seriously, are you? Having a child with her to get a donor for Gillian?"

"Don't be ridiculous." Desmond thrust his arms up, breaking Philippe's hold. "I know you can't understand this, but I've never felt anything like what I feel for Rebecca."

Desmond smiled, remembering the bond between them. He didn't have the words to do the feeling justice, but he tried to explain it to Philippe anyhow. "She's like my other half, sharing my thoughts, my desires. I think we could be happy together. It's not impossible, Philippe. I need to give it a chance."

"Uh-huh. Tell me, in all this sharing, did you happen to tell her about your curse?"

Philippe's words destroyed Desmond's wistful mood. Philippe was too blinded by his own bitterness to listen to anything he said. Fine. He wouldn't waste any more time trying to convince him.

But the worries raised by Philippe's question made Desmond answer more sharply than he intended, "It hasn't come up yet, no."

"It's never going to just *come up*. Voodoo isn't generally a topic of casual conversation. How many cocktail parties have you been at where people say, 'These canapés are lovely. By the way, are you cursed?'"

Desmond turned away in disgust, but Philippe grabbed his shoulder and jerked him back around.

"Damn it, Des. You can't hide your head in the sand on this. Think."

"About what?" Desmond clenched his fists, struggling to keep his temper. They'd only just repaired their friendship. Another fight might drive his half-brother away for good.

"About Olivia."

Desmond froze, Philippe's words catching him by surprise. Philippe stepped back, nodding, certain now that he had Desmond's attention.

"What about Olivia?" Desmond asked.

"How long were you married?"

"Five years." Desmond didn't like the self-satisfied smirk on Philippe's face, especially since Philippe had argued against Desmond's first marriage, too. What sort of underhanded trick was he trying to pull?

"Five years. And in five years of marriage, did you ever tell her you were cursed?"

"No."

"You didn't only not tell her. You went out of your way to conceal the fact. You disguised your needs. You explained away your reluctance to go out in the sun."

Desmond nodded impatiently. He knew all that. But he'd had his reasons. Then Philippe sprung his attack.

"You let her die."

"No!" Desmond surged forward, forcing Philippe to backpedal. Then the thread of guilt felt by all survivors knotted around his heart and stopped him cold. Had he really done everything he could for Olivia? If he hadn't pressured her for a family, she wouldn't have been pregnant when she discovered her disease. Taking the treatments earlier might have saved her life. She'd refused to risk Gillian's life to save her own. How much had his outdated views, forged in the 1800s, influenced her choice?

He'd never know. They'd made the choices they believed in at the time. Once he'd found out about her illness, he'd done everything he could to save her. Everything she'd let him do. He had.

Desmond felt behind him for the desk, and sagged against it, speaking to himself as much as to Philippe. "It wasn't like that. By the time we found out she was dying, her disease was too advanced. I couldn't have saved her. I couldn't. Telling her at that point would have been cruel."

"You don't know that. Cursing her might have saved her. You weren't willing to take the chance. And why? Because on some level, you agree with me. You know what happens when a woman finds out that she's married to a freak of nature. And you preferred that she be in love with you and die, rather than have her hate you and live."

"No! Damn it, Philippe, I *loved* her!" If cursing her could have saved her, he would have offered to do it, no matter how repellent he found the idea. But it couldn't. He'd researched her form of leukemia enough to be sure of that. The cursed agents in her blood would have been killing off sickly cells as quickly as the diseased agents killed off the healthy ones. Not only that, but both agents worked to transform cells whenever possible. She'd have been reduced to a cellular-level battlefield. And like a battlefield in a nuclear war, it didn't matter which side eventually claimed victory. The field was destroyed.

That assumed the curse could even be transferred. Philippe had spent years trying to reconstruct his grandmother's magic. They knew the words of the curse, but without the rest of it, the sacrifices and invocations, they'd be guessing. The results would be completely unpredictable.

"I did everything I could, Philippe. You know I did." Desmond's anger burned with a white heat that blistered away any other considerations, as he finally said what he should have said a hundred years ago. "My father's lust and cowardice made you an orphaned bastard. As his only surviving heir, I had everything you didn't. But don't you think I'd have given up the plantation in an instant if it meant my brothers would come home from the war? That I would have sold all the jewelry if it could stop my sister from going to New Orleans that summer? That I would have willingly worked twenty hour days in the fields if it kept my mother from stepping in front of that coach?"

Desmond advanced on his half-brother, driving him across the room until he backed into the bookshelves. First editions tumbled to the floor at his feet.

"You're not the only one who lost someone you loved, Philippe. I will not continue to pay for my father's sins. He was your father, too. Bear your own guilt."

Philippe's eyes widened at the magnitude of his attack's backfire. But the genie had escaped, and nothing Philippe said or did could ever bottle it again.

"Des—"

"I'm through listening to you. Find Rebecca's car. Return it to the airport."

Philippe stayed silent for a long minute. When he finally spoke, his voice was laced with bitterness. "Yes, master. Whatever you say. Is there anything else this most lowly, humble servant can do for you?"

"You've done enough."

"Yes, master. At once. I live to serve you." Philippe stalked out of the room, slamming the door behind him. Desmond waited to hear the front door close before sinking down in the chair behind his desk and burying his face in his hands.

Was that it, then? One hundred and fifty years of friendship, gone, as if it had never happened?

Desmond rubbed his throbbing temples. He remembered the night Philippe came to the plantation, demanding to see Edouard Lacroix. Then his son, Etienne. His wife. When Desmond burst out, "They are dead. They are all dead, except for me," Philippe had stared into his eyes and answered, "Then you shall pay your father's debt."

Desmond sighed. He hadn't understood. He'd listened in horror as Philippe explained the curse, then tried to pay him off, tried to bribe the Voodoo gods. Philippe had laughed bitterly. "I suffered my whole life, and still I was cursed to feel my sons' deaths and watch my wife try to kill me. You've had everything. You could not begin to pay enough."

But Desmond had done what he could. He'd opened his home to Philippe, and they had become friends. Now he'd repaid Philippe's unswerving friendship over the years by turning on him. Philippe only wanted to protect him from suffering a betrayal similar to his own. Why had Desmond reacted so strongly? Philippe had given the same basic argument against marrying Olivia. What was it about Rebecca that made Desmond so unreasonable?

As much as he hated to admit it, he knew the answer. He'd loved Olivia. But he needed Rebecca in a way that went beyond love. He'd touched her soul when they made love, and knew she was the only woman who could ever be his true partner. No matter how many hundreds of years he lived, he'd never find anyone who matched him so equally. Unfortunately, that meant she was his equal in all ways, including the arrogant assumption that she knew best and the steely determination to follow through on her decisions. He had to find a way to convince her of how right they were for each other. But he feared she'd leave without ever giving him a chance to prove himself.

REBECCA REACHED for another sheet of paper from the stack at the foot of her bed. Lying on her stomach, with her notes and half-finished article spread around her, all she needed was a stick of chewing gum in her mouth and a telephone plastered to her ear to look exactly as she had in high school. It had taken her most of the morning, but now that she'd found a comfortable position to work in, she didn't care what she looked like.

A quiet knock on the bedroom door interrupted her train of thought, and she put down her pen.

"Come in."

The door opened a few inches, but she couldn't see anyone on the other side. Then she looked down. Gillian's face peered through the opening.

"Come in, Gillian."

Gillian nudged the door open further, but stayed in the doorway. "Daddy says you're sick."

She wasn't sick. She was recovering from an operation. But would a three-year-old understand the difference? She had no idea. She'd never had much experience with kids. It was probably best to follow Desmond's lead.

"Yes, that's right. I'm sick."

Gillian nodded. "Daddy's worried. He worries when I'm sick, too."

"There's no need to worry. I'll be fine."

Gillian frowned. Obviously, that was the wrong thing to say. This was the girl's first overture of friendship, and Rebecca didn't want to ruin it. But what else should she say?

"It's kind of your father to worry about me."

Gillian smiled and nodded again. Rebecca had hit on the right answer. Pushing the door all the way open, Gillian entered the room and held out a coloring book.

"Daddy gave me this when I was sick."

"It's lovely." Rebecca smiled admiringly at the coloring book. Gillian shook her head, raven curls bouncing with her frustration, and pushed the book closer.

"No. You take it."

"Thank you." Rebecca reached out and took the coloring book, winning a smile from Gillian. "But don't you want it?"

"No." Gillian waved her hand dismissively. The gesture, obviously copied from her father, reminded Rebecca of Desmond. Her chest tightened.

Gillian continued, "I'm all better. No more shots for me. You got shots. You got sick."

Rebecca doubted that's how Desmond explained it, but Gillian obviously believed the reason she didn't need to take medicine any longer was because Rebecca was taking it for her. Given her luck communicating with the girl so far, Rebecca wasn't about to try and correct her.

"Thank you. I'm sure I'll enjoy the coloring book."

Gillian turned to go, and Rebecca realized how lonely she'd been cooped up in her room.

"Gillian, wait. Will you stay for a little while and talk to me?"

She considered, then smiled radiantly. She'd be as much of a heartbreaker as her father when she grew up. "Okay."

"Great." Rebecca patted the bed. "Come sit up here."

Gillian hopped onto the bed, and immediately picked up the papers to look at. "What're you doing?"

"I'm writing an article. For a magazine." Gillian looked blank. Rebecca tried to recall any magazines she'd seen in the apartment, but there hadn't been any. Only books. She tried a different explanation. "A very tiny story, for a thin book."

Gillian hopped off the bed and ran out of the room. Rebecca stared after her in confusion, just as confused when the girl raced back into the room all out of breath. Then she saw the Big Little Book in Gillian's hand. Gillian clambered back up onto the bed and presented Rebecca with the book.

"Tiny story. Thin book."

"You're right. That's a tiny story in a thin book." Rebecca had better stop trying to explain things, or she'd end up totally confusing the poor kid. Then she had an inspiration. "Would you like me to read the story to you?"

"Yes, please." Gillian held out the book, and lay down on her stomach next to Rebecca so she could look at the pictures. Rebecca discovered reading the book consisted of equal parts reading the text, and asking Gillian questions about the pictures. If Rebecca didn't ask questions, or asked the wrong ones, Gillian would stop her and point out all the important things in the picture before letting her turn the page.

"That's the sun, and that's a tree, and that's grass, and that's the puppy, and that's a fence, and that's another puppy," Gillian said, pointing to each object in the picture. Then she looked up at Rebecca and said, "You're sick. You can't see them any more."

"You want me to stop reading to you?"

"No." Gillian shook her head and frowned at Rebecca's inability to grasp the obvious. Rebecca wondered if this was another mannerism she'd copied from Desmond. "You can't go outside. It's bad for sick people."

Rebecca darted a glance at the black glass window. In the few days she'd been here, she'd already adjusted to the odd lighting arrangement. Leaving the overhead light constantly on had become a reflex, and she no longer thought about the reasons behind her actions. There were so many more important things to wonder about, like her relationship with Desmond.

With the egocentricity of children, Gillian continued, "I can go out now. Daddy said so. Mrs. Waters is taking me next week. We're having a picnic."

"How nice for you. You'll like that." Rebecca let Gillian prattle on about her picnic, nodding when it seemed required. Sick people couldn't go outside. Gillian was going on her trip with Mrs. Waters, not Desmond. Why? The only answer that made sense was that he couldn't go with her. He was still sick, and could not venture outside.

Rebecca remembered her earlier conjecture, that much of the medicine stocked in the refrigerator belonged to Desmond. How sick was he? Was he dying? Is that why he was in such a hurry to get married?

"Gillian," Mrs. Waters called. "Time for lunch. Where are you?"

"Here!"

Mrs. Waters looked into the room, frowning at the sight that greeted her. She hustled over and grabbed Gillian by the arm, snatching up the book in her other hand.

"Ms. Morgan doesn't want to be bothered reading to you, Gillian."

"Oh, it was no trouble. I enjoyed it." Rebecca's smile faded beneath the other woman's stern glare.

"Come along, Gillian. It's time for your lunch. I've made you your favorite, grilled cheese. And for desert, animal crackers."

"Yummy!" Gillian hurried from the room. Mrs. Waters followed at a more sedate pace, pausing in the doorway to send a withering look over her shoulder at Rebecca.

"I'll see that she doesn't bother you again."

Before Rebecca could correct her, Mrs. Waters had closed the door. The housekeeper's words had all been perfectly correct, but her tone clearly warned Rebecca away from Gillian. Rebecca relaxed her arms and dropped face first into the covers. Mrs. Waters knew what had happened last night. She wouldn't allow her innocent young charge near such a scarlet woman, afraid of what unsavory attitudes Gillian might pick up.

Rebecca sighed, and twisted her head so that she could breathe. So far, only the housekeeper's reaction made any sense. The situation worried her, demanding an explanation she couldn't give.

Yes, she and Desmond had made love. And it had been wonderful. He'd transported her to a reality she'd never dreamed of. But in retrospect, she had trouble believing she'd been so carried away that she'd agreed to marry him. And lovemaking, no matter how wonderful, wasn't enough of a reason for a man to propose marriage. She could understand if he'd asked her to stay on as his lover. Or suggested they keep in touch, or visit each other. But not marriage.

No, the key piece of the puzzle remained a mystery. If only she could remember his exact words. They contained a clue. She was sure of it. But her memory blurred last night's images of passion into an impressionistic montage of ecstasy.

She sank into the memories, revisiting the heights to which he'd taken her. When she surfaced, she lacked any clearer view of the puzzle, but recalled all too clearly the feel of his hands and lips against her skin. Alone and lonely, she longed to see him.

The thought made her push herself into the closest approximation of a sitting position she could manage. Was that true? Did she really long to see Desmond again, not just because of the way they'd made love, but because she missed him? Somehow, despite her best intentions, she'd already started to rely on his quiet presence.

She remembered how frightened she'd been before the operation, and how she'd instinctively reached for his hand. The way she'd turned to him for comfort. Even how she'd readjusted her schedule for him, staying up later at night so she could talk with him after he'd put Gillian to bed.

That was wrong, all wrong. She'd learned from her parents' example, that trust too easily bestowed ended in betrayal. She'd promised herself not to fall into that trap, to enter every relationship with her eyes wide open and her partner's motivations clearly understood. For ten years she'd kept that promise. Now, she'd stumbled into a pit, and had no idea how to climb back out.

She should leave, before she started to trust Desmond. That way, he wouldn't have a chance to turn on her. The thought chilled her as completely as a spring downpour. Had she become so cynical, then, that she expected betrayal?

If only she understood him better. Unless she knew his position, unless she understood his reasoning, how could she trust him not to cast her aside? For all their talking, she knew nothing about him. Oh, she knew a few snippets of information about his past, like his father had died when he was very young, and he had a sister and a number of brothers, including his half-brother, Philippe. But he refused to speak of anything that happened between when he was a boy and the time when Gillian had been born.

He doesn't want to lie to you. The answer came to her in a flash of insight, the same way the answers to puzzling aspects of her articles often came to her. She'd learned to trust her insights, but still sought corroborating evidence. That's what she did now.

Casting her mind back over their conversations, she sifted through Desmond's words. He'd never lied to her. He'd given vague and ambiguous answers, or shifted the topic of conversation, but never outright lied to her. Rebecca shook her head. No. He never lied to her, that she knew of. That didn't mean he'd never lied. She hadn't suspected her mother's lie, either. His apparent truthfulness supported her insight, but it didn't prove it. She needed more, before she could trust him.

For instance, what secret was he hiding? It must be something big, for him to believe any mention of his adult years might reveal it. But other than that, any possible explanation could be nothing more than supposition on her part. She had no evidence, not even a clue as to what took place during those years.

Maybe she didn't need to know what had happened to him. Maybe it was enough to know he was hiding something from her. She'd ask him tonight, when he came home. If he refused to tell her, she'd know he couldn't be trusted.

DESMOND STRUGGLED through the pile of paperwork before him. He should have finished this hours ago, but he couldn't concentrate. Philippe had left the rental car receipt for him on his desk, avoiding a direct confrontation. He'd avoided Desmond's attempts to reach him all day.

Desmond didn't know what he would say to Philippe if they did see each other. A lot of pain and resentment could build up in a hundred years. Their argument last night had forced them to face the blight on their friendship, and Desmond's words had pierced the protective skin of denial covering the sore spot. But he'd be naive to think it would heal quickly. That would take much longer, if it happened at all.

And what about Rebecca? Had Philippe been right? Had Desmond's cursed blood led to Olivia's disease? The thought of Rebecca wasting away made Desmond's heart falter in its beat. He wouldn't let that happen.

A breath of cold wind wrapped around his soul. Olivia's cancer had been caused by a malfunction of her immune system. For some unknown reason, it overresponded to a simple cold, producing far too many white blood cells. The problem was compounded by the white blood cells themselves, a diseased variant that did not go away when the need for them was over. They filled her blood stream, preventing the red blood cells that carried nutrients and removed waste from doing their job. Or so it had been explained to him.

The doctors hadn't known of his special condition. He'd never thought to mention it. But what if her body had been fighting an infection? An infection caused by his cursed blood?

If his cursed blood could cause disease, there was no telling how small an amount of blood was necessary. But it would have to be caused by an exchange of actual blood. Unlike most diseases of the blood, an exchange of bodily fluids in general couldn't cause infection. If it could, Olivia would not have taken five years to become ill.

Desmond groaned. He would have to be very careful with Rebecca. He needed her, needed her passion, her strength. He couldn't bear the thought of living without her. But he couldn't bear the thought of risking her life, either.

It didn't matter that he found ecstasy in her arms. It didn't matter that making love with her transported him to another world. All that mattered was that he couldn't endanger her. He couldn't let himself make love with her again. Ever. He prayed that would be enough, and that he hadn't already infected her.

Chapter 11

REBECCA ADDED the finishing touches to her article and read it over one more time. Perfect. Now she could devote her attention to planning the most important interview she'd ever done. Desmond Lacroix. She needed to discover what secrets lay in the years he'd refused to discuss, without having him realize she was probing for information.

Then again, some interest on her part was surely called for. What sort of woman wouldn't want to know about her prospective husband? But she couldn't act too curious. Interested, but not inquisitive. She frowned. It would be easier to prompt Desmond for information if she had some idea of what she wanted to know.

Rebecca relaxed, and tried to clear her mind of distractions. Sometimes she could provoke one of her flashes of insight that way.

A mental picture formed instantly. Of last night's lovemaking. As if it were happening now, she could feel the heat of Desmond's presence against her passion slicked skin. His hands gripped her as he filled her, pulling her closer, even as her fingers dug into the corded muscles of his back in an effort to fuse them closer still. He tossed back his head, his thick black hair clinging damply to his shoulders, and opened his mouth to cry out. Echoes of last night's ecstasy shuddered through Rebecca, and the memory shattered into cascading flecks of brilliant green light. The floating specks of light slowly faded, melting like snowflakes when they touched her, leaving her alone in the present.

She struggled to catch her breath. Gradually, her lungs settled into a steady rhythm, and her heartbeat slowed to match it. Nothing like that had ever happened to her before. The memory had swept her away completely, as thoroughly as if she'd been transported back in time to experience her night of passion again. Except for one thing. That wasn't how it had happened.

Rebecca tried to concentrate, but her mind buzzed with a happy afterglow. The recent experience slipped away from her every time she focused on it, so she concentrated on last night, instead. She remembered the same contented glow, the feeling of being simultaneously so full of emotion that she was the size of a house, and so focused that she'd become no bigger than an ant. She remembered running her hands lazily over Desmond's back, smooth and relaxed after his own passion had been spent, and opening her eyes to gaze upon his smile.

Opening her eyes? Rebecca replayed the scene in her mind. Yes, last night her eyes had been closed. So she couldn't know how Desmond looked as ecstasy claimed him. Whatever had just overcome her, it wasn't a memory.

Much as she would have liked to spend longer thinking about last night, she resolutely pushed the thoughts aside. That interlude, no matter how enjoyable, got her nowhere closer to her goal of uncovering Desmond's past. Unfortunately, nothing else did either. When he arrived home a few hours later, she still hadn't thought out a way to systematically probe his background without rousing his suspicions. She'd have to wing it, and hope for the best.

Gillian squealed happily in the next room, and Desmond asked a question too softly for Rebecca to make out the words. Mrs. Waters answered him, and he chuckled, a rich sound that made Rebecca's heart pick up its pace. A moment later, he knocked on her door and looked in. Gillian clung to her father, obviously uncertain if being in Rebecca's room was forbidden or not.

"How are you feeling after a full day of bed rest?"

Desmond rested one hand lightly on top of his daughter's mop of curls, simultaneously blessing her presence in the doorway and preventing her from entering further into the room. Strangely, he showed no interest in coming any closer, either.

Rebecca twisted her neck to see his expression better, and caught her breath at the smoldering desire in his eyes. But even as his gaze exchanged silent promises with Rebecca, he dropped his hand down to Gillian's shoulder and protectively drew her closer. Hot shame flooded Rebecca's cheeks, and she lowered her face into the softness of the covers to hide her reaction.

"I'm fine," she mumbled into the covers. "And sick of staying in bed. I'm getting up tomorrow."

"If you feel ready for it. I don't want you rushing things and injuring yourself."

She lifted her face enough to sneak a quick peek at him. Something about his tone hinted that he wasn't referring to the aftereffects of her operation. But his expression revealed nothing, not even his previous desire.

"I'll be okay. I know how to take care of myself."

"I hope you do." He smiled. "I'll bring you in a dinner plate, tonight. I'm sure you'll feel well enough to eat with us tomorrow."

"I'm sure I will."

He and Gillian left the room. He returned alone, with Rebecca's dinner, but didn't stay long enough for any discussion. She'd have to wait until Gillian went to sleep before she could hold a conversation of any length with him. Rebecca picked at her food, inactivity and nerves destroying her appetite, and waited for Gillian's bedtime.

Finally, Gillian went to bed, and Desmond returned to Rebecca's room.

"Are you finished? You didn't eat very much."

"I wasn't hungry." Rebecca ignored the plate she'd set on the floor and patted the bed beside her. "Come over here. I want to talk to you, and you're giving me a crick in the neck looking up at you like that."

Desmond crossed the room warily. He stopped at the edge of her bed, and after a moment of hesitation, slipped off his shoes. He stretched out next to her, but kept a careful distance away. The warm glow of his presence brushed her skin, stinging like nettles, since he so obviously refused to admit to any similar attraction. She longed to turn and pull him close, but forced herself to concentrate on her interview. She still wasn't sure of how she could get him to open up about his past, so she focused on trivialities and hoped she might build it into something bigger.

"Your mother must have taught you well. You took your shoes off before putting your feet on the bed."

"My sister, actually. She was quite liberated for a woman of her time, and insisted we boys wash our own linens. I learned quickly to keep things clean."

Rebecca grabbed at the opening he'd left her. "Liberated? Because she had you do your own laundry? You can't be that much older than me."

"But I'm much younger than my sister," he cut in. Before she could ask how old his sister was, he added, "Veronica was practically an adult while I was still a toddler."

Rebecca did the math in her head. With a fifteen year difference in ages, if Desmond had been born in the early sixties, his sister would have been born right after World War II ended. She'd have grown up with the Donna Reed model of virtuous womanhood, where men never lifted a finger toward any domestic chore. Compared to that, asking her brothers to help with the washing was a big step. But it didn't explain why she assigned the household tasks in the first place.

"So your sister was in charge of all the domestic chores, rather than your mother?"

"Yes." Desmond turned to get a better view of her face. "But you had something to say, and here I am going on about my sister. What was it you wanted to discuss?"

Rebecca admired his smooth deflection of her questions. If this had been a casual conversation, she would never have noticed how, after his first comment, Desmond had provided only enough of an answer to forestall further questions. But this wasn't a casual conversation, and his evasiveness only added to her conviction that he had something to hide.

"Actually, we were discussing it. I wanted to know more about your family."

"Why?"

Desmond's closed and guarded expression sent a shiver through Rebecca. She no longer doubted that he was hiding something. Now, she needed to discover what.

"Because you've asked me to marry you, that's why. Isn't it natural I be a little curious about your family?"

"I asked you to marry me, not them."

"But they're part of what went into making you who you are."

He frowned, but she stared him down. Finally he admitted, "I suppose you have a point." Rolling onto his back, he put his arms beneath his head and studied the ceiling. "It doesn't seem relevant because they're all gone now."

Rebecca waited. She wanted to find out about his past, and what had happened during the years he didn't discuss. But her reporter's instincts to pry open his secrets were muted by a wave of protectiveness that swept through her. She wanted to take him in her arms and comfort him, let him know that whatever troubled him, she would soothe him. She wouldn't pry, or do anything to make him uncomfortable. At least, not yet. After another minute of silent contemplation of the ceiling, he took a deep breath and began his story.

"I was the youngest of five children. Four boys and a girl. They are all dead now."

"How?" she whispered.

"My eldest brother, Etienne, joined the army. He was a great idealist. His country called him, and he rushed to fight for her. He led recognizance missions into enemy territory. One night he didn't come back."

"I'm sorry."

Desmond shrugged off her sympathy. "My other brother, Jean-Michel, joined the army with him. He couldn't bear to think Etienne would have all the excitement. Jean-Michel lasted a few days longer, but without Etienne to stop him, he took too many risks."

"It was a terrible war."

Desmond turned to look at her. She thought she saw a flash of fear in his eyes, but it must have been a reflection of the light, as his voice showed no trace of concern. "Yes. It was. Even after the war ended, nothing was ever the same."

A chill shivered down Rebecca's back. The war had shaped her world, too, in ways she didn't like talking about. Desmond didn't need to remember more about it for her sake. She was interested in other areas of his history. "What about your other brother?"

"Roderick was the artist of the family, with the weaknesses common to that temperment. He was killed in a bar fight."

"Your sister?"

"Illness." Desmond's voice had turned completely flat and unemotional.

Rebecca swallowed, and fumbled for something she could ask that would not cause him any further pain. "What interesting names. I'd guessed Lacroix was French, and so are Etienne and Jean-Michel. Where did Roderick and Desmond come from? Aren't they British names?"

Desmond smiled, and his shoulders relaxed. "They are the names of my maternal grandfather and uncle, respectively. My parents alternated which side of the family we were named after."

Rebecca counted off the names. Etienne—French, Roderick—British, Jean-Michel—French, Desmond—British. The only place for another British name was before Etienne.

"So your sister, Veronica, is the oldest."

"Oh, no. Being a girl, she didn't count." He realized his mistake immediately. "I mean, my father named the first boy, and they took turns after that. My mother named the first girl. If they'd had another, my father would have named her. Veronica came after Etienne but before Roderick."

"It must have been hard for your sister when you were a teenager." Rebecca tossed the comment out, hoping to guide Desmond's recollections to his missing years.

"No, by that time she'd already started running out. At first, she'd be gone for a day or two. Then she stayed away for a week. Finally, months would go by between visits. And then she stopped coming home at all."

"That's terrible! How could she do that to you?"

"I didn't blame her." A sad smile tilted Desmond's lips. "She needed her freedom. She would have returned eventually, had she not taken ill."

"I see." Rebecca studied the comforter, and picked off a piece of invisible lint, strangely unwilling to meet the truth in his eyes. Or maybe afraid he'd see the naked fear in hers. "Is this need for freedom something that runs in your family?"

"Rebecca." Desmond turned her face to look at him. "If you're asking, will I run out on you, the answer is no. Never. Absolutely not. I know what it feels like to be the one left behind. I couldn't do that to you."

He'd left his hand against her cheek when he turned her face. Now he started stroking her jaw with a feather light touch, and dusting around her ear with soft caresses. He stared into her eyes, and she watched as passion darkened his eyes from a light jade to a fiery emerald. Her lips seemed to go dry under the heat of his stare.

She moistened her lips. The quick movement attracted his attention, the way a hawk is attracted by the movement of a hare that breaks and runs. The weight of his gaze settled on her lips, and he traced their contours with his thumb. She closed her eyes, concentrating on the ripples of pleasure set off by his touch. But it couldn't last. She had to get back to her interview, to discovering his secret.

She opened her mouth to tell him so, the movement giving him access to the tender inside surface of her lips as well. He glided the tip of one finger across the moist lining, sweeping back across the edge of her lower teeth, again and again, until she abandoned all thoughts of an interview. She stopped his relentless caress by closing her mouth and wrapping her tongue around his finger. She tasted traces of her own shampoo, the citrus flavor almost masking Desmond's subtle musk, and drew his finger deeper.

He groaned. "Rebecca, we can't."

"Can't what?" She kept his finger lightly imprisoned between her teeth, and flicked the edge with her tongue as she spoke. He twisted on the bed, but made no effort to break away.

"I dare not risk your health," he protested.

"We'll go easy. After all, last night didn't hurt me any."

He jerked his hand free so quickly her teeth snapped together. She pushed herself up and glared at him.

"What is your problem?"

He ignored her, his head bent and eyes closed in an internal struggle for control. When his eyes opened, he kept his expression carefully neutral.

"I told you, I don't want to endanger your health."

"One little kiss is no risk to my recovery," she snapped. He looked at her lips, and smoldering passion flickered in his eyes as he trailed his gaze lower, skimming her breasts and hips with palpable heat.

"Do you honestly believe it would stop there?"

She swallowed, thrown by the husky catch in his voice, and allowed her gaze to drift downward from his face. He might be able to school his features to show no emotion, but his body betrayed him. He wanted her. Very much. At the sight, an answering need flared to life within her.

"Would it be so bad if we didn't stop?" she whispered.

"I don't want to hurt you."

"You won't." She smiled, a knowing, predatory grin, and reached for his pants. The zip rasped open, freeing him, and her hand closed around him. He pressed forward, sliding through her fingers in a soft caress that left him trembling. Echoes of his pleasure rippled back through her, tightening her own tension and quickening her pulse.

"Rebecca." Desmond struggled to focus pleasure-glazed eyes on her. "Be careful. You mustn't—"

His words dissolved in a groan as she replaced her hand with her lips. As if she'd pressed them against a newly minted steel bar, his molten heat fused her flesh to his. His pleasure became her pleasure, tremors of sensation rising from a single epicenter to quake through them both. And when the passion raging through them burned too brightly to be contained, they melted into liquid heat together.

Thoughts and images spun dreamlike through Rebecca's mind. She pictured herself, recast as a buxom redhead, dancing a fiery tango with Desmond, the smoke of countless cigarettes screening them from everything but the pulsing beat of the band. The image shifted, and she transformed into a giggling flapper, leaning against a cool plaster wall. Her beads clicked and chattered against the wall as she swayed beneath Desmond's masterfully orchestrated caresses. The picture melted and ran, reforming as two naked bodies tangled in the throes of passion, thrashing back and forth on the jade silk of his bed. Desmond arched back, then bent to bestow another kiss on the soft skin of her neck.

Rebecca snapped back to the present as suddenly as if she'd been doused with cold water. Desmond held her, fitted together like the Tango dancers in her dream, although she didn't remember moving. Her cheek rested against his, a faint hint of stubble proving this time, the contact was real. His breath steamed rhythmically across her neck in the soft pattern of sleep.

She turned and reached for a pillow. When she turned back, Desmond was staring at her with unblinking green eyes that reflected the light like a cat's. The look unnerved her. He didn't seem to move, even to breathe, just watching, waiting for the chance to pounce upon his unwary prey. She chuckled, dismissing the thought as another dream fancy.

"I didn't mean to wake you," she said softly.

"That's all right. I wasn't asleep." He smiled, a long slow smile that gradually transformed his face and kindled the banked embers in his eyes. A flush of heat swept over Rebecca, following the path of Desmond's gaze, until it covered her completely. She knew she looked like a giant candy apple, but he didn't embarrass her further by commenting. Instead, he hooked up a sheet with one foot, then pulled it over them.

"I don't want you to catch cold, on top of everything else," he teased.

"Thank you."

She nestled more comfortably into his embrace, and they lay together in companionable silence, their hearts and breath moving in the same slow rhythm. He trailed a hand through her hair, ploughing idle furrows, while she toyed with the dusting of black hairs that softened his chest.

Still looking at his chest, she asked, "Why did you ask me to marry you?"

His hand stopped in mid-furrow and the muscles that sheathed his ribs tensed. Rebecca held her breath, then let it out when he relaxed with a dry laugh.

"I must remember investigative journalism isn't just what you do. It's who you are. But since you ask," he pushed himself up on one arm so that he looked deep into her eyes, "I asked you to marry me because having met you, having made love to you, I couldn't bear to lose you."

"Like you lost Olivia?" Rebecca wanted to take back the words as soon as she'd said them. She seemed to be going out of her way to provoke him, and she had no idea why.

"No." Cold fire glittered in the depths of his eyes, and honed the edge on his voice. "Not like I lost Olivia. I will not lose someone to that death again."

Rebecca shivered, frightened by his expression. His words suggested denial, but his face hinted at something more sinister.

He forced a smile. "Are you reluctant, Rebecca? I speak of marriage, and you bring up death. Not exactly encouraging."

"No." She tried to return his smile, but the expression felt pasty and false. With a sigh, she turned her face away from his disturbingly perceptive gaze. "I'm afraid. I don't understand what it is I feel for you, and I don't know how you can be so calm. It scares me witless."

He gathered her into his arms and held her, the heat of his body driving out her cold fear. She relaxed beneath his gentle caresses as he stroked her back and whispered soothing murmurs into her ear.

"I guess I'm being silly, huh?" she mumbled into his shoulder.

"No. Just human." He pulled her closer and pressed a soft kiss against her temple. "But you have nothing to fear. No harm will ever come to you through me. I swear it."

"I believe you." A punishing grip she hadn't been aware of released her chest, and her heart began beating at a normal rate again. She turned her head, and met Desmond's lips with her own. She might not have all the answers, but that was all right. She didn't need them. She trusted him, and that was enough for now. The answers would come.

Their lips lingered in a kiss until Desmond broke it off. He pulled back far enough to look at her, his eyes shining with a naked hope he was too proud to voice. She answered him anyway.

"I believe you. And I will marry you."

He grinned and swept down to claim her mouth in a searing consummation. The heat of his passion rose between them, but she no longer tried to analyze the sensations. She committed herself wholly to the flames, and let the conflagration carry her away.

REBECCA TURNED in her sleep, bumping Desmond awake. She slept on, oblivious, as he enjoyed the feeling of waking up with her in his arms. He glanced at the window—the stars had begun to fade, but the sky hadn't started to lighten. Well past midnight, but not yet dawn. Although with that damn meeting at six o'clock to review new procedures, there was no point in going back to sleep.

He shifted his weight to look at the woman still held in his loose embrace, and smiled. Rebecca looked little older than Gillian, holding his arm close as if it were a favorite stuffed animal. He brushed her hair away from her face to study it, amazed at how sleep stole all traces of anxiety or cynicism away from her expression. She had the unlined, guileless face of a child. *And could have that face forever.*

He pushed the thought aside. He mustn't give credence to Philippe's insidious suggestions. How could Rebecca believe in his curse? He'd barely gotten her to believe he wouldn't leave her.

A chill premonition wiped away his smile. What would she think when she woke to find him gone? Would she believe he'd abandoned her? He'd told her about the meeting this morning, but he'd mentioned it as she drifted off to sleep. She might not remember.

He swore softly under his breath, afraid of waking her. She needed her sleep, to recover from her operation. And to build up her strength. He'd been careful last night, so very careful, not to risk infecting her. But surrounded by her scent, enslaved by her passion, she'd overwhelmed his senses. He hadn't been able to stop himself from taking her blood. At least he'd kept the site free of contamination.

Bunching up the covers, he leaned over to check again. The wound, too small to notice unless you were looking for it, had already closed up. He needn't worry about more mundane forms of infection, either.

That was a relief. But it didn't address his other problem. He needed to convince her that his thoughts were still with her, even if he was not. A note, perhaps?

He shook his head. No. Aside from being hopelessly passé, a sample of his handwriting would only give her another thing to question. His penmanship had changed over the years, the more elaborate flourishes dropping away as he adapted to the faster pace of the world around him. But it still bore more resemblance to the engraved inside of a greeting card than contemporary script. No, he needed a way to give her his message without words.

Flowers. He'd say it with flowers. He grinned, certain that he'd solved the dilemma. A bouquet of hand-picked flowers, left on the pillow, would convince her of his feelings. All he had to do was go out and pick them before the sun came up.

He slid his arm gently out of her grasp. Rebecca mumbled in her sleep and reached for him, but seemed content with the corner of her pillow she'd grabbed. He dropped a light kiss at her temple.

"Sleep well. I'll be back before you know I'm gone."

Moving silently, he eased out of bed, then located and put on yesterday's clothes. He didn't have time to shower and find the suit he wanted to wear to the meeting. He'd do that when he got back.

The door opened with a faint click, and he slipped into the living room. Gillian was sound asleep, burrowed under her covers, but he left her door open so that Rebecca could hear her if she cried out.

He held his breath as he triggered the front door lock, but either it was too far away or Rebecca had grown too accustomed to the noise for it to disturb her. He stepped out into the hallway and guided the door closed. Then he turned and ran for the stairwell. Few wildflowers bloomed on the Institute property, and he didn't have much time to find them. The sun would be coming up soon.

He laughed, appreciating the irony. His gesture proved how important she was to him, but because she was so important to him, he couldn't risk driving her away in order to explain the reason why.

Chapter 12

DESMOND CUT the timing close, waiting until the sky began to grow light before he returned. He'd hoped to find something better for Rebecca, but aside from the flowering cacti whose prickers seemed to send the wrong message, he'd seen only flowering weeds. He'd gathered a big bouquet of the prettiest blossoms, a double handful, yet still lingered outside in case the pre-dawn light revealed another flower he'd missed.

It didn't. He shut himself safely away bare minutes before the distinct glow of sunrise gilded the eastern horizon.

Gillian was still fast asleep, although she'd kicked her quilt onto the floor. Desmond picked it up with his free hand and settled it over his sleeping daughter. She mumbled something around the thumb in her mouth, and tightened her stranglehold on her beloved Pooh. He watched her sleep for a moment longer, then eased her door shut and slipped into Rebecca's room.

He intended to leave the flowers on the pillow beside her, but while he'd been outside she'd preempted his pillow, and now held it tucked tight against her chest. He pushed the blankets down to clear a spot beside her, and piled the flowers there. She didn't seem to have moved much while he'd been gone, except to steal his pillow. She probably wouldn't roll over on the flowers.

He considered the tableau a few minutes longer, then plumped the covers beside her to form a gentle ridge. That should be enough to discourage her from turning over. Satisfied that his gift would remain safe, he left her and went to take his shower and get dressed.

Half an hour later, he strolled into the kitchen, a towel slung around his neck to protect the raw silk of his jacket from his still damp hair. He put a pot of water on to boil, and took one of his medicine bottles out of the refrigerator. The liquid needed to be kept in cold storage, but he preferred to warm it before drinking it if he could.

He caught the refrigerator door with his elbow before it could close. He'd stayed out late. Very late. How much sunlight had he absorbed? Enough to damage his skin? He pulled out a second bottle, just to be on the safe side, and put them both in the pot of warm water.

While he waited for the medicine to heat up, he busied himself making coffee.

By the time Mrs. Waters arrived promptly at five forty-five, he'd already drained both bottles, rinsed them, and stacked them to be returned and refilled. Sipping his second cup of coffee, he walked into the living room to greet her when she buzzed herself in.

"Good morning, Mrs. Waters. Thank you for coming early."

"Pish." She dismissed his thanks with a wave, and set her knitting supplies on the couch. "You know I'm more than happy to look after Gillian any time you need me. I love that child like she was my own daughter."

Desmond glanced at his daughter's room, fighting the urge to push open the door and check on her again. He'd looked in on her less than ten minutes before.

"I hate not being here when she wakes. The mornings and evenings are our special time together."

"It's only once a month."

"I know." He sighed. "And it's the only hour all the doctors can fit into their schedules. I'll make it up to her, though. I'll be home for lunch today."

"I'll have it ready for you when you arrive." Mrs. Waters paused, then asked, "Will it be just the two of you?"

"No, Rebecca will join us. I expect her to be tired this morning, but I think she'll manage to get up by noon." He smiled, remembering how enjoyably they'd tired each other out. Then he recalled how cranky she'd been the other morning when he'd woken her for the operation. "You'd better keep the coffee warm for her. She'll be needing it. And put off anything noisy, like laundry or vacuuming, until after she wakes up."

"Whatever you say. What about Gillian?" Her face showed no expression, and her surface thoughts only repeated the same question in an endless loop.

"What about her?" he asked.

"I just wondered if you wanted me to keep her quiet, too?"

"Of course not! I mean, don't encourage her to be noisy, but this is her home. Rebecca may as well start getting used to that."

"But surely she won't be staying with us that long?"

Desmond smiled, his hands curling around his coffee mug to embrace the last of its heat. She would be staying. She'd accepted his proposal last night. And he'd destroyed the only possible reason for sending her away when he proved that they could make love safely. He could send her over the maddened edge of pleasure again and again with no fear, so long as he withheld his own release.

"Oh, yes, she'll be staying. I hope forever." He turned his attention back on Mrs. Waters. "Of course, things will be different after she's recovered from her operation."

"Of course."

Desmond frowned at her icy tone, but he didn't have the time to pursue her comment further. He was already running late.

He swallowed the last of his coffee, and placed the mug on the glass-topped table. "I've got to go. Remember, tell Gillian I'll be home for lunch."

"I will, Mr. Lacroix."

REBECCA WOKE slowly, aware first of the sheets resting against her bare skin, then of the circle of warmth created by the overhead light. She stretched languorously, arching her back and rippling her muscles like a cat. A satisfied smile pulled at the corners of her mouth, and she turned toward Desmond. He was gone.

She surged into full wakefulness. He'd mentioned something last night about a morning meeting, but she couldn't recall what. She never could think clearly before her first cup of coffee.

She glanced at the clock—quarter after nine. She'd slept late. The satisfied smile crept back onto her face as she remembered what had tired her. Desmond had refused to do anything that might aggravate her injury. But he was an inventive lover, and that prohibition hadn't stopped him from giving her a night of passion unlike anything she'd ever known. He'd taken her to the heights of ecstasy, only waiting until she started her descent before lifting her to an even higher peak.

Still smiling, she tossed the covers aside. The motion uncovered a bouquet of wildflowers. Broad green centers, bristling with rolled purple-pink petals, topped spindly stalks and dagger leaves. Rebecca had never seen more beautiful flowers. Wondering if they had an aroma as distinctive as their shape, she held them to her nose. Lingering traces of Desmond's cologne overpowered any scent the flowers normally had. Rebecca inhaled deeply, savoring the reminder.

She showered and dressed quickly, then headed for the kitchen clutching the bouquet. She needed a vase for the flowers and a cup of coffee for herself, not necessarily in that order. Then she could start making calls, and find out what it would take to move out of her apartment and transfer her business contacts to an answering service out here.

As she left her room, she spotted Gillian playing quietly in the living room and called out, "Good morning, Gillian."

Gillian looked up and smiled. "Wanna play?"

A jumble of blocks and tiny dolls snaked around the little girl, carefully arranged in some order only she understood. Rebecca didn't recognize the game Gillian was playing, and knew better than to try and learn anything before her first cup of coffee.

"Maybe later."

Gillian nodded and turned her attention back to her dolls. Rebecca watched her for a moment, trying to puzzle out the rules of the game, then gave up and pushed open the kitchen door.

"Good morning, Mrs. Waters." Rebecca practically sang the words.

"Coffee's on the counter," the housekeeper replied without looking up from her piecrust. "Mr. Lacroix said you'd most likely be tired this morning, and I was to keep the pot warm for you when you woke up. If you'll be making a habit out of sleeping in, let me know, and I won't start the coffee until later in the day. It's better if it doesn't sit so long."

"Oh." Rebecca's cheeks burned. She'd be even more embarrassed if the housekeeper could see her reaction. Rebecca tried to keep her voice casual as she poured out a cup of coffee. "Did he say anything else?"

"He suggested I change my schedule. I normally clean in the morning and do my baking in the afternoons. I suppose he thought my vacuuming would disturb your beauty sleep." She slammed the dough against the pastry board hard enough to raise a cloud of flour.

Rebecca busied herself with adding milk and sugar to her coffee. Desmond must not have mentioned their wedding plans to Mrs. Waters, or she would have said something about it. Since he hadn't, Rebecca wouldn't mention it either, although the opportunity tempted her. Maybe knowing she and Desmond weren't just having a casual affair would ease the housekeeper's disapproval. Rebecca took a bracing sip of her coffee.

"Thanks. It's delicious."

Mrs. Waters grunted affirmation.

"Do you have a vase I can borrow? I'd like to put these flowers in some water."

"Flowers?" The housekeeper looked up for the first time. "Those are just thistles."

"They're still flowers. And *I* think they're pretty."

Mrs. Waters sighed, and dusted her hands off on her apron. "It's in the china closet. I suppose I'd better get it. Wait here."

She left the room, returning a few moments later with a cut glass bud vase. Turning on the tap, she filled the vase half way with water. Then she snatched the thistles from Rebecca and stuffed them into the vase.

Rebecca grabbed the vase away from Mrs. Waters. Holding it protectively close to her chest, she fluffed the leaves and readjusted the stalks. Mrs. Waters frowned, but didn't comment.

"If there's nothing else...?"

"Actually, there is one more thing." Rebecca glanced up from her flowers. Not surprisingly, Mrs. Waters was looking away from her.

"I thought there would be."

"I need a telephone book."

Mrs. Waters turned to her, eyes narrowed. "Who are you going to call?"

"I won't know that until I have a chance to look in the yellow pages." Rebecca fought to control her temper. Mrs. Waters worked for Desmond, not her. He might be able to talk to the woman about her attitude, but there was nothing Rebecca could do without making the situation worse.

"There's a directory in the study. It's in the drawer under the phone." Mrs. Waters shrugged and returned to rolling out her dough. "Not that it will do you any good. None of the shops deliver out this far. There's not much for a woman to do here, unless you're a doctor like Mrs. Lacroix was. I can't imagine what possessed you to say you'd stay on."

Rebecca gripped the vase and ground out a stiff, "Thank you." But as she left the kitchen, the housekeeper's words continued to echo in her mind. Possession. She remembered her first few confrontations with Desmond, and the sense that she didn't control her own words and actions. She leaned heavily against the living room wall.

She'd had that feeling of being out of control more recently, too. Last night, when she and Desmond made love, she'd felt that way again. Looking back, it seemed ominous that she hadn't questioned the gaps in her memory, when he'd been awake and she apparently hadn't. She'd also given in far too easily when he'd sidestepped the issue of his missing years. She recognized the symptoms, but questioned the underlying cause. Was she a woman in love, or a woman possessed?

Rebecca shook her head and marched into the study. She was letting Mrs. Waters get to her. She needed to treat the situation like one of her stories, uncovering the facts and exposing all the angles. Then she'd be able to make an informed decision.

She opened the desk and took out a legal pad, then sat down and started making notes. What evidence did she have? Desmond's lovemaking made her feel out of control and larger than life. He could coax responses from her body that she'd never even imagined existed. He'd asked her to marry him. He'd never told her he loved her. She'd saved his daughter.

She filled the page with facts, but was no closer to an answer. If he'd made love to her and asked her to marry him before she'd donated bone marrow to Gillian, Rebecca might suspect an ulterior motive. But after the operation was over? He had no reason to keep her around, except the obvious.

He loved her. Just as she loved him. The only power clouding her thinking was her own fear of betrayal. She had to trust him. She had to believe she could depend on him. Because if she couldn't trust the man she loved, she'd never be able to trust anyone. And a world without trust was as bleak and unappealing as a world in which no one ever helped anyone, and no one loved anyone. She'd spent the last ten years in that world. She didn't want to go back.

DESMOND WALKED into the board room, already filled with the doctors and researchers heading up the various branches of Institute activities. He took his seat, as the individual conversations slowly faded into silence, and swept his gaze across the assembled division heads. He stopped, staring at the man sitting halfway down the right side of the table. Philippe.

Damn. Of course Philippe would be there. As Head of Operations, he oversaw the Institute's residential housing, building maintenance and procurement departments, among other things. He presented monthly status reports and fought for his share of the budget along with the medical and research department heads.

Maybe Philippe wouldn't make any trouble. If they could get through the meeting on a strictly business footing, there would be no opportunity for him to cause a scene. Desmond stood and called the meeting to order.

Each department head stood in turn and presented charts outlining successes and detailing why they needed additional funding. Desmond hid a smile. In all the meetings he'd attended since the founding of the Institute, no department head had ever admitted to a failure, or asked for less money. But none of the increases surprised him, and he nodded acceptance after each presentation. Until Philippe spoke.

"And we need thirteen hundred to repair the west elevator shaft in building three," Philippe finished his summation.

Desmond frowned. "We repaired that shaft a few months ago. Why does it need more repairs?"

"Because the side bracing buckled again."

"What? When?" He leaned forward. "Why did you wait until now to tell me?"

Too late, Desmond realized he'd given Philippe the opening he'd been looking for. If Desmond didn't stop him, Philippe would try to enlist the doctors in his fight against marriage to Rebecca. Desmond had to keep Philippe's comments in neutral territory. Or better yet, get Philippe to sit down and shut up.

"It happened the morning after your daughter's operation," Philippe announced. Then he added, in a thought directed at Desmond, *When you were busy screwing around.*

Desmond gripped the table hard enough to bruise the wood, but allowed none of his fury to color his voice. The other attendees hadn't heard Philippe's thought, only his words. Philippe was trying to provoke a reaction, but Desmond refused to be baited.

"You should have contacted me."

"I tried. Your housekeeper said you didn't want to be disturbed." *We'd already taken care of the problem by the time you finished taking care of—*

"We'll discuss this later. After the meeting."

Philippe sat down, abandoning for the moment his attempts to force a confrontation. But he'd try again. The same persistent attention to detail that made him such a valuable administrator made him an infuriatingly obstinate opponent for a disagreement.

The last two department heads responded to the reverberating tension by whizzing through their presentations in record time. As soon as they finished, the meeting disbanded, with department heads jostling each other to be first out the door. Not one stayed behind to argue for more funding or resources.

Philippe waited until the door closed behind the last researcher, then resumed his attack. "I told you that woman was getting to you. You're paying more attention to her than to the business of the Institute."

"A business you're sabotaging. Why didn't you tell me about the elevator? Someone could have been hurt. Would you have told me then?"

"Would you have cared? Admit it, you've gotten what you wanted out of this place. They bought Gillian more time."

"That's not what I wanted," Desmond snapped.

"You didn't want them to help her?"

"No!" Desmond took a deep breath, and struggled to regain his composure. "I mean, of course I wanted them to help her. But that wasn't why I originally started this venture. I started it to find a cure for us. And I'll keep the Institute going until they do."

"Yeah, well, that'll be mighty hard to do when we're both dead."

"Philippe—"

"You just don't get it, do you? No matter what she says now, as soon as she finds out what you are, she'll turn on you. If you're lucky, she'll just leave and not try to kill you, or expose us so others can kill us."

"She won't—"

"Yes, she will."

"Don't judge Rebecca by the standards of your wife! She won't turn her back on our relationship. She won't turn her back on me."

Philippe snorted and gathered up his presentation. "You owe me vacation days. Well, I'm taking them. Now. I refuse to work for you when you're so irrational. But I'll make sure you know where I am. So you'll have no trouble finding me to apologize when she leaves you."

"Go to hell."

"I've already been there." Philippe stalked off, slamming the conference room door on his way out.

Desmond returned to his own office, hoping Philippe might cool off and see reason. But when the Assistant Director of Operations showed up later that morning with the division's follow-up paperwork, she confirmed that Philippe had gone.

Desmond gave the papers only a cursory glance before carving his signature across the bottom of them. He pushed the signed authorizations back across his desk to her. "You know what all of these are for?"

"Yes." She picked up the pile and stuffed the papers into her already overflowing briefcase. "Philippe and I discussed all the open action items yesterday, when we reviewed his presentation for today's meeting."

"Good." He paused, not sure how to phrase his question without offending her. "Philippe left suddenly. Will you be able to absorb the additional workload?"

"Of course." She straightened, indignant that he dared to question her capability. He didn't try to defend his question, only looked concerned, and she relaxed with a laugh. "You're right. It won't be easy. But I've got a great staff who can pick up parts of my job while I do his. Although...."

"Yes?"

"I know we've asked for a lot this month already," she blurted out in a rush, "but if you could just authorize some discretionary award money? They'll be putting in a lot of overtime on this. I'd like to give them a little bonus, as a way of saying thank you."

"Of course." He should have thought of that. This fight with Philippe had gotten to him. "Just tell me who and how much, and I'll authorize it."

Desmond smiled. If she asked for too much, he could always take it out of Philippe's check. He deserved it for running out on them like this.

She thanked Desmond and left. He glanced at his watch, and discovered it was already eleven. He didn't have anything urgent to keep him in the office. If he left now, he'd have three hours with Gillian before he had to return.

Desmond smiled as he locked up his desk. Honesty forced him to admit Gillian wasn't the only one he was looking forward to seeing.

When he opened his front door, Gillian didn't run to greet him. He hoped she was busy, and not angry with him for leaving her earlier. It hadn't been that long ago when she'd throw tantrums over the slightest change to her schedule. He thought she'd outgrown that, but he wasn't sure.

He walked inside, and was relieved to see Gillian and Mrs. Waters engrossed in a brightly colored game spread across the coffee table. Candyland, it looked like. Gillian looked up and smiled, then turned her attention back to the game.

"Blue. Orange. Green. Red!" She grabbed her red plastic game piece and slammed it down triumphantly on the red space. "I passed you!"

"That you did," Mrs. Waters agreed. "You're so good at this, Gillian. I don't think I have any chance of winning."

Gillian giggled and smiled at her father. "I'm winning, Daddy! See?"

He strolled over and examined the board. "Yes, you are. By quite a bit, too."

Mrs. Waters turned over a card and handed it to Gillian. "Could you find where my piece is supposed to go, dear?"

Gillian studied the card carefully, and began tracing the board with her finger, reciting the colors.

Mrs. Waters looked up at Desmond. "You're home earlier than I expected. Lunch isn't ready yet."

"That's all right. You and Gillian finish your game. I'm in no hurry." He paused, then asked, "Where's Rebecca?"

"In the study." Mrs. Waters lowered her voice to a stage whisper, and added, "Making phone calls."

Desmond frowned at his housekeeper's obvious suggestion of impropriety. He couldn't image what she objected to about Rebecca using the phone. But the tone of her words sent a sliver of apprehension down his spine, and he approached the study with caution. He pushed open the door in time to hear the end of Rebecca's question.

"And how soon can you have a vehicle available?"

He froze in the doorway. Was she calling for a taxi? A rental car to take her away? Had Philippe been right?

"Okay. You're sure delivery this far out in the desert won't be a problem?" she continued.

"Rebecca?" He hated how hesitant his voice sounded. But it was enough to startle her.

She spun around toward the door, her eyes wide. Then she recognized him, and a huge grin spread across her face.

"You're home," she whispered. A loud squawk from the phone recalled her to her previous conversation, and she babbled into the receiver, "Yes, well, thank you for all your help. I'll let you know. I've got to go now."

She hung up and turned back to Desmond, the smile spreading across her face and lighting her eyes. "I was trying to arrange for a moving van. I already called my landlord and gave notice. But I'm going to have to go back to New York and pack up my things before the end of the month. When were you thinking of having the wedding?"

Desmond felt an answering smile warming his face. He was an

idiot to have doubted her. He'd let Philippe's fears poison his mind when he should have known better. Nothing could separate Rebecca from him.

"I was thinking Saturday."

"This Saturday?" she squeaked.

"Yes. Is that a problem?"

"But...but...that's less than a week away! Where will we hold it? When will we get the rings? What will I wear?"

He leaned over and gave her a lingering kiss. "You're adorable when you're flustered. Did you know that?"

"No. And don't change the subject. How on earth were you planning to get ready by this Saturday?"

"Las Vegas isn't that far from here. I thought we could reserve one of the wedding chapels, drive up Friday night, get the license and the rings, and get married Saturday morning."

"Las Vegas?" Rebecca pulled back in horror.

"You don't like the idea?" He tried to keep the panic out of his voice. If she refused to get married in Las Vegas, he didn't know how he was going to explain or obtain the services of a Justice of the Peace willing to marry them during the hours of darkness.

"It just seems so...tacky."

"It won't be."

"But why not wait and do it right? A real church service, with family and friends in attendance."

He tilted his head and studied her, trying to see beneath her calm veneer. If only he could pry into her mind for the answers, this would be so much easier. "Is there anyone in particular you'd like to invite? I thought your parents were both dead."

"My father's dead. I said my mother was gone. She's gone to Florida. I don't talk to her anymore." Rebecca smiled sadly. "I guess I don't have any friends or family to attend me. It's just that I'd always pictured a storybook wedding. A big stone church, full of stained glass, and crammed to the rafters with people who'd watch me process down the aisle in yards and yards of white lace."

Desmond caught up her hands and covered them with gentle kisses until she gave him her attention.

"Rebecca. Dear heart. I'll find you a chapel with stained glass, and a wedding dress with yards and yards of lace. Don't you know I only want you to be happy? But I'm selfish. I don't want to wait any longer to make you my wife than I have to."

He ignored the edge of guilt scraping at his conscience. Marrying her would please him, and he'd do everything he could to make the marriage a happy one for her, too. But he couldn't forget that she'd be better off with a normal man. One who could grow old alongside her, and who could give her nice, normal children that weren't likely to die before they'd ever had a chance to live. Someone who wouldn't threaten her safety by his very existence.

She laughed, and the shadow lifted from her features. "What did I ever do to deserve a man like you?"

You angered the gods, he thought, but didn't say it. She wouldn't understand his bitterness. Instead, he asked, "Are you finished with your calls? Lunch should be ready soon."

"You're staying for lunch?"

"Yes. Didn't Mrs. Waters tell you?"

"No." Rebecca frowned, then forced a smile. "I'm sure it just slipped her mind."

"Rebecca, what is it?"

"What is what?"

"Why were you upset that Mrs. Waters didn't mention it?"

"I wasn't upset." She stood up and started for the door. "Are you coming?"

"Not yet." He placed a hand on her arm to stop her, and turned her to face him. "Tell me why she upset you."

Rebecca tilted her chin up, prepared to fight him, but almost immediately her shoulders drooped and she lowered her head again. "Mrs. Waters doesn't want me here."

"What? How can you—"

"She barely talks to me, won't let Gillian near me, and constantly reminds me that I'm not worthy to so much as speak your late wife's name."

Desmond stiffened. Scraps of images cascaded through his mind, projected by Rebecca's distress. She might have exaggerated a little, but he didn't doubt that his housekeeper had gone out of her way to make Rebecca feel unwanted and unwelcome.

"She's wrong. And from now on, she's going to treat you with the respect and courtesy you deserve. Or she can find another job."

Chapter 13

HAVING DESMOND home for lunch was an obvious treat for Gillian, and she monopolized him throughout the luncheon conversation. She insisted on telling her father everything about how lunches were normally prepared and eaten, and reminded him several times that she'd helped set the table. Each time, Desmond agreed that the napkins were folded wonderfully, each one under the knife just so, or that the water glasses held just the right amount of water, or that she was extremely clever to have remembered both the salt and the pepper.

Rebecca was glad when the meal was finally over. Desmond had occasionally tried to draw her into the conversation, but between Gillian and Mrs. Waters, he'd rarely had the chance. And Rebecca wasn't sure how to behave around Gillian. She'd never had much experience with kids.

When the other girls had been playing with dolls, Rebecca had explored the woods and creeks. They'd baby-sat to get pocket money. She'd delivered papers and helped after school at the library. Although some people claimed parenting was an instinct, considering what a mess her own mother had made of it, Rebecca wasn't willing to bet too heavily on that.

So she sat quietly, smiling occasionally at Desmond and Gillian, and avoided looking at Mrs. Waters. Gillian frequently asked the housekeeper for confirmation as she spoke to her father. Each time she did, Mrs. Waters darted a smug look at Rebecca. Rebecca wasn't sure what game Mrs. Waters thought they were playing, but the housekeeper clearly believed she was winning.

After lunch, Desmond took Gillian away to get cleaned up, and Mrs. Waters started gathering up the dishes.

"You'll want to be getting back to your phone calls, then?" Mrs. Waters asked over her shoulder as she carried the plates to the sink.

Rebecca slapped the table and shoved herself upright. "I've had as much of this as I can take. I don't know what your problem is, but you better tell me now."

Mrs. Waters added soap to the water and swirled the bubbles over the dishes. "Or what?"

"Or when Desmond puts Gillian to bed for her afternoon nap, he's going to ask you the exact same thing. And if he doesn't like the answer, he's going to fire you."

A plate slipped from the housekeeper's fingers and crashed into the stack of dirty dishes. Mrs. Waters gripped the counter with soapy fingers.

"You're lying. He wouldn't do that."

Rebecca stopped and counted silently to ten. She'd lost her temper and rushed into this confrontation, but she could still get control of the situation. And that's what she needed. Picking a fight with Mrs. Waters wouldn't accomplish anything, other than forcing Desmond to get rid of someone his daughter clearly adored. A chill washed over Rebecca as she drew the parallels between her wish for a peaceful homelife by getting rid of Mrs. Waters and her own father's banishment. She couldn't hurt Gillian the same way she'd been hurt.

"You're right. He wouldn't fire you. At least, not until he'd tried every other solution. But how can we find a solution if we don't know the problem?"

"The problem? The problem is you." Mrs. Waters steamrollered over Rebecca's indignant response. "Nothing personal, you understand. It's been over two years since Mr. Lacroix's wife passed on. I don't blame him for moving on. But whatever's between you should stay between you. You don't belong here, and you don't belong with Gillian."

"You think I'm having an affair with him?" Rebecca smiled, anticipating the look on the housekeeper's face when she learned the truth.

Desmond walked in before Rebecca could deliver her coupe de grace. He sized up the situation as soon as he entered the room, and turned to her with a frown. "I see you entered the fray without waiting for me."

"Did Gillian go down for her nap all right?" Mrs. Waters asked.

"Perfectly. She's more well-behaved than the so-called adults around here. Care to explain what you were fighting about?"

"She said I was sleeping with you!"

Desmond smiled, a slow indulgent smile that drove everything from Rebecca's mind but his presence. He was so near, she could feel the heat radiating from him. She stepped toward him, drawn to him with a single-minded desire to lose herself in his fire. He wrapped his arm around her shoulders, pulling her closer still.

"You are sleeping with me," he whispered to her. When he turned aside to speak to Mrs. Waters, the separation caused an almost physical shock. "You've mistaken the nature of our relationship. Rebecca and I are going to be married."

"Married! But...that is...I mean...Congratulations," Mrs. Waters finally stammered out.

"Thank you. This isn't how I intended to tell you." He favored Rebecca with an irritated look that dissolved into another indulgent smile.

She grinned back at him. "Years from now we'll look back on this and laugh, right?"

Mrs. Waters interrupted them. "When will the ceremony take place?"

"This Saturday," Desmond answered.

"Saturday?" Mrs. Waters pulled out one of the kitchen chairs and slumped into it. "So soon?"

Rebecca snuggled closer to Desmond. "We didn't want to wait."

"Besides," Desmond added, "you've already agreed to spend the day with Gillian."

"I'll miss her," Mrs. Waters said.

"Miss her?" Rebecca asked, just as Desmond asked, "Why?"

Mrs. Waters looked at them in confusion. "Well, I just naturally assumed..."

"Good grief, you didn't think *I* wanted to take care of her, did you?" Rebecca couldn't help laughing. "I mean, she's a nice kid and all, and I really like her, but I don't know the first thing about caring for children. And when would I have time to learn? I'll still be traveling a lot for my stories."

"You will?" Desmond quirked an eyebrow.

"Uh, yeah." This seemed to be her day for blurting things out. She'd meant to present her future plans to Desmond in an orderly, rational way, outlining why they'd both benefit from her career, and why her career would be improved by traveling. Instead, she'd handed him a *fait accompli*, like it or lump it.

"Why don't I leave you two alone to discuss your plans," Mrs. Waters suggested, heading out the door.

Desmond sighed and settled into one of the chairs. "Rebecca, your independence is one of the things I admire most about you. But there's such a thing as being too independent."

"Meaning what? You don't want me to have a career?" She balled her hands into fists, and glared at him. "I'm like your sister—I'm a girl so I don't count?"

"Not at all!" His eyes darkened with anger, but he kept his voice level. "Being a reporter is part of what defines you, it's part of who you are. Taking that away from you would be destroying part of what makes you so special. I'm not an idiot. I can see that."

"Then what's your problem?"

"Marriage is supposed to be a partnership. You're making decisions that affect both of us without any input from me."

Rebecca stared at him in disbelief. "And how much of what you do every day do you ask for my input on? I bet there's a lot of things you never told me about."

He didn't answer.

"That hit a nerve, didn't it?" Rebecca snarled. The sudden chill of fear warred with the heat of her anger, and she lashed out to keep the fear at bay. How serious were his secrets? Would he end up betraying her after all?

"You are like my sister, but not the way you meant," Desmond said slowly. He toyed with the salt and pepper shakers, avoiding Rebecca's gaze. "She was also very independent. Whenever the confines of family duties became too much for her, she'd head for the city. I never knew what she did, or how long she'd be gone."

Rebecca's anger drained away. He was just as scared as she was. She pulled out another chair and sat beside him. They sat in silence, punctuated by the clink of the salt and pepper shakers touching, until she reached out and folded his hands in hers. He looked up, into her eyes, and she saw the sad and frightened little boy he'd been.

"I never knew if she was coming back," he whispered.

"Desmond." She tightened her grip on his hands. "I'll always come back. I love you. And every time I leave to go out on a story, it'll rip me up inside. But to stay here, to be no more than an extension of you, that would tear me up worse. I *have* to go."

He straightened, squaring his shoulders and lifting his head with his customary confidence, and she knew he believed her. He gave her fingers a light squeeze, then favored her with a crooked grin.

"Well, that was particularly maudlin, don't you think? Can we try and keep these little scenes to a minimum after we're married?"

"Sure." Rebecca stood up and grinned back at him. "Don't disagree with me."

Desmond rose to join her, sliding his arm around her waist. "Good advice. If I pick a fight with you, I'll probably lose."

"You can count on it."

AS THE WEEKEND, and wedding, approached, Rebecca worked to get her affairs in order via long-distance. She wanted a minimum of loose ends left to take care of in person, so that she didn't have to spend any more time away from Desmond than necessary. She'd suggested he might want to return with her and help close things up, but he'd merely smiled his enigmatic grin and assured her she could handle it.

She sighed and hung up the phone, placing a check mark next to "Cable company." Only two more calls and she'd be finished. She'd accomplished more this afternoon than she'd expected.

A glance at her watch revealed the reason she'd accomplished so much. It was after eight o'clock. Desmond was late, again.

She gathered up her notes and placed them in the desk drawer she'd garnered for her use. As late as he stayed in his office, Desmond would still put in some time at home, working on files. She didn't know where he got the energy.

Or rather, she did. He used the energy that otherwise would have gone into their lovemaking. Sighing, she admitted her concern was not just that he was wearing himself out. She was jealous of his work.

To his credit, he hadn't ignored her. His kisses and caresses transported her to heights she'd only dreamed about. But it wasn't the same. She wanted to make him happy, too.

The study door opened and Desmond entered. She rose to meet him, exchanging a soul-deep kiss and crushing embrace. They broke apart when lack of oxygen or the nearness of Desmond made her lightheaded, and even then, they only separated enough to draw breath.

His eyes sparkling with merriment, he said, "I've got something for you."

"Oh?" Rebecca smiled, hoping he meant he had more energy. Instead, he pulled a plastic card from his jacket pocket.

"It's one of the Institute's keycards. You're in the system now, so I can find you wherever you are."

Rebecca took the card and examined it. It was laminated plastic, with a magnetic stripe on the back. On the front, plain black letters printed across a pale blue background read, "Rebecca Morgan Lacroix."

A warm glow settled over her. Desmond had merely appended her future married name at the end, not replaced her maiden name. He understood how important a separate identity was for her.

She turned the card over in her fingers, then glanced over at Desmond. He looked even paler than usual, and his face had become disturbingly thin. He was wearing himself out past the point of exhaustion. If he didn't take time to rest and recover soon, he'd make himself sick. Maybe she could distract him from thoughts of business. She moved closer.

"How's it work?"

"The keycards? You remember—"

"No. I mean using them to locate people."

"Oh. Every time you run the card through one of the scanners, the change in your position is recorded in a computerized database." He walked over to his desk and flipped the power switch of his personal computer. "Then you just use the Access program to locate the person's last known position."

Rebecca came up behind him and peered over his shoulder. The computer blinked quietly, prompting for a password.

"I can't use the program if I don't know your password," she reminded him.

Desmond chuckled. "It's SERAPHIM."

She watched in disbelief as he sat down and typed the letters, and the computer screen sprang to life. "Seraphim? Like the angels?"

"Why not? It's easy to remember, the right number of letters, and I can guarantee you wouldn't have guessed it."

The computer hummed and beeped for a minute, finally displaying a dark blue screen filled with pictures used to start various programs. He pointed to a picture of a compass.

"That's the Access program." Tapping keys, he selected and started the program, filling the screen with a map of the Institute.

"I didn't realize how big this place is." Rebecca traced her finger across the four topside buildings and the three levels of the complex underground. "No wonder taking care of it is using up so much of your time."

He lifted her hand away from the screen and pressed a brief kiss into her palm, but didn't comment on her thinly veiled reference to his recent added hours. He described the map of the Institute, instead.

"It's color coded. The research areas are white. Common areas are yellow. Residential areas are blue. High security areas are pink."

"High security?" She leaned closer, resting her hand on his shoulder for balance. One of the topside buildings and half of the lowest level of the complex glowed pink.

"The generators, communications and air filtration systems," he elaborated, tapping the topside building. With his other hand he reached up and covered her fingers in a light embrace. "The pumps, water, and computers are down on the bottom level."

She cuddled closer to him, resting her cheek against his thick mane of hair. The information he'd just given her was detailed enough that anyone she gave it to could shut down the Institute, but Desmond wasn't the least bit concerned. He trusted her. Completely.

She ran her hands over his shoulders in a soft caress, but the rough weave of his jacket interfered. Not to be deterred, she slid her hands around to the jacket's open front. When she reached inside to stroke his silk clad chest, he closed his eyes and let his head tip back against her breasts.

"Mmm," he sighed. "That's nice."

"I don't want to be nice," she whispered back, stroking his chest in rhythm. "I want to be wicked."

He laughed. "And you do it so well."

She reached inside his shirt to tease his hardened nipples, her own breasts swelling in sympathy. The weight of his head against her tender flesh was a delicious agony, and she leaned closer.

He reached back and guided her around the chair, sitting her on the desk before him. With excruciating patience, he unfastened the buttons of her blouse and pushed it aside, then cupped both her breasts in his warm, capable hands. She leaned into the caress, her eyes closing as she exhaled in a soft whimper. His touch excited and inflamed her until she could barely think. And yet, she wanted more. She wanted him.

He reached inside her bra, freeing her breasts to the gentle torture of his thumbs flicking across her nipples. When he replaced one hand with his mouth, she grabbed his head and forced him closer, aching for the union they could achieve if only he wasn't so exhausted.

She closed her eyes and tipped back her head, overcome with a rush of desire. A broken sigh escaped her lips as he pulled her from the desk into his lap, and she felt the strength of his desire for her. He nuzzled the tender underside of her jaw, his warm breath steaming across the sensitive skin of her throat and making her quiver with need. He tightened his arms around her and pressed a hot, openmouthed kiss on her pulse point, overloading her already straining nerves.

The world turned black and fell away, leaving only the blazing trail that ran from the fire between her legs to the miniature inferno at her throat. She lost herself in the raging wildfire of emotion burning through her, a fiery cataclysm she'd never experienced in anyone else's arms and that seemed to grow stronger each time they embraced. It seemed impossible to contain so much passion and pleasure within one person, yet Desmond's every touch only stoked the fires higher.

When she gradually drifted back to awareness, the telltale soreness in her breasts and neck reminded her that this bout of lovemaking had gone the way of the others. He had given her more pleasure than she used to dream existed, and she hadn't given him anything. She opened her eyes to find Desmond smiling down at her. He didn't seem as drawn and peaked as he had before. Maybe their lovemaking had been just what he needed, after all.

Desmond shifted his hold on Rebecca so that he could better see her face. He loved watching that sated expression she had after making love, her eyes barely half open, shining with a glint of starlight, a slumberous smile weighing on her lips. Reaching out, he brushed back the lock of hair that never stayed where she wanted it, letting the soft strands float across his fingers. So fine, like a chestnut cloud.

He smiled, knowing she'd laugh if he told her that. Having grown up in a far less poetic era, she had no patience for his more lyrical expressions. She'd probably tell him it was the shampoo she used, a honey and lemon blend that reminded him of spring. She must be running low on her travel size tube by now. They'd have to buy some more for her in Las Vegas.

He intended to stop in a drug store, anyway. He wasn't about to settle for this hands-off mental lovemaking on his wedding night.

Her eyes opened, darkening to the troubled gray of storm clouds off the Maine coast. She was feeling guilty again. He wished there was a way he could convince her that his sudden abstinence wasn't her fault, that he loved and desired her as much as ever. But how could he, without explaining what he was? He couldn't. But at least he could reassure her.

He reached out again to stroke her hair, and whispered, "You have no idea how happy you make me."

"Really?" The sparkle returned to her eyes.

"Really. Just having you near me is all I need."

She laughed nervously and glanced away. "Funny, I was just... Sometimes, I almost feel you can read my mind."

"Because I am devoted to pleasing you," he answered, too

quickly. Damn! She'd given him the perfect opportunity, and he'd wasted it. The instinct to hide, to protect his secret, had been too strong. But maybe he could still recover. "We're united by—"

"Were you going to show me how to use this computer program?"

She didn't want to listen. Very well. He wouldn't push it. Sooner or later, the topic would come up again. In the mean time, he'd show her his feelings in another way.

"Yes. It's pretty basic. Type in the name of the person you're looking for, and the person's current location lights up on the screen." He demonstrated, typing her name. A blue dot blinked on the map. He continued by typing Mrs. Waters' name. "You can even pick a second person, and find the fastest way to get from the first person's location to the second's."

"Wow! Look at that!" Rebecca leaned closer to the screen, tracing the line between her blue dot and the red dot blinking in the residential section. "It does stairs and everything."

"It's quite a program, all right." Desmond shut down that program and started another. "But I think you'll like this one better."

She relaxed in his arms, watching the screen. When she turned back to face him, a galaxy of stars shone in her eyes.

"A word processing program."

"Mm-hmm." He couldn't help himself. He brushed her lips with a light kiss. It took so little to please her. She didn't realize he'd hire an army of skilled craftsmen to hand set movable type if that's what was needed to keep her happy, and with him. "And it has built-in fax capabilities. So you can send in your stories without ever leaving home."

She laughed. "I should have known you'd have an ulterior motive."

Turning away, she put the program through it's paces.

"Do you use it much?"

"No. I draft the occasional report or announcement. Nothing much."

"From what I've seen, that's still pretty rare for an executive. Most of them prefer the personal touch of a secretary slaving away for them."

"I guess I'm unique, then. I've always been fascinated by computers. I remember when the first one was invented—" He stopped himself, but she didn't seem to notice his slip. She must have thought he was talking about personal computers.

"Me, too. We had one in our school. The old kind, that used a tape recorder to store programs. That's part of the reason I decided to become an engineer."

"An engineer?" He swiveled her away from the computer so he could see her face. No wonder she'd been so inventive in breaking out of her suite. "You studied to be an engineer?"

"For two years." She shrugged. "I thought I'd like engineering, because it was about absolutes. Equations worked the same every time, and the numbers didn't lie."

"So why'd you switch to journalism?"

"Engineering's only absolute in theory. In practice, it's all about compromises. I didn't want to compromise."

A chill rolled down his back at her steely expression.

"You don't compromise in journalism, do you?"

"No. Never. I tell the story, the best way I can. I'll take an editor's suggestions when I'm writing, of course, if it won't destroy the article. But after I've sold the story, they're free to make whatever other changes they want. That's why I only work with editors who I know respect the truth as much as I do."

He smiled and nodded and said something polite about sticking to one's guns. But his heart felt as if it had just been dipped in ice water. He'd been right not to trust her. Because no matter how much he loved and trusted Rebecca the woman, he could never forget she was also Rebecca the reporter.

Chapter 14

REBECCA DROPPED the last armload of her clothes on Desmond's bed. Gillian had helped ferry things from one bedroom to the other, until Mrs. Waters became concerned that the girl was tiring herself out. So Rebecca had completed the last few trips on her own.

She looked around the bedroom. After tonight, it would be *their* room. A thrill of anticipation raced through her, and she glanced at her watch. Only eleven o'clock. Hours yet until they left for Las Vegas.

Hours. With no reason to hurry, she could take her time and thoroughly investigate the room. She smiled, looking forward to what she might learn about her husband-to-be.

Picking up an armload of socks, she walked over to the dresser. The ebony and inlaid green marble top shone from a recent cleaning. On the left side, a shallow stone bowl held a set of car keys, and a natural-bristle brush and double-toothed comb sat neatly beside it.

She dropped the socks on the empty right side of the dresser top, and turned her attention to the drawers. Three drawers wide, and three high, the black dresser bowed out in a graceful curve. The top three drawers were shorter than the others, and the center drawers were narrower, with the stylized curves of green marble that acted as drawer pulls sized accordingly. The top left drawer contained socks, and the center drawer held handkerchiefs.

Momentarily distracted from her quest for an empty drawer, she lifted up the socks and handkerchiefs to search beneath them. Nothing. Not that she'd really expected anything. Desmond was too clever, or too security conscious, to choose the most popular hiding place for personal valuables.

She opened the top right drawer and found it empty, so she swept her socks into it. The few pairs she'd packed for her trip seemed lost in the vastness of the drawer, and she couldn't wait until the rest of her things arrived from her apartment. Then she'd look like she belonged here.

The other two drawers on the left contained Desmond's turtlenecks, underwear, and a few plain white T-shirts. The four remaining drawers were bare, chilling Rebecca with an uneasy premonition. Had he already made space for Rebecca's things, or was he honoring his wife's memory by keeping the room the way it had been when they'd shared it? Rebecca knew how little time he'd had this past week. He hadn't done any reorganizing. They'd been his wife's, and he'd never filled them.

She hurried to the closet. The black sliding doors, set in both top and bottom tracks, glided smoothly at her touch. A thin strip of insulation kept the doors from touching, making their movement eerily silent. She pulled the chain on the overhead light bulb, illuminating a deep closet with a double row of clothes. The back row held darker, heavier suits and shirts, while the front held spring and summer clothing. Desmond had used both rows, rather than hanging anything on the other side of the closet.

Rebecca shoved open the other closet door, and hung as many of her clothes as she could on the empty bar. She even hung shirts and pants she'd normally fold and keep in a drawer. Anything to occupy that ominous space.

Trying to fill more space, she spread some of Desmond's suit coats further along the rack. Then she stopped, and really looked at them. She was no fashion expert, but she knew styles changed, lapels became wider or narrower, suits changed from single- to double-breasted and back. The suits hanging in this closet couldn't be more than five years old.

She flipped through the shirts, finding mostly washable silk and rayon blends no more than a few years old. The one exception was a dark green chamois shirt that looked well-worn. But she didn't know if it had come that way, like acid-washed jeans, or if it had actually been in service for more than five years.

She thought back on her discussion with Dr. Chen. He'd been one of the Institute's first researchers. And he'd been working there for five years.

Desmond had purchased an entire new wardrobe when he took this job as Director of the Institute. Why? What had he been before that? Rebecca didn't know, but she was certain it had something to do with the secret of his missing years, and why she'd been unable to find references to him in any of her normal background searches.

She sat down on the floor of the closet, appreciating the softness of the deep pile throw rug covering the wood, and tried to think this through. A pair of extra pillows lay in the corner of the closet, and she picked one up to lean against, revealing a brassbound travel case that had been hidden beneath the pillows.

She grabbed the case and examined it. Small, no more than a foot in each direction, the brass fittings and reinforcements made it heavy. The top clasps had keyholes indicating they could be locked, but when she touched them, they sprang open. A narrow tray, lined with velvet, held cuff links, tie tacks, and two antique pocket watches. Hooking her fingers into the loops on the sides of the tray, she lifted it out. The tray beneath held a variety of men's jewelry, from a delicately crafted gold watch chain to a chunky gold nugget bracelet of the kind that had been popular a few years back.

Intrigued, she pulled out that tray to see what was beneath it. A bulky suede bag filled the tray. She opened it and poured out a jumble of necklaces, earrings, pins and bracelets. Kitschy items from the dollar store mingled with items easily worth a few hundred dollars. Then she spotted a necklace whose delicate tracery spelled out "Olivia."

Rebecca crammed the jewelry back into the bag, tying it shut with a savage knot. The game had soured. She wasn't sure if she wanted to know more about Desmond's past. Not if it was a past that included another woman.

She might not want the information, but she needed to know it. You couldn't change the truth by pretending it was something else. Her mother had tried that, and look where it had gotten her. No, she had to know the answer, even if she didn't like it. Reaching into the case, she lifted out the tray.

The next tray held only construction paper cards from Gillian; Birthday, Christmas and Father's Day. Penciled in the corner of each card was a notation, such as "Gillian at 2 years."

She broke off her investigation of the box to compare the writing on the cards. It was obviously penned by the same hand, in a perfect antique bookplate script. She'd suspected Desmond of taking voice lessons to disguise his accent. Had he also studied calligraphy to disguise the personality clues inherent in handwriting?

She'd hoped to learn answers to her existing questions, not uncover more puzzles. Desmond managed to overturn her plans again, without even knowing. With a sigh, she replaced the cards and turned back to the travel box.

The next tray was empty, with no loops to lift it out by. It had to be the bottom level. Rebecca glanced at the outside of the case, then measured the depth of the tray with her hand against the outside wall. No, there was still room for one more tray below this one.

She sunk her nails into the velvet corners and pulled. Moving at a grinding slowness, the tray slid up the walls of the case and popped out. She peered inside. A gray and maroon cloth, the kind sold on late night television to preserve silver services, shrouded a thin rectangle. She lifted out the bundle and unwrapped an antique silver picture frame.

The picture seemed equally ancient, a family portrait of stern, unsmiling people. A middle-aged woman garbed in a dark burgundy gown and a younger woman in a similar gown of shimmering lavender sat in two high backed velvet chairs, flanked by two young men standing at stiff attention. Two boys, one a teenager and the other still a child, sat on stools in the very front. The detail of the picture was incredible. Rebecca could see the pattern of the women's lace collars and count the hairs in the teenager's unruly cowlick.

But who were they? The men's features were similar to Desmond's, and the young lady in the middle bore a striking resemblance to Gillian, so they were obviously relatives. Rebecca's attention was caught by the expression of the youngest boy. Although his face was as unmoving as the others, his eyes blazed with the hunger of barely restrained curiosity as he stared at the photographer. She recognized the expression, just as she recognized the same hunger to know more in the man's library shelves filled with science fiction and popular science books. The boy was Desmond.

Rebecca put names to the other faces. His mother and Veronica in the middle. The older son, with the stern expression, was Etienne. The younger one, with a slightly bruised expression, as if the world had hurt him badly and he hadn't quite recovered, must be Roderick. The teenager perched precariously on the edge of his stool had to be Jean-Michel. But what were they doing in such ridiculously old-fashioned clothes?

She frowned, trying to remember other old photographs she'd seen. They'd been brown, and rather blurry. Not crisp and in color like this. So it must be a new picture, with the family dressed in old clothes for some reason.

Of course. Historical sites had photographers that would take your picture in antique costumes. This must be a souvenir from a family vacation. If the rest of his family was as adverse to photographs as Desmond, this might be the only picture he had of them. Carefully rewrapping the heavy frame in its protective cloth, Rebecca replaced the picture where she'd found it. Then she replaced the other trays, and finally put the pillow back on top of the case. Her intuition told her she'd just learned something important, but Rebecca had no idea what it was.

DESMOND TIMED their departure to the minute. He arrived home half an hour before sunset, packed his bag, put two bottles of medicine in a cooler, made sure both Gillian and Mrs. Waters knew what was expected of them in his absence, and escorted Rebecca through the employee elevator to the underground parking garage just as night claimed the sky.

She carried her own suitcase and held tightly to his hand, although she did scan the parked cars, muttering numbers under her breath.

"Three hundred eighty-seven," he whispered, amused to see she was still trying to find answers to the questions she'd posed when she first arrived.

She blushed.

Desmond's car waited at the curb. He turned to see Rebecca's reaction.

She glanced at him, the car, then back at him. "It's a very pretty car."

Picking up their bags, he chuckled at his own foolishness, like a raw boy trying to impress her with the power and speed of his chosen vehicle. "You don't even know what kind of car it is, do you?"

"Of course I do! It's a...sports car."

Still smiling, he dropped the bags in the trunk. Rebecca tried again. "An expensive sports car."

He shut the trunk and came back to open the door for her. "It's a Lamborghini."

Settling into the leather interior, she smiled up at him with a devilish twinkle in her eye. "So I was right, then."

He leaned down to kiss her, captivated anew. A moment later, he lost himself in her honeysuckle sweetness, letting his mind drift with hers. She broke off the kiss with a mental wrench that staggered him.

"Enough of that. We don't want to be late to our own wedding."

"Don't worry." He patted the car's hood as he circled around to the driver's side. "That's the advantage to a car like this. You can make up lost time."

Her laughter rang out like a carillon of bells. "If we got involved now, the car doesn't exist that could make up that much time."

He slid into the driver's seat and strapped himself in place. Firing up the engine, he paused to carry her hand to his lips for a brief kiss.

"What can I say? Where you're concerned, I'm insatiable."

She drew in a sharp breath, and images of the two of them entwined rushed over him. He felt himself hardening in response to her desire, and jerked his hand away. Throwing the car into gear, he squealed out of the garage. It was going to be a long drive.

They rolled through the night, the headlights picking out stands of aspen like pale ghosts in protective circles amid the darker blackness of the ponderosa pines. Rebecca thumbed through his assortment of CD's, looking for suitable background music.

"I can't believe this. Big Band tunes, jazz, folk trios, rock music, and new age instrumentals."

"So? I have eclectic tastes."

"I'll say." She snorted and pulled out another CD. "I've never even heard of half these people."

"Expand your horizons." He reached over and pulled out a CD at random. "Have you ever heard this one?"

She looked at the casing. "Vangelis? No. What's he do?"

"Listen and find out."

Shrugging, she opened the case and popped out the CD. A few moments later, the first invigorating notes of an instrumental piece cascaded through the car's sound system, and she was hooked.

Like a child with a new toy, exploring Desmond's music collection kept her occupied for the rest of the trip. He'd convinced her of the merits of Mozart and Vangelis, and she'd agreed to reserve judgment on swing and barbershop, by the time the lights of Las Vegas appeared in the distance.

Not only was the horizon bathed with the multicolored glow he remembered from his last trip, a beam of pure white shot straight into the sky with a luminescence so bright it was blinding.

"Do you want to go to the hotel first?" Rebecca asked. "Or should we get the license first?"

"The hotel. And then we need to buy rings. I'm sure there must be a store still open. The court house is open all night, so we don't have to rush." It seemed too amazing to be true, that in a few short hours, Rebecca would be his wife. She sat with her head bowed, silently shuffling the CD's.

Desmond reached out and clasped her hand. "Nervous?"

"A little." She gave a shaky laugh. "I thought it was the groom who was supposed to get cold feet."

"I planned ahead and wore thermal socks."

"Oh, you—" She chuckled with real humor, and playfully swatted at his arm.

He pulled off the highway, and onto Tropicana Boulevard. Rebecca leaned forward in her seat and scanned the darkened streets.

"I thought there'd be more lights."

"Don't worry. There will be." A quick left and a right looped them around the airport, bringing them out almost at the end of Las Vegas Boulevard. Before them stretched a shimmering vista of rainbow hued light.

"Look! It's a pyramid! And a castle!" Rebecca leaned past him to gawk, then spun to look out her window with a giggle. "A Polynesian village. Oh, look at that gate, made out of light. It's beautiful! Is that another pyramid?"

He kept silent, letting her enjoy her first sight of the hotels and casinos. He'd been here twice before, and each time it seemed to get larger, louder and brighter. After a lifetime spent trying to avoid notice, such blatant plays for attention made him uncomfortable. But he had to agree, in its own way, the city was truly amazing.

"It's a lion!" Rebecca laughed and squeezed his arm. "What's next?"

"What's next is a traffic jam," he muttered.

After spending fifteen minutes watching the same ads scroll by in foot high letters on ten-foot tall screens, the city's lights no longer seemed so glamorous. In fact, Desmond and Rebecca made a game out of finding the missing light bulbs in the signs, with Desmond looking for missing red bulbs and Rebecca looking for blue ones. Green bulbs counted for either one of them.

"Finally," he sighed, turning across traffic into the hotel's driveway. The backlit Roman statues and lighted water fountain would have been garish in any other surroundings. Here, it seemed tasteful and subdued.

He helped Rebecca out of the car, while a bellman emptied the trunk and an eager looking valet held out his hand for the keys. The fresh-faced boy looked out of place, as if a Mormon native of Utah had migrated southwest for the winter and had been unable to complete his return trip in the spring. Desmond handed him the keys wrapped in a ten dollar tip.

The bellman advanced on them with a smile. "Welcome to Las Vegas. Are you here to get married?"

"Yes," Rebecca answered. "How'd you know?"

"You had that look about you. When's the happy occasion?"

"Two o'clock in the morning," Desmond told him, nudging Rebecca toward the door. "We really need to get checked in."

"Congratulations! If there's anything you need, you just call down to the front desk. Or I can bring it up to your room with your luggage." The man's grin widened.

"Actually," Rebecca said, "we need to find a jewelry store that's open."

"You're in luck! Our Forum Shops stay open until eleven o'clock, and we have some wonderful jewelers. If you'd like, I can point them out to you on the map."

"Thank you. That won't be necessary." Desmond pulled Rebecca through the doors into the blinking, flashing, clanging foyer. Slot machines jangled their happy melodies and poured change into steel buckets, all the while advertising their wares in colors as bright as they'd seen on the Strip. The registration area off to the side was slightly more subdued, but the cling and clang of winning spins provided a constant background accompaniment.

"Welcome to Caesar's Palace. May I help you?"

"We're checking in. The name is Lacroix." Desmond placed his credit card on the marble counter.

"That says Prescott Institute," Rebecca whispered.

"It's a corporate card. I don't have a personal one."

She nodded to herself. It was almost as if he'd just confirmed something for her, but he didn't know what. Why would she care about his credit cards? Of course. Not his credit cards, his credit.

He grinned. "You little minx. You tried to run a credit check on me before you came out here, didn't you?"

"You can't blame a girl for being careful," she tossed back.

The clerk shuffled slowly through a pile of papers. When Desmond and Rebecca didn't say anything else scintillating, the woman handed them a hotel folder.

"These are your room keys. Instructions are on the back." She slid one of the plastic cards out of the folder and flipped it over, then tapped the circled number on the folder. "This is your room number. Memorize it, don't write it on the card or on a piece of paper you carry with the card. Your room is in the Olympic Tower, straight through the casino. You see the Emperor's Club booth? Head for that. The elevators will be on your left. The bellman will bring your luggage up."

"Thank you," they chorused. Sharing a laugh, Desmond wrapped his arm around Rebecca, and she nestled close against his side. Her thoughts curled just as closely against his, in a tumult of anticipation, proving how deeply she trusted him by lowering her mental barriers. He snatched the packet off the desk and hurried her toward the elevator. He wanted to drop his own shields and melt into her. But they needed to reach the room to merge together properly.

He stopped, halfway across the casino, chilled by his near lapse of judgment. Surrounded by blinking, beeping, clanging distractions, he couldn't see the walls, let alone look for the sundries shop he knew must be somewhere in this lobby.

"Hon? Is something wrong?" Rebecca asked, leaning close to be heard over the din.

"No. I'm just looking for the gift shop." He started walking toward the elevators again. Once they got out of the casino, they could skirt the edges until they found it.

"The gift shop?"

"Mm-hmm." They exited the casino, into a quieter area of shops and restaurants, and he pulled her aside. "Gillian's more than enough to handle. I don't really want another child right now. Do you?"

Rebecca's blush scalded her cheeks, paling to an adorable soft pink by her ears. "I, uh, hadn't thought about it. But, yeah. You're right. We should, um, do something about that."

"Why, Rebecca," he teased. "I never would have thought someone with your voracious sexual appetite would be a prude."

"I'm not! I'm just—" Realizing he was teasing her, she frowned and tugged him toward the elevators. "We can stop at any late night drug store for that. We need to get our luggage, then go out and buy the rings before the jewelry stores close."

He sighed melodramatically, but followed readily. "Dear heart, sometimes you can be too practical for your own good."

THEY ARRIVED at their room before the bellman. Opening the door, Desmond's gaze was immediately drawn to the huge king size bed dominating the room. Bright neon colors played across the spread, shining through the window from the displays on the Strip. Rebecca strolled over to the window and stared out.

"Oh, look. It's like a giant riverboat paddling down the street. Come see."

He joined her at the window, but his attention was on the draperies. The sheer gauze privacy curtain wouldn't shield any sunlight to speak of. The thicker, primary curtain might block most of it. But it was alarmingly thin compared to the reassuring blackness of his tinted windows back home.

"Will the neon light come in, even with the drapes drawn, do you suppose?" he asked her. Without waiting for a reply, he pulled the privacy curtain closed on his side of the window, then fumbled for the cords to draw the drapes.

She pulled her side of the sheer curtain closed, and stepped out of the way of the drapes. "Not much on scenery, are you?"

"I'm sorry." He opened the drapes again, and parted the curtains. "What was it you wanted to show me?"

"There. The big boat."

A knock on the door saved him from having to answer.

"That must be the bellman. I'll get it."

The man unloaded their bags, and Desmond hastened him out with a generous tip. They could settle in later. They needed to get to the jewelry store before it closed.

Desmond and Rebecca took the elevator back down to the lobby. Turning in the other direction, they walked through a different casino to reach the Forum Shops. They stepped through the archway separating the two areas, and it was like stepping into another world.

The marble paving stones beneath their feet lasted only as long as the gold-plated, marble-fronted slot machines. Then the ceiling lifted, painted midnight black and shining with tiny Christmas-light stars. The storefronts became two or even three stories tall, with elaborate frescoes and statues on their roofs, and the floor changed to a cobblestone street with raised stone sidewalks. They came out on the village square, in the center of which sat an elaborate fountain depicting plunging horses, cavorting sea creatures, and a selection of Roman gods.

Desmond stepped closer, amazed at the detail and lifelike nature of the statues. They must have paid a fortune to get such skilled sculptors. Not to mention the sheer cost of all this marble. He ran his hand over the hoof of one of the horses.

"It's Plexiglas."

"Of course it is," Rebecca answered over her shoulder, heading around the fountain for the jewelry store. "What did you expect? This is Las Vegas. Everything's an illusion."

"I should have expected it. But I've never been inside Caesar's before. With all the marble on the floor and walls, it was an honest mistake."

She chuckled. "Uh-huh. And I've got a bridge I can sell you...."

He caught up with her, and they entered the jewelry store together. The only customers in the store, they had the salesman's full attention.

"We'd like to buy a set of wedding rings, please," Rebecca told him.

"Gold, nothing too fancy, but more than just a plain band," Desmond clarified.

"Of course. If you'd please take a seat, I'll bring out our selection. I'm sure you'll find just what you're looking for."

After a minimum of debate, they selected rings with an ivy vine etched on them. The salesman wrapped the rings, congratulated Desmond and Rebecca on their upcoming wedding, and put a significant dent in the corporate card's credit line.

"You don't have cheap tastes, do you?" Desmond asked as they headed for the door.

"Of course not. I chose you, didn't I?"

He couldn't help but laugh. How could he argue with that line of reasoning? "Why do I even bother trying?"

"Beats me." She grinned. "You know you're never going to win."

They stepped out into the plaza. It seemed lighter than before, brighter. Desmond cast a reflexive glance upward, then stared, unable to believe what he saw. The stars had faded, and the midnight black sky had been replaced by pre-dawn gray.

Oh, God. They'd been in the jewelry store far longer than he'd thought. It was almost dawn. He had to get back inside.

He lengthened his strides, pulling Rebecca along with him.

"Hey! Where's the fire?"

Her words acted like a tonic, snapping him out of his knee-jerk panic. He was already inside. The sky above him was an illusion. But what an illusion!

He stopped, so suddenly she ran into him, and turned to face the east. The first tender fingers of rosy pink were stretching out, tinting the gray sky around them a soft baby blue. Was that really what it looked like? It had been so long since he'd seen a sunrise.

He felt the warmth of Rebecca's presence beside him, and pulled her close. He wanted her to share this beautiful sunrise with him.

"Desmond?" she whispered. "Hon? You're crushing my hand."

He loosed his grip on her fingers, and whispered back, "Isn't it amazing?"

A golden glow edged the buildings, sliding up into the sky. The rays of sunlight slid from pink, to peach, to orange, to gold, and the sky deepened from a cold pale blue to a brilliant robin's egg blue. Fluffy white clouds drifted across the sky, blocking the sun from his sight. But he could see the light, burning, lighting the entire sky.

Rebecca tugged on his hand, and he forced his gaze away from the beautiful sunny sky. Her gray eyes were dark in her pale face.

"What is it? You're frightening me."

"Wasn't that sunrise beautiful?"

"It's just a trick. Special effects. Lights and mirrors." She reached up and touched his cheek. "My God, are you crying?"

"No, of course not." He blinked, and struggled to get his feelings under control. Normal human beings didn't react this way. "I was staring at the light for too long."

"Yeah, I noticed." She tilted her head and studied him, not quite mollified. "But why were you staring at it?"

"I'd never seen anything like it before."

"Oh." She chuckled, and turned the same soft rose as the sunrise. "You just seemed so blasé about the other sights of the city. I forgot you've seen them before."

He returned her smile, even though he didn't feel like smiling. A cold knot of fear was growing in his stomach. When he'd seen the sunrise, he'd been inspired. She was so close to him, almost a part of him, that he'd instinctively tried to share the experience with her. Thank God her mental shields had been up.

Without that mental communion, she hadn't understood the meaning behind his comments. Which was a relief. If she had, it all might have been over. If she found out what he was before they were married, she might run back to New York and leave him forever.

No, he had to keep his secret hidden. He couldn't tell her until he was sure the knowledge wouldn't drive her away from him. He only hoped the day would come when he could tell her. And that the day did not come too late.

Chapter 15

REBECCA KNEW she'd remember this moment forever. Desmond, handsome as the devil in a black tuxedo, framed against a backdrop of scarlet and pink lilies and the delicate white wedding bells of lilies-of-the-valley, taking her hand in his strong, warm fingers. Sliding the cold metal of the ring onto her finger, and clasping his hand around hers until the gold heated beneath his touch. Staring deep into her eyes as he intoned his vow.

"With this ring, I pledge my love to you. I will honor and cherish you, for better or for worse, for richer or for poorer, in sickness and in health. We shall be as one, all the days of our lives."

The minister turned to her, and prompted, "Miss Morgan?"

She was drowning in the emerald sea of Desmond's eyes, sparkling jewels that shone with his love for her. She could lose herself in those eyes, drown and never come back up for air. And she wouldn't mind in the least. United, heart and soul, for eternity.

The minister coughed, and Desmond gave her fingers a quick squeeze. She blinked, and felt a hot flush cover her cheeks. Taking the ring from the minister, she lifted Desmond's hand. Following the minister's prompting, she repeated the vow.

"With this ring, I pledge my love to you. I will honor and cherish you, for better or for worse, for richer or for poorer, in sickness and in health. We shall be as one, all the days of our lives."

The gold band slid on smoothly, nestling at the base of his finger. She wrapped her fingers around his hand, needing to feel the ring's solid weight. It was real. They were married.

The minister continued speaking, but she ignored him, watching Desmond. The rosy light from the stained glass panel gilded his features, highlighting the rich fullness of his lips. Lips which smiled, and parted, as he bent his head toward her. Closing her eyes, she lifted her face to his and received his lips in a kiss that was as much promise as offering.

He pulled back, smiling down at her. She smiled back, deliriously happy. Everything was perfect.

"Congratulations," the minister interrupted. She smiled at him, too. She'd smile at the whole world, but the chapel held only the witnesses needed to make the ceremony legal. So she smiled at them.

"Thank you," Desmond answered, his voice soft and husky. Their wedding had affected him as deeply as it had her.

He released her hand long enough to shake hands with the minister, and receive the payment envelope. While Desmond filled the envelope, the minister shook her hand, too, and kissed her cheek. Then Desmond was leading her down the aisle, between the ribbon-festooned benches, and out to the car.

He kissed her again before settling her into her seat, and again before starting the ignition. They stopped at the light by the mall, and he took the opportunity for a long, lingering kiss that left her breathless. Sliding his hand up her new white stockings, he pushed aside the layered white chiffon skirt of the dress they'd bought just a few hours ago. The heat of his hand burned her thigh, sending a flash fire skittering across her skin. He pulled his hand back to shift the car, and his absence chilled her like a January midnight. Then he was back, sliding his palm even higher, cupping her in heat and touching off a firestorm of need.

She shifted in her seat, pressing against him. "Are we there yet?"

"Almost." He sounded as breathless as she did.

He jerked the wheel, making a one-handed turn that got them into the hotel's driveway, but almost clipped one of the fir trees pillaring the drive. Slamming on the brake, he threw the car out of gear as soon as it stopped. He cut the ignition, opened the door, and was helping her out of the car before the valet had closed half the distance to their car. They abandoned it, trusting that the valet would know what to do with it, and hurried through the hotel doors.

The clinking and blinking machines sounded like an angelic choir, come to serenade them on their special day. Holding hands, they hurried to the elevators, not quite breaking into a run. When the elevator came, Desmond took advantage of their privacy to lean her against the mirrored wall and kiss her senseless.

The elevator chimed. Desmond stepped away, leaving her dazed with passion. She had a brief vision of how she must appear to him, her gray eyes glittering with desire beneath half-closed lids, her lips swollen and dark red from the force of their kisses. His strong fingers twisted in the silk of her hair, pulling her closer, and then the doors slid open.

They ran from the elevator, pelting down the hall to their room. Desmond fumbled to work the lock as she wrapped her arms around his waist and rubbed herself against him.

"Hurry," she whispered, her breath steaming against his ear. She slid her hands lower, and felt his trembling reaction to her touch.

The door opened and they fell inside, stumbling toward the bed. She unzipped her dress and pulled it over her head, and he pulled off his topcoat, tie and cummerbund. He unbuttoned his shirt, while she stripped off her slip. She reached for her bra strap just as he unbuttoned his pants. Then they stopped. And looked at each other.

"Curtains," she said, just as he said, "Condoms."

They rushed to the far sides of the room, he to wrench closed the drapes, and she to retrieve the box of protection they'd purchased with her stockings. Coming together again, they finished undressing each other, trembling hands slowing them down and adding to their urgency. Finally, they both stood naked in the center of the room. He was so handsome, she could die from looking at him. And he was ready for her, too.

She slid the condom over him, making him groan at the agony of her whisper soft touch. Grabbing her shoulders, he threw her to the bed and tumbled on top of her.

The past week of denial had only inspired her longing, and now she arched and writhed against him, unable to get enough of him. Wrapping her arms around him, she clawed at his back, trying to draw him even closer. They branded each other with kisses, scorching marks across shoulders, chests and necks.

He plunged inside her, and she screamed in need. His hands were behind her, pulling her closer, and she raked his back, striving to be closer still. He bent his head to kiss her neck, hot, liquid kisses that fueled her passion to an intensity she'd never dreamed of. She couldn't see. She couldn't think. She was consumed by need, a wildfire blazing out of control. And only one thing would satisfy her. Opening her mouth wide, she pressed a heated kiss to the pounding vein in his throat. And then drove her teeth through the skin.

Hot, salty blood spilled out of him as he collapsed on top of her, his seed bloating the condom. She kissed and nuzzled, transported by their communion, even as he kissed and nuzzled her. She no longer knew where she stopped and he began. They were truly united as one.

Then the rhythmic stroking of his tongue faltered. A shudder ripped through him, shaking them apart, and he pulled back to stare at her in wide-eyed horror. She blinked, not understanding, and reached for him, only to have him recoil away from her.

"No. Oh dear God, no." All the color drained from his face, and she saw for the first time the ragged cut on his neck, and the blood smeared across his shoulder and chest. He leapt from the bed and ran into the bathroom, slamming the door behind him. But she still had time to see the mass of fresh red welts scarring his back.

She sat up in the bed, and looked at her hands. One of her nails was broken, and a thin layer of sticky crimson covered her fingertips. She brought it closer, fascinated by the gleaming red surface. Then she popped the tip of one finger into her mouth, drawing off the sweet warmth.

She yanked her finger from her mouth and started shivering. What was wrong with her? What had she done?

Closing her eyes, she let a brokenhearted moan escape her before plunging her head into the pillow, and muffling her sobs beneath another pillow. She'd ruined everything. Desmond thought she was some sort of psychopath, a deranged Black Widow who literally wanted to devour him. If he wanted an immediate divorce, no judge would refuse him after seeing the injuries she'd inflicted on him. The one man she'd ever love, and she'd chased him away in horror. But why? Why?

Stifling a sob, she let the tears course down her cheeks and wash away the blood staining her face. If only she could as easily wash away the memory of what she'd done.

DESMOND CROUCHED on the floor of the bathroom, the cool tile wall soothing against his back. He was probably staining it with blood. It didn't matter. Nothing mattered except Rebecca, and what he'd done to her.

He'd lived with the blood thirst for so long, he'd ceased paying attention to it, much as normal human beings drink water as a matter of course, and only think about it on long trips or after exerting themselves. But she'd been unprepared for the fierce craving.

They'd wanted to be close to each other. Whether he'd lowered his shields too far, or she'd mastered her telepathic powers enough to break through them, didn't matter. The result was the same in either case. A complete merging of thought, so that they truly had been united in body and mind. And while he could control his cursed needs, she could not.

He buried his face in his hands. And to think he'd been worried about protecting her from accidental infection. Instead, she'd chosen the most direct source of contamination, by drinking his blood. The memory of her hot tongue, lapping at his neck, flooded him with desire. He wanted nothing more than to go back out there and rip open a vein, filling her with his essence. And he would no longer confine himself to tasting her sweetness. No, he would plunder her spirit, and absorb her into himself. They'd share each other so deeply, they'd be transformed by the experience.

He'd already stood and walked halfway to the door, but that phrase stopped him cold. Transformed.

Clutching the marble sink top, he bent his head. No. He couldn't risk it. He could control his own urges, but it was a control won after decades of effort. She couldn't afford that kind of time to master her desires, not when one mistake could mean her death. The only solution was complete and total abstinence. Not only couldn't he touch her, he couldn't even open his mind to her. He didn't dare risk anything less comprehensive. This was one error he couldn't repeat.

A sudden cold chilled him from the inside out, as he realized it might already be too late. She could have already become infected. What if she was dying now?

He threw open the bathroom door. She lay face down on the bed, naked and still, a pillow over her head. A brief fear that she'd smothered herself slashed through his heart. But no, she was breathing, and her heart beat steadily. Her mind held only the blank fog of a dreamless sleep.

Not daring to touch her, or even go any nearer to the bed, he pulled on the clothes he'd worn earlier, before changing into the tuxedo. Grabbing one of his medicine bottles, he left the room. He needed to think, and he couldn't do it near her. With any luck, the shopping arcade was still open, even if the stores were closed. He'd like to see the sunrise again.

He was forced to settle for a secluded back booth in the 24-hour cafe. After ordering a cheeseburger, rare, and a pot of coffee, he opened the medicine bottle and took a swig. It had warmed to room temperature. He drained the rest of the bottle, feeling the kick of renewal as his body started converting the liquid.

He set the empty bottle on the table and stared at it. Plain black glass, nothing to reveal the dark secret it contained. Modernized, sanitized, it was as far removed from a living, breathing human being as his coming cheeseburger was removed from a steer. But it hadn't always been that way.

In the early days of their curse, he and Philippe wore masks and robes to drink sacrificial blood at Voodoo ceremonies, restoring the strength sapped daily by the sun. Then one day, after too many hours riding under the harsh summer sun, they killed a man.

That night, Desmond made a vow. He would never allow his need for blood to blind him to others' humanity. He vowed to take only that which was freely offered, and no more. It was a vow he'd never broken in all the years that followed, no matter how desperate his situation had been.

His order arrived, recalling him to the present.

Not two hours ago, he'd made another vow. To Rebecca. He'd promised to love, honor and cherish her. Less than two hours, and he'd already failed her. Or maybe not. He didn't knew how the blood he drank made it into his bloodstream, but there was no similar route in normal human beings. It was possible that the infected blood Rebecca had swallowed hadn't been able to contaminate her system. When Desmond stopped to consider it, the odds were fairly high against his cursed blood surviving intact in her system. But even a million-to-one chance was too much risk to ever take again.

He glanced at his watch. They'd never make it back to the Institute before sunrise. Then he smiled grimly, remembering his earlier comment to Rebecca. The Lamborghini had a top cruising speed of 196 miles per hour. They'd make it.

REBECCA PULLED her head out from under the pillow and glanced sleepily around the room, wondering what had awakened her. The bathroom door was open, and the room beyond was empty and dark. Desmond. She sat up and searched the room. His clothing was gone. He was gone.

She threw off the sheets and climbed out of bed. The time for tears had passed. It was time to take action. She wasn't sure exactly what she'd do, yet, but she'd start by taking a shower.

When she flipped on the bathroom light, she saw blood stains, smeared down the white tile wall. She looked at her hands, seeing the dark brown stains beneath her nails, and remembered the way she'd clawed at Desmond's back. Dear God.

She stepped closer to the wall, then screwed up her courage and touched the stain. Flakes of red-brown fell from the tile. Spinning around, she grabbed a wash cloth and doused it with hot water. The stain yielded to her scrubbing, and in no time at all, the wall was clean. No trace remained of what she had done to Desmond.

Stepping into the shower, she blasted herself with scalding hot water, trying to erase all signs of what had happened. The dried blood washed away, even the stains beneath her nails. But no matter how hard she scrubbed, she couldn't remove her own horror at her actions.

She conceded defeat, and toweled off. She dressed in clean clothing, and put away the clothes she'd worn earlier. The wedding dress seemed to mock her, with it's virginal white. She'd been anything but timid and innocent.

Finished with her own clothing, she folded and put away Desmond's tuxedo. She traced the satin edging of the lapels with her fingers, and sighed. It was supposed to be so different. This should have been the happiest day of her life. But she'd ruined it. The script didn't call for her to attack her new husband and send him fleeing in horror.

She stuffed the tuxedo into a drawer, and turned her attention to the bed. The stains wouldn't come out, but she could hide them. Struggling to make the bed, despite sheets that stuck to each other where the blood had matted, she tried to puzzle out the twist of her psychology that had made her react like this.

Since she'd made love to Desmond before without attacking him, the difference had to be that they were married now. And the only explanation she could think of that made any sense to her was that deep down, she was reinforcing her childhood image of marriage, by trying to kill her husband. When she got back to the Institute, she'd look up a local psychiatrist, and make an appointment to try and work this all out. But in the meantime, it would be safest for both of them if she didn't get too close to Desmond.

The hotel room door opened, and Desmond walked in, a black medicine bottle in his hand. She winced. He suffered from a blood disorder. Maybe she'd remembered that, subconsciously, and attacked him at his weakest point.

Desmond glanced around the room, but didn't comment on her cleaning. Instead, he asked, "Are you packed? We're leaving."

"Now? In the middle of the night?"

For an answer, he just stared at her. His eyes, always so bright and glittering with emotion, were the flat green of antique bottle glass. She pulled her suitcase from the closet and started emptying the drawers into it.

She heard him making phone calls to the front desk, bell captain and valet parking. Apparently their guests did not usually check out at this hour, since he had to repeatedly assure them that he was not dissatisfied with their service. Rebecca finished packing her bag, and turned to where his suitcase sat on the folding luggage stand. The only thing he'd taken out had been the tuxedo, and she repacked that while he was arguing with the parking attendant.

He hung up the phone. After a long moment of silence, he turned to face her.

"The bellman will be up in a few minutes. They should have our car ready by the time we get down to the lobby."

"Good." She twisted her wedding ring around her finger, and added, "I packed your suitcase, too."

"Thank you."

She stood by the suitcases, waiting for him to say something about what had happened. He didn't. Finally, she couldn't take the waiting any longer.

"About what happened earlier—"

"I don't think anything more needs to be said." His face had the rigid determination Rebecca remembered from when he'd first described Gillian's disease. "We made a mistake, and we won't make it again."

She loved him more in that instant that she ever had before. Instead of reviling her for what she'd done, he was willing to take a share of the blame. He couldn't have any idea why she'd acted the way she did, yet he didn't accuse her. He didn't want to get rid of her. He was sticking by her, just as he'd promised to do in his wedding vows, for better or for worse. A horrible new interpretation of his words occurred to her.

"By a mistake, did you mean...?" Unable to finish the sentence, she held out her left hand so that the light reflected off of her wedding ring.

"No! I will not forsake my vow." He started to take a step towards her, then checked himself.

She turned away so that he wouldn't see the relief in her face. Relief and shame. She shouldn't have doubted him.

A knock at the door spared her from having to answer him. "I'll get it," she said, and opened the door for the bellman and his cart.

"Just these two bags, ma'am?" he asked.

"Yes. No, wait." She searched the room for the cooler, but didn't see it. Reluctantly, she turned to Desmond. "Where's the cooler?"

"I put it out of the way." He retrieved the small plastic case from where he'd stowed it under the desk, and handed it to the bellman.

The elevator ride down to the lobby was accomplished in awkward silence. Rebecca couldn't help contrasting it to their earlier trip in the elevator, when they'd been unable to keep their hands off of each other. Now, they stood in opposite corners, like boxers before the starting bell.

They reached the car, and Desmond tipped the valet and bellman. He spoke to each of them. But he didn't say anything to her.

He opened her door and held it for her, but he didn't extend a hand to help her in, or draw down the seat belt for her. She'd started to expect his chivalrous signs of affection, but they were gone now. He couldn't be chivalrous when he was afraid to touch her. A dull ache started to pound in her temples, and at the base of her neck. Discovering she'd clenched her teeth together, she forced her jaw muscles to relax.

He wheeled onto the Strip, and she shut her eyes against the garish intrusion of light. She didn't want to be reminded that she was surrounded by happy, laughing people. She especially didn't want to be reminded that only a few short hours ago, she'd been one of those happy people.

She felt the car turn and bump over a slight curb. Opening her eyes, she saw a small gas station, dwarfed by the huge casino complexes surrounding it. Desmond pulled up to the pumps, and got out of the car.

"This won't take long," he assured her. At least he was still speaking to her.

"Take your time." She put the seat back and closed her eyes. It was very late, almost three o'clock, and the events of the day had tired her out. Since it had taken them five hours to get to Las Vegas, they should get back to the Institute around eight in the morning. She wasn't going to wait until then to go to sleep, especially since she and Desmond weren't likely to say anything to each other the whole ride back.

The car shook as he climbed back in, lightly scented with gasoline fumes, and slammed his door closed. He revved the engine, and accelerated into traffic. Rebecca kept her eyes closed, feigning sleep, until a sudden swerve tossed her against the door frame.

Desmond glanced over at her, his eyes unreadable in the highway darkness. "Did I wake you?"

"I wasn't really asleep," she admitted. "Just resting."

She glanced outside, but wasn't able to see anything. At first she thought it was too dark, but then she realized the scenery was moving by too quickly to focus on. She sneaked a peak at the speedometer.

"One hundred and forty miles per hour! Are you trying to kill us?"

He turned to answer her, and she shrieked, "Don't look at me. Look at the road!"

He sighed, but kept his attention fixed on the road where it belonged. "No, I am not trying to kill us. I am trying to get us home in the shortest time possible."

"You can take longer. I don't mind." She risked another look at the speedometer. One hundred and fifty. She gripped the dashboard, even though she knew it wouldn't help her if they got into an accident.

"But I do. Besides, you have nothing to worry about. Both the Lamborghini and I are perfectly capable of handling these speeds. And the roads are ideal driving conditions—well paved, straight, and empty."

She had to admit, he wasn't having any problems controlling the car. He handled a slight curve with ease, and she relaxed enough to let go of the dashboard. It didn't feel that fast. If she closed her eyes, she could pretend they were only moving at sixty miles per hour.

Desmond's voice interrupted her thoughts. "If you're not going to be sleeping, and I assume you want me to keep both hands on the wheel at all times, could I trouble you to put a CD in?"

"Sure." She leaned down and pulled the case out from under her seat. They wouldn't be discussing the music, this time. The lighthearted mood of their earlier car trip had been destroyed. She had destroyed it. "What one do you want?"

"Edvard Grieg's Piano Concerto in A Minor."

She found the disk he wanted and slipped it in. The melancholy notes of Grieg's music wafted out of the speakers, and she shivered. If Desmond was hoping to be cheered up by that music, he must be feeling as miserable as she was. And it was all her fault.

Leaning back in her seat, she closed her eyes again. At the rate he was driving, they'd be home in two hours. Recalling the twisting roads around the Hoover Dam, she adjusted her estimate up to two and a half hours. It would probably be the longest two and a half hours she'd ever spent.

She grimaced, and turned her face toward the door. That music wasn't helping her mood any, either.

Chapter 16

REBECCA AWOKE with the feeling that something was wrong. She glanced around her room and saw nothing out of place. The overhead light burned steadily, and yesterday's clothes lay neatly folded on a chair.

Yesterday! With a rush, memories of the beautiful wedding and its hideous aftermath filled her mind. She must have dozed off in the car, and Desmond put her to bed when they got home.

She tossed off her covers and got out of bed. Her bed. Not the bed she and Desmond were supposed to have shared. Just another indication of how badly she'd ruined everything between them. Shrugging into last night's shirt as a makeshift bathrobe, she took a moment to gather her courage before knocking on the connecting door to his room.

When he didn't answer to a second, louder knock, she pushed open the door and peeked inside. The room was dark, and the bed showed no signs of having been slept in.

She leaned her forehead against the cool tile wall of the bathroom. It was even worse than she'd thought. Not only couldn't Desmond stand to sleep in the same bed as her, he couldn't bear the thought of sleeping in the same apartment. She had to find him. They had to discuss what had happened last night, or it would fester between them, poisoning their marriage. That is, if they still had a marriage.

She scoured the silent apartment for any trace of her husband. Nothing. He wasn't only gone, but in a telling lack of consideration, he had left no note to indicate where he could be found or when he expected to come back.

Standing in the middle of the living room, she admitted the truth. He didn't want her to find him. She'd driven him away, just as her mother had driven away her father.

Rebecca stiffened her shoulders and set her jaw. She wouldn't let it happen again. She'd find Desmond, and force the issue. Yes, she'd behaved horrendously, but that didn't give him the right to leave her. She could get counseling, straighten herself out. Maybe even just understanding her motivations was enough to get rid of the problem. They could make their marriage work, if only Desmond stayed committed to it.

She could convince him when she saw him. But her first task was to find him. Perhaps he'd joined his daughter at Mrs. Waters's?

Remembering the Access program he'd shown her, as soon as she was dressed she went into the study and turned on the computer. When the locator prompted her for the name of the person she was searching for, she entered Desmond's name. A blue dot blinked into existence on the map, three levels down in the lab section of the Institute. After experimenting with different keys, she managed to enlarge the display of that section of the map, labeled "Administrative Offices." The room surrounding the blinking blue dot was labeled "Office of the Director."

He'd gone to his office. A sudden relief swept through her, leaving her limp. Faced with the terrible things that had happened last night, he'd turned to his work. It was a reaction she could understand, a reaction she sympathized with. He hadn't abandoned her.

A sharp knock on the apartment door startled her out of her musings. As she stood up and went to answer it, she wondered who it could be. Not Desmond. She'd just seen he was in his office. Gillian, back from her picnic? No, she would be with Mrs. Waters. What about Evan? Desmond might have sent him over to check on her, or to deliver an explanation for his absence.

Her steps speeded up and she reached for the door, only to stop short at the sight of the keycard reader.

"Wait a minute. I forgot my card," she called through the door.

"You don't need it," a muffled voice responded. "Press the authorized entry button, and my card will open it."

She studied the scanner, and found an unlabeled black button on the corner of the panel. She pressed it. The lock rewarded her with its customary buzz-click, and she opened the door. To Philippe.

"Good morning, Rebecca." He slid his foot forward just enough to keep her from slamming the door shut in his face. His vacation had been good for him, as he looked calm and relaxed. "Is Desmond at home? I need to speak to him."

"No. He's not." She tried to shut the door anyway, but only succeeded in banging his shoe.

He pushed the door back open. "It's important. Do you mind if I wait for him?"

"Yes."

He caught the door as she tried to close it, forcing it back open with easy strength. "I realize I made a poor first impression on you. But since you're going to be here until Gillian makes a permanent recovery, we'll have to at least learn to tolerate each other."

She let go of the door and stared at him, feeling the blood drain from her face and icy foreboding close around her heart. "What do you mean?"

"I mean that's a long time to carry a vendetta, especially one that doesn't accomplish anything."

"No. What did you mean about Gillian?"

"I'm sorry. I thought you knew. The bone marrow transplant was a temporary solution. She'll need another in a few years. And until a more exact donor can be found, she'll keep needing transplants every few years."

"A more exact donor?" She studied him with all her senses, even that vague intuition she sometimes had about people, searching for signs that he was lying. He was telling the truth.

"Doctor Chen told Desmond that if the two of you were to have a child, it would—"

"Stop!"

Philippe broke off in mid-sentence, widening his eyes in surprise. "I'm so sorry. I thought you knew that's why—"

"Liar!" She fisted her hands at her sides. Philippe's wide eyes and contrite tone of voice didn't ring true. He was neither surprised nor sorry. But the patent falseness of his apology only underscored the truthfulness of the rest of his words. Shaking with suppressed rage, she whispered through clenched teeth, "Get out. Now."

As soon as he stepped back, she slammed the door shut. He was a vicious, hurtful snake in the grass. He'd known she was here alone, probably using the same locator program she had. So he'd come over, with his lame excuse, just to tell her the truth about why Desmond had married her.

Rebecca sank into the soft folds of the leather couch, stunned by the magnitude of Philippe's revelation. Desmond had already proved he'd do anything for his daughter. He was more than capable of marrying someone he didn't love, just to keep her nearby.

Her reporter's instincts digested Philippe's story, searching for flaws, even as Rebecca puzzled over what she would do if he was right. She had no doubts that he'd spoken the truth, as far as it went. Gillian wasn't permanently cured, and would need a future transplant. Dr. Chen probably had mentioned that a sibling of Gillian's would make a better transplant donor than Rebecca. But just because the facts were true, didn't make the interpretation of those facts true.

She bolted upright. Philippe insisted Desmond had married her to have a child, who could act as a donor for Gillian. But Desmond had emphatically insisted they take precautions so that Rebecca didn't get pregnant.

Her shoulders slumped. That didn't prove anything. He might have hoped he'd already gotten her pregnant. Or he might have wanted to wait until a certain time to have another child.

The way she saw it, she had two choices. Believe Philippe, believe the worst about the man she'd sworn to honor and cherish all the days of her life, or confront Desmond and demand to know the truth of the situation, the whole truth, without any prevarication. When she put it like that, it was obvious that there was no choice, not if she wanted to break out of the pattern set by her mother. She had to confront Desmond.

Going back to the computer, she printed out a copy of the route she should take to reach him. The path highlighted two sets of stairs, reminding her that she'd be going underground. She clenched the piece of paper in a tight fist, and fought against her memories.

She'd been eight years old. A heavy rain had shifted a block of shale, exposing a cave. Always adventurous, she'd crawled in for a look, but hadn't been able to pull herself back out. The shale had crumbled and splintered as she tried to hold it, slicing her hands until she had to take a rest. Then the rain had returned, shifting the block of shale again and closing the mouth of the cave to a narrow crack she could never escape through. Worse yet, the saturated walls of the cave started crumbling and collapsing, covering her in cold, wet mud. Unable to see in the darkness, she'd groped for another exit, and her questing hands had encountered the bones of the last creature to fall into the cave.

She'd screamed herself hoarse, but no one came to rescue her. She spent the longest night of her life, waiting to die, convinced she would die alone. When the searchers had arrived the next morning, she barely had the strength to call to them.

She hated going underground. Every time, no matter what she told herself beforehand, she suffered through those anguished fears of dying a slow, lonely death, and her body being abandoned to rot.

Startled by a new interpretation, she repeated it aloud. "Being underground is just the trigger to the real fear, of dying alone and forgotten."

If she allowed her fears and insecurities to separate her from Desmond, that's exactly how she would die, alone and unremembered. No matter how much fame she achieved through her work, when the moment came, there would be no one by her side to mark her passing.

Terrified that she might already have waited too long, she grabbed up her keycard and rushed out of the apartment.

DESMOND FOLDED yet another piece of paper embodying a pointless tenet of bureaucracy into an origami bird. Setting it next to the analysis of projected demand versus actual use of various supplies, whose wings drooped sadly, he picked up another memo. This Japanese paper folding had been a great fad a few years back. He couldn't recall exactly how many years it had been, but he'd been rather skilled at the time. The only forms he remembered now were the bird, a jumping frog, and a piano.

He added the newest bird to the flock already collected on his desk, and picked up the paper scrap he'd torn off when he'd squared up the memo. A frog would make for a nice change of pace.

Five frogs later, the amusement value of jumping them over each other had worn thin. His thoughts turned back to the problem he'd been struggling with since he retreated to his office. What was he going to do about Rebecca?

He could tell her the truth, the full truth. Despite Philippe's predictions, Desmond didn't think she'd pronounce him an agent of Satan and try to cut off his head or burn him alive. That kind of thinking had gone out with hoop skirts and powdered wigs. He wasn't afraid for his life. He was afraid for the quality of his life.

What would it matter if she spared him, if he had to live with her revulsion and contempt? Oh, she tried to hide her feelings behind a mask of cynicism, but at heart she was a loving, compassionate woman. That's why her mother's betrayal had hurt her so deeply. She'd loathe and despise him; for what he was, what he was forced to do to survive, and most importantly, for lying to her. After all, he'd had plenty of opportunities to correct her misapprehension of his nature. He hadn't. Not even when they'd made love.

He snatched up another piece of paper and started folding. It kept his hands busy while he thought, and he needed that. Otherwise, he feared he'd start breaking things, just to relieve some of his frustration.

His other choice held even less appeal. He could refrain from telling her, go back to her and pretend that everything was normal. No doubt he could concoct some sort of explanation for why she'd bitten him while they made love. She'd stay with him, and love him, until the disease claimed her.

He remembered Olivia, lying wasted in her bed, too weak even to lift her head when her daughter was brought into her room. If Rebecca had any sort of open cut, even just biting her tongue or the inside of her cheek, and they made love...he forced aside images of her dying in his arms. He couldn't go through that again. He wouldn't go through that again. More importantly, he couldn't betray his wedding vow to her that way. He could not be the agent of her death.

There was always a third option. He could send her away, without telling her the truth. That way, he'd preserve her life, and keep the Institute and its work secret. But with her insatiable curiosity, she'd uncover the truth behind any story he tried to tell her. With her telepathic powers, he couldn't even try to use mental suggestions. She'd break through them eventually, and be twice as determined to discover what he'd been hiding. The most he could gain in that situation was time. Time for the researchers to find Gillian's cure. Time to establish a new life and a new identity someplace where Rebecca would never find him.

He jumped paper frogs over paper birds. He'd have no trouble losing himself in New York City. Or Chicago. Desmond sighed and pushed aside the frogs. It was a perfect solution, except for one thing. He couldn't do it.

He'd vowed to honor Rebecca. How much honor was there in taking away her freedom of choice? In forcing foreign thoughts into her mind? In denying and decrying their love for each other? The answer was obvious. None.

Whatever path he chose, he'd spend the rest of his life without her. But there was only one option that would let him live with himself. He had to tell her the truth. And pray that his daughter wouldn't suffer for it.

Looking around the room, his gaze was caught by one of his brother's paintings. Ancient trees dripping Spanish Moss screened a darkened plantation house. Trees, moss and building were all painted in shades of gray. In the painting's only spot of color, field hands in gaily patterned clothes danced with wild abandon around a blazing fire. If you looked carefully, you could just make out a shadowed face in one of the house's windows, watching the merriment below. The panoply of life, from which the cursed were forever excluded.

Desmond buried his face in his hands. It wasn't fair. Given time, of which he had an abundance, he could find someone else to love, a brief dalliance to take his mind off of the woman he'd sent away. But he'd never find anyone else like Rebecca. She was his one true love, his soul mate, his completion. She was the other half of his heart. Life without her would be mere existence, as colorless and devoid of light as the painted plantation.

He could torture himself by watching her from afar, spying on her life without ever being a part of it. But even so, how long could that last? Another fifty years? Then she'd be gone, forever. And he'd go on, eternally alone.

He'd have Philippe, if they could ever work their differences out. But that thin companionship paled beside dreams of a wife to love and cherish. All the things he loved about Rebecca, the way she could raise his spirits with a witty comment, encourage him with just a word or a touch, comfort him just by being there; he would lose it all. Never again would she whisper to him after they'd made love. Never again would she come to him, eyes shining, and tell him of the articles she'd written. He'd even miss her early morning, pre-coffee grizzly bear antics.

He had to tell her. But he could put it off for a little while, yet. He could go home, take her in his arms, and finally tell her he loved her. He could see the light in her eyes one last time. One last time before her love changed to horror and disgust.

The outer door buzzed. Bernice wouldn't be working on a Saturday, so it must be Philippe, returning from vacation. Desmond sat up straight. He couldn't let Philippe see him like this.

The inner door opened.

"Rebecca," he breathed. He rose and stepped around the desk, drawn to her despite his best intentions.

She glanced around the office, refusing to look at him, her hands shoved into the pockets of her jeans. "Nice office. Directing a research institute must pay well."

"It has its benefits."

He stood in front of her, unsure of what to do. He wanted to take her in his arms, or at least hold her hand. But he couldn't. Not with her hands stuffed in her pockets like that. She clearly didn't want him to touch her. Instead, he gestured toward the painting she was admiring.

"It's one of my brother Roderick's. Take a closer look if you like."

"Thank you." She slipped her hands out of her pockets as she walked. "He wasn't a real cheerful guy, was he?"

"No. Not really." His heart was breaking, but she could still make him smile.

Rebecca reached out to touch his cheek, but pulled her hand back before she brushed his skin. She stared down at the floor. "I'm sorry if I insulted your brother."

"Rebecca. Dear heart." He caught up her hand and carried it to his lips, pressing a kiss against her fingers. He continued to hold her hand tightly, while she lifted her gaze to look at him. The pain and doubt in her eyes slashed at his heart. He kissed her fingers again. "You did no more than speak the truth. The truth can be unpleasant, but no matter how much it hurts, knowing the truth is better than believing a fantasy."

She tightened her fingers on his, and gave a sad smile. "I said that, didn't I? When we were discussing the transplant operation for Gillian."

"Yes. And I think the time has come for you to hear the truth."

She pulled away from him and paced the perimeter of the office, her arms crossed before her as if she'd caught a sudden chill. "I had a surprise visitor a little while ago. Your half-brother, Philippe. He had some truths for me, too."

"Philippe?" Desmond felt the same chill wash over him. "What did he have to say?"

Rebecca spoke without looking at him. "When I first came here, you refused to let me leave. Because of your daughter, and the help you thought I could provide. Please, tell me the truth. Is she the reason you married me?"

"No!"

"So you didn't want me to donate any further bone marrow transplants?"

"If she needed any, and there's no guarantee she will, I'd naturally assumed you'd want to help her. But—"

"And Doctor Chen never told you a child of ours would make a better donor?"

Damn Philippe. He could kill him for this. "Yes, he told me that. But I never seriously considered it. I only mentioned it to Philippe as an example of how divorced from reality a researcher could become."

It was bad enough that Desmond had to tell her he was cursed. He didn't want her thinking he was a monster even while she still believed he was a normal human. He spun her around to face him. The shimmer of tears silvering her eyes nearly undid him.

"Please, Rebecca. You must believe me. I never intended to hurt you or use you in any way."

"You married me because you loved me?" she asked, an unsteady quiver shaking her voice.

"I did," he agreed, trying to put the weight of his emotions into his words.

She closed her eyes and swallowed, then whispered, "And I ruined that."

"No!" He grabbed her shoulders, shaking her eyes open. "No, you must never think that. You have been all to me that I could ask for. More than I had any right to dream of. No fault lies with you."

"Then why are you speaking in the past tense?"

It was his turn to swallow and look away.

"Desmond, I know what happened last night upset you. It upset me, too. But I've been thinking it over, and I've figured out why it happened."

A bitter laugh escaped him. "You have no idea."

"No, I—"

"Do you remember the tour you took when you first came to the Institute?" He spun to face her.

His apparently arbitrary change of subject creased her forehead with confusion, and she took a moment to collect her thoughts before answering, "Yes."

"Do you remember our discussion at the end of the tour? When I asked you to stay, and you refused?"

"Yes. But I don't see what—"

"Think carefully. You originally refused. Why did you change your mind and agree?"

She frowned with the effort of remembering. "You had a very persuasive argument."

"I never said a word." He sighed, seeing that she still wasn't following him. "Later, when I escorted you to the guest suite, I convinced you to stay put even though you wanted to leave. Do you remember how?"

A shadow of doubt crossed her face. "No. But I was very suspicious, after you'd gone. I thought you'd hypnotized me."

"Close. Very close." He forced himself to go on, even though he could see the first stirrings of fear in her eyes. It would get far worse before he was done. "I can both read others' thoughts, and implant my own thoughts in their minds. That's how I was able to convince you."

"Don't be silly." Her tentative grin faded at his expression.

"You're serious."

"Yes."

"Prove it. What am I thinking now?"

He'd known it would come to this. If he lowered his mental shields enough to touch her inner mind, but kept his own thoughts strictly controlled, she shouldn't be in any danger of picking up on his ever-present blood lust. Sighing, he reached out to touch her mind for the last time.

"You're thinking he can't possibly do this. There's no way he could know that I'm thinking about a lemon chiffon pie. With whipped cream. On one of Mama's blue and white Corelle serving dishes."

"Enough! You proved your point." Her eyes widened, and she took an involuntary step backward, away from him. She put one hand to her head, as if she could feel where the treacherous thoughts had leaked out. "Do you do that all the time? Listen in on people's thoughts?"

"No. I'd go mad from the constant chatter. One of the first things a telepath learns to do is to put up mental shields, keeping their thoughts in and everyone else's thoughts out. I've had a lot of practice, so I can control whether that shield is more like a brick wall, or like tissue paper." He stared into her eyes, hoping she'd make the connection with her own gift. "For an untrained telepath, the shield is more likely to stay as a brick wall, or to fluctuate unpredictably."

She watched him with the blank look that said she was amassing information, but had not yet formed an opinion. He tried again.

"Haven't you ever wondered where your sudden flashes of insight come from?"

"You mean you think I'm a telepath, too?"

"I know you are."

Her eyes slid out of focus, and he watched as she replayed scenes in her memory, testing this new theory against the facts. She was so beautiful, so intelligent, so open to everything life had to offer. How could he give her up?

She focused on him again. "Even if that's true, what does it have to do with last night?"

"Do you believe me?"

"You didn't answer my question."

"And I won't, until you answer mine. Do you believe that you have the telepathic gift?"

She strolled around the office, her fingers trailing over the backs of chairs and across book cases. Returning to her starting point, she tipped up her chin with determination and announced, "I won't dismiss the possibility. That's the best you're going to get."

"Good enough." He looked down at his desk, stirring the paper birds with his finger. He had no idea how to say this. "That's why you're not to blame for what happened last night. You let your mental shields down, and were overwhelmed by my thoughts and desires."

"*Your* desires? You wanted to kill me?"

"No. You weren't trying to kill me, whatever it looked like."

"Then what—"

"You wanted to feast on my blood. Just as I passionately desired yours."

Chapter 17

"YOU'RE TRYING to tell me you're some kind of a vampire?" Rebecca chuckled. "Yeah, right."

Desmond's eyes glimmered the wet color of a stormy sea, and his lips lifted in a soft smile of pity. He believed what he was telling her. Dear Lord, she'd married a madman.

"You're not a vampire." She edged away from him, around the chair and toward the door. "You're not dead. I've seen you eat and drink. You have a daughter for heaven's sake!"

"I'm not a vampire. I'm cursed. My father angered a Voodoo priestess, and I'm paying his price." He stepped toward her, stopping when she backed away. "I'm not insane."

He was reading her mind!

"And I'm not reading your mind," he added. "You have a very expressive face. Your thoughts are clear for anyone to see."

She reached the door, and the knob pressed against her hip. Desmond watched her as she reached back and turned the knob, but made no move to stop her. He just sighed and looked down at the floor.

"I didn't expect you to stay once you knew."

Her hand froze on the door knob. What was wrong with her? This was Desmond, the man she loved. So he thought he was cursed. Maybe it was his way of dealing with all the death that had surrounded him.

She crossed the office to where he stood, and laid her hand against his cheek. He jerked back his head, eyes wide and nostrils flared, then just stared at her. Quivers of emotion rippled through him, but he stood rooted to the spot. Silent. Staring.

"Hon." She forced herself to touch his cheek again. His control looked about ready to snap, and she had no idea what might set him off, or what he might do if he lost control. Remembering the scene between him and Philippe, she feared she might not have done the wisest thing. "It's all right. We can get help."

He winced as if she'd struck him, and pushed her hand away. Turning aside, he whispered, "You don't believe me."

"Of course I believe you. You think you're cursed."

"That's *not* what I meant."

"You've suffered a terrible number of tragedies, and I'm sure it feels like you're cursed sometimes. But it's not too late," she told him. "We can find some professional help for you."

"Damn it all!" He turned and slammed his fist onto the secretary's desk. "What will it take to convince you?"

"Desmond, calm down. You'll hurt yourself."

He spun around, a strange glint in his eyes. "Yes, maybe that will do it."

"What?" Her heart speeded up, and she swallowed with a too-dry mouth. "What are you thinking?"

"One aspect of my curse is that I'm immortal. If I demonstrate that, you'll have to believe me."

"Desmond, please. This has gone far enough." She had a vision of him blowing out his brains to prove his point.

"No it hasn't. Not until you believe me." He opened the center drawer of the secretary's desk, and took out a wicked looking letter opener. Gripping it in his right hand, he placed his left hand flat on the desk.

Rebecca ran towards him. "No! Desmond, stop! I believe you!"

"No you don't." He drove the letter opener through his hand, closing his eyes and hissing at the pain. Blood welled up around the wound, but not as much as there might have been. He hadn't punctured any of the larger veins.

"Desmond, honey. We're in a hospital. They'll be able to treat that. Just, don't touch it. It'll be okay."

He blinked, and forced a weak smile. "Well. That hurt." He took a deep breath, and looked down at his hand. A glimmer of hope sparked within her, that the pain had snapped him out of his delusion.

He cradled the wounded hand in his good hand, bumping the tip of the letter opener, and she winced in sympathy at his sudden intake of breath. Following behind him as he walked to the sink, he surprised her by turning and holding out his hand.

"Do you agree that the letter opener goes all the way through?"

She looked away, her stomach turning at the sight of the bloodstained steel tip protruding from his perfect flesh.

"Yes, but it's not bleeding much. If we get you to the doctor, they'll be able to bandage it up for you. You might not even need stitches."

He laughed, a short bitter sound. "Dear heart, I won't even need the bandage. Watch."

Unable to stop herself, she watched in sick fascination as he slid the letter opener out of his hand, and rinsed them both under the water. Shaking the water off of his hand, he held it out for her inspection.

She took his hand, turning it over to look at the back. A thin pink line marked where new skin had formed, but it faded to pale alabaster even as she watched. In moments, no sign of his injury remained.

She grabbed his other hand, thinking she'd been mistaken about which hand he'd injured. Both hands were perfectly formed and whole.

"You were telling the truth," she whispered. Then a wave of fury swept through her. "You lied to me!"

"I didn't lie."

"You knowingly let me believe something that wasn't true, and didn't correct me. That's the same thing."

"But I had to."

"There's no excuse for lying." She turned to leave, only to have him catch her arm and pull her around to face him.

"I love you."

She stared at him. He'd finally said the words she'd longed to hear, the words she'd thought he'd never say. She whispered, "Why now?"

"I was trying to keep you safe. I thought I could protect you from the curse if I didn't say that I loved you. But I couldn't let you leave believing the lies Philippe told you. You are the other half of my heart. I love you more than I knew it was possible to love anyone."

He loved her. He'd loved her all along. All the time she was doubting his motives and suspicious of his actions, he had loved her. If she had trusted him, if he had believed he could tell her such an amazing story without being forced to prove it wasn't a fanciful cover-up for an even worse crime, would he have? If she had encouraged and supported him, would he have told her the truth in the beginning? Was it her actions that had driven him to lie?

He caught her just as her knees buckled.

DESMOND HELPED Rebecca to sit down in Bernice's chair, tilting it back when she looked in danger of fainting. Her gray eyes had gone glassy, and he feared her reaction when she eventually regained her senses. He took the opportunity to smooth a lock of her soft hair away from her face, knowing it might be the last time she allowed him to touch her.

Her eyes focused on him, then she surged out of the chair to pace the room, rubbing her hands together in time to her steps.

"Okay. So. You're cursed. You're some kind of voodoo vampire. The blacked out windows in the apartment are for you, then."

"Yes. But also for Gillian, as I told you. The sunlight aggravated her condition, just as it does mine."

"That's why we traveled to Las Vegas at night. And why you drove so fast to get back, before the sun came up."

"Yes." He turned in a slow circle in the center of the room, facing her as she paced. Her lack of reaction puzzled and alarmed him. Was she still denying the truth?

She continued pacing, head down in thought. Then she turned and faced him.

"When I was moving my clothes in to your closet, I thought that it had a very strange construction. It makes a seal, doesn't it? In case the windows ever fail?"

"Yes." Her perception surprised him, and for the first time he allowed himself to hope that her rational mind would be able to accept his condition without emotional prejudice. He grabbed the glimmer of hope, and struggled to find the right words to explain his situation without frightening her. "I've never used it for that purpose. But I feel safer knowing the option exists, should I ever need it."

"You said your sister was liberated for her time. What time exactly was that?"

"The mid 1800s. And before you ask, the war that claimed my brothers' lives was the War between the States."

"So you were born when?"

"1853."

She nodded, as if this line of questioning made sense to her. He could only wonder where it was leading, and hope he was answering her questions correctly. When she crossed her arms and tilted her head to stare at him, his heart plummeted to his feet. Somehow, he'd failed her test.

"But if that's the case, one thing doesn't ring true. The photograph of your family. It's in color."

He sighed with relief, not caring how she'd found the picture.

"It's not a photograph, it's a daguerreotype. They were individually printed on silver plates, and hand colored after the initial image was fixed."

"Oh." She seemed to deflate, and he longed to go to her and comfort her. But he didn't dare.

She started to wander around the room again, picking up items for a brief inspection before putting them down and moving on to the next thing that attracted her attention. Her silence weighed on his nerves, but he had to let her make the next move. He couldn't risk intimidating or frightening her. Striving to maintain a casual attitude, he leaned against the desk.

"So, how similar is your curse to a real vampire? Do you have to drink blood?" she asked.

"Yes." Unsure what had triggered her question, he almost stopped with that simple answer. But honesty compelled him to give the full picture. "The researchers created a transfusion liquid to prevent accident victims from going into shock. It has all the nutrients I need. If I'm quiet, and don't use my mental powers, I can get by with one dose every other day. If I use my telepathic powers, or sustain some sort of injury, I might need two or more doses in a single day. The fluid replaces the cells that are destroyed in my body, so my need for it depends on how strenuously I push myself."

She stopped her restless pacing and approached him, standing so close that he could smell the lemon and honey fragrance of her shampoo.

When she placed one of her hands lightly on his, he thought his heart would stop from the shock. She still loved him. His needs did not disgust her.

His smile died stillborn. Needs were one thing. She hadn't yet learned the rest of his curse.

He looked down at their joined hands, noting that he'd automatically twined his fingers through hers. He tightened his grip, as if that could keep her by his side after he revealed the complete truth.

With her free hand, she brushed the hair off his forehead and caressed his cheek, tipping his face to look at her.

"There's something else, isn't there?"

"Yes." He led her back to the chair, then took his turn pacing. There was no easy way to say this, but he was determined that she hear nothing but the truth from him. "My father seduced the daughter of a Voodoo priestess, and in revenge the old woman laid a curse upon him and all of his future descendants. They would live forever surrounded by death, sharing the last hideous moments of those they loved as they died in agony."

He ran a hand over his face, appalled to discover he was trembling. The memories...

"That's how I learned of my telepathic skills. I felt the bayonet pierce Etienne's lung and his bubbling struggle for breath. I felt the bullet shatter Jean-Michel's leg, and the amputation fever that burned his life away. I was with my mother when she learned of their deaths and stepped blindly into traffic, and felt the horses' hooves that trampled her. I felt every blow of the drunken gamblers that beat Roderick to death. I choked and sweated with my sister as she succumbed to Cholera. I dared to hope that the curse had run its course, that I had gained enough control to defeat it, but I felt every moment of Olivia's pain and frustration as she wasted away."

Desmond closed his eyes, unwilling to see the expression on Rebecca's face as he told her, "I will not cause your death."

The gentle touch of her hand on his arm startled him. He turned to find her smiling sadly at him.

"The members of your family died tragically, but you didn't cause those deaths. You didn't hold the bayonet or drive the coach."

"But I killed Olivia."

"What do you mean, you killed her? I thought you said she had a hereditary form of cancer. Or did she request euthanasia?"

"She had cancer."

"Then how did you kill her?" Rebecca was staring at him, clearly not comprehending what he was trying to say. He sighed, wishing she would just take his word, and not make him relive the pain. But she wouldn't give up until she understood everything about his curse.

"Doctor Chen explained to you about Gillian's unique blood chemistry?"

"She has both the regular leukocytes and something he called neukocytes."

"Yes." Desmond shoved his hands into his pockets and paced back and forth in front of the desk. "In normal humans, the leukocytes are part of the immune system that identifies foreign bodies in the blood stream, and marks them for destruction. Another function of the same system is to identify cells that have been damaged beyond repair, and mark them for destruction, as well. When the number of damaged cells being destroyed outpaces the number of new cells being created, you see the affects of age."

"Since you obviously haven't aged, that can't be how it works for you," she interrupted him.

"You're right. The neukocytes do more than just identify foreign bodies in the blood stream. They convert them, so they are no longer foreign. If the conversion succeeds, the bloodstream carries them to where new cells are needed. If the conversion fails, the leukocytes mark them as unhealthy and they are destroyed." He raised his hand, forestalling her next interruption. "If a normal human being is infected with my cursed blood, the neukocytes begin their work in a new host. They begin trying to transform the blood cells they encounter. If the person's own immune system is functioning correctly, the neukocytes will be destroyed before they can cause much damage. But if they take hold..."

He shut his eyes, seeing a memory of Olivia, wasted by her disease, needing his help to hold Gillian in her arms. He couldn't let that happen to Rebecca.

"So we'll practice safe sex," Rebecca said. "I don't see what the problem is."

"Don't you?" He leaned forward, bracing his hands on the desk top. "What about Las Vegas?"

She shrunk back into the chair. "Las Vegas?"

"Yes. Rebecca, you are a telepath." He cut off her protests before they were fully formed. "While we were making love, you tapped into my thoughts. My desires. For blood."

He saw understanding dawning in her eyes, and a growing horror spread across her face.

"Yes. You understand now. When your mental powers remained dormant, I could shield my thoughts and contain my blood lust. But now, the risk is too great that you will be overcome by the desires I've struggled for years to subdue. If that happens, and you drink my blood...."

He couldn't bring himself to finish the sentence, fearing that saying the words might give them the power to come true.

"What if it's already too late?" She raised her fingers to her lips, as if she could feel the blood on them even now. He seized on the change of subject with relief.

"We would know by now. The first sign of infection is a raging fever, a few hours after contamination. You worried me when you passed out in the car on the trip home, but it wasn't a fever, just exhaustion."

Tilting her head to the side, she studied him in silence. He knew that look. She was fitting together facts, building a story. Any moment now, she'd test her theory by asking him a question. And he was sure it would be a question he didn't want to answer. It was.

"Are you speaking from experience?"

"Yes." He tried to wait her out, but she just kept looking at him. Staring at him with those big gray eyes, as if she expected literal pearls of wisdom to fall from his lips at any moment, and didn't want to miss any of them. He couldn't resist her, no matter how painful the memories were that she called up. It was something she needed to know, anyway.

Taking a deep breath, he explained. "When Gillian's condition was first diagnosed, we attempted a blood transfusion. We didn't know about the neukocytes then. It nearly killed her."

Rebecca reached out and stroked Desmond's cheek in a reassuring caress. He smiled, leaning into her touch.

"That must have been awful for you," she said.

"Yes." He closed his eyes, luxuriating in the silken feel of her palm and the whisper of her fingertips. She hadn't meant to upset him, only to understand what she was up against.

He jerked away from her, throwing up his mental barriers. Touching her mind had been an instinctive response to the intimate discussion and comforting gesture. But it proved that they must avoid any sort of physical relationship, not just making love.

He stood up and poured himself a mug full of water as an excuse to get away from her. Glancing over his shoulder, he saw her standing in her head-tilted "thinking" pose. He waited for her next question.

She folded her arms, and fixed him with a look of stern resolve. "You didn't know the dangers then. Now you do. I don't see why we can't just be careful."

She still didn't understand the seriousness of their situation.

"I can only guarantee your safety if we refrain from physical contact. *All* physical contact."

She frowned. "I touched your cheek not five minutes ago, and nothing disastrous happened. Don't you think you're overreacting? Just a little?"

"You weren't using your mental powers at the time. If you had been, who knows what might have happened."

"Why can't you just use this mental shielding you've spoken of before to keep my thoughts away from yours?"

"Because a shield like that takes conscious control." He shook his head, wishing she'd understand this and make the denial easier for him. "Rebecca, despite my curse, I'm still just a man. I don't have that kind of control. When I hold you, when I touch you, God, even when I just *think* about holding you or touching you..." He wrenched his thoughts away from images of the two of them tangled in passion.

She stepped away from him, linking her hands behind her back to prevent herself from offering any unwanted gestures of compassion.

"That's it then. A platonic relationship."

"At least until you can control your gifts enough to provide some shielding for your thoughts."

"How long will that take?"

He hated her desperate, pleading expression. Even worse, he hated destroying the slim thread of hope he'd just handed her. "To be able to control my thoughts even during moments of extreme mental or physical stress, took me thirty-five years."

"You expect me to wait until I'm more than sixty years old before I touch you again? No. There's got to be another way."

Chapter 18

REBECCA WRACKED her brain for a solution on the silent walk back to the apartment. Desmond hovered beside her, jumping away with a guilty start whenever he brushed against her. It was clear to her that he was fooling himself if he thought he'd be able to stay away from her.

No, they'd make love again. Probably sometime soon. Despite their best intentions, the magnetism that drew them together was too primal to overcome with rational arguments. If they were anywhere near each other, they'd come together. They wouldn't be able to help it. She needed to find a way to live through the experience before it happened.

She imagined dying in the agony he'd described, and shivered.

"Cold?" he asked.

"A little." She rubbed her arms, even though the chill that permeated her came from within.

Desmond took off his jacket and draped it around her shoulders, careful to avoid touching her. "Better?"

She snuggled into the raw silk, still heated with his warmth. It was almost like a caress, and she could imagine the sleeves that held her so securely were really his arms. The warmth behind her was really his body, pressed close to hers.

"Rebecca—" Desmond's voice vibrated, just short of a groan.

"What?" She stopped walking and glared at the flesh and blood man beside her, annoyed that he interrupted her pleasant fantasy with harsh reality.

"You were projecting." He took a deep breath and motioned her forward, falling into step beside her. "If you're going to control your powers, you have to learn to control two things. The first are your mental shields, which keep other people's thoughts from getting in. You've naturally developed strong ones, but when you concentrate on people, you instinctively lower them. That's one of the things that makes you such a good reporter, but in this case, you can't afford to do that. The other thing you need to control is projection, or sending your thoughts out to other people. If your thoughts are as explicit as yours just were, they could get you in a lot of trouble."

"Not only can't I touch you, I'm not even supposed to think about you for the next thirty years?"

"That's how long it will take for you to gain full control of your powers. You should be able to master the basics in a few weeks."

She bridled at his overly patient tone, and snapped back, "So then you'll stop jumping around like water on a skillet, afraid to come anywhere near me?"

His expression didn't change, but she felt a chill wind brush across her mind. She instantly regretted taking out her anger on him. The situation might be driving her half mad with frustration, but he was suffering just as much.

"I'm trying to keep you safe," he reminded her.

"I know. I'm sorry. This is hard for you, too." She sighed, and wrapped his jacket's arms tighter around herself. They continued the walk in silence.

When they reached the apartment, Desmond headed straight for the kitchen and pulled a medicine bottle from the refrigerator. She watched with mingled fascination and horror as he boiled a pan of water to warm the liquid, then turned and faced her.

"Now that you know what I am, there's no reason to hide this. Is there?"

"No." She recognized his challenge, his subtle insistence that his needs could frighten her into leaving him. She hadn't backed down from a challenge yet, and she wasn't about to start now. "Let's stop pussyfooting around the issue, and cut straight to the point. You're a cursed immortal. I'm not."

He dropped the bottle into the pan with a clatter, turning to look at her. She'd gotten his attention. Good.

"Now, as I see it, there are only three possibilities," she continued. "You can become a normal human being, we can leave everything the way it is now, or I can become like you. Let's take the easy option first. Is it possible for you to turn back into a normal human being?"

Desmond stared at her, opened his mouth to reply, and then just blinked. Chuckling, he shook his head. "You're remarkable, do you know that? I think you took all of five minutes for recovering your wits before you were back to being the scrappy little terrier, worrying the truth out of your story."

"Oh, thanks. Every woman longs to have the man she loves call her a dog."

"You know that's not what I meant, dear heart. Don't get your hackles up." He laughed, and reached out to draw her closer for a conciliatory kiss. His hand stopped just short of her jaw as he realized what he'd meant to do, and he stepped back, out of reach. All traces of humor were gone from his voice when he added, "To answer your question, no, I can't become a normal human being, not without killing all the neukocytes in my system. And the only way to do that is to kill me."

"That's not an option, then." She didn't want him to even consider the possibility that the best way to protect her would be by eliminating the danger, in this case him. "How about the other extreme? Could I become like you?"

"You wouldn't want—"

"That's not what I asked. I asked if it was possible."

He considered for a long moment, before admitting, "I don't know. Philippe has been trying to reconstruct his grandmother's curse for over a hundred years, but hasn't finished it yet."

Rebecca blinked, sidetracked by this new information. "Philippe's grandmother was the Voodoo priestess? She cursed her own grandson?"

"Why not? Her curse killed her daughter. She died in childbirth. My father committed suicide immediately after, I assume because he felt her death."

Rebecca hesitated, but she had to know. "You said you drank blood, before the researchers created their potion. Did you ever... kill anyone?"

"Yes."

She clutched the table behind her, and refused to back away from him. Then she watched his eyes mist with remembered pain, and she only wanted to soothe him. She held onto the table to keep from going to his side.

"The first death was an accident," he said quietly. "A blood sacrifice got out of hand. I vowed that it would not happen again, that I would take no more than what a person was willing to give. After that, I haunted battlefields, offering easy deaths to those dying in pain."

"Did you feel their pain?"

"Yes. Giving them peace helped me as much as it helped them." He smiled sadly. "Of course, I was the only one who survived the experience. Later, I worked the night shift in a hospital. I would bring the newly dead to the morgue, with an unauthorized stop on the way. It was easy to convince the coroner to overlook the evidence. For over a hundred years I've surrounded myself with death so that I could live."

"A hundred years?" With everything else he'd told her, she'd forgotten he'd also said he'd been born in 1853. The rare first editions of Jules Verne and H. G. Wells lining his study supported that claim, but viscerally, she couldn't believe Desmond was that old. She examined his features from a table length away, but found no hint of lines or wrinkles, not so much as a single gray hair marring the luxuriant waves of black surrounding his face. She flexed her fingers, remembering the feel of every inch of his exquisite body. There had been no signs of aging, no sagging or wrinkles, anywhere on him. Only firm, muscular flesh.

She clenched her hands by her side, fighting not to reach for him. Imagining the feel of him, skin slick with passion, his body hot with desire, she felt an answering flame kindle within her. But she could not touch him. She must not reach for him. Her fingernails dug into the palms of her hands as she tightened her fists.

"Does that upset you?" He must be shielding his mind from hers. Without his telepathic powers, he misinterpreted the cause of her tension.

"No. I don't care that you're over a century old. You don't even look thirty." Her face flared hot then cold as she realized what that meant for the future. "Actually, it does upset me. I bet you looked a lot like you do now, a hundred years ago."

He nodded. "Much the same."

"Uh-huh. And a hundred years from now, you'll still look pretty much like this?"

"Yes."

"You know what I'll look like a hundred years from now? I'll be dead."

"Rebecca—"

"Even twenty years from now, you'll look thirty, and I'll be pushing fifty. In forty years, I'll be seventy. You'll still be thirty. Do you see a problem with this? The lines in that famous poem are 'Grow old along with me, the best is yet to be,' not 'Watch me grow old, the good times are gone.'" She bowed her head, closer than she'd ever been to admitting defeat. "Maybe you're right. Maybe it is best if I go."

"Go? I never said anything about you going."

"Well I can't stay here. Don't you see what it would be like? Day after day, night after night, denying ourselves the most casual of touches, not even thinking of each other in case that triggers a vampire response. Celibacy is one thing, but you're asking for monasticism. I'm not cut out to be a saint. I know I can't do that. I don't see why we should suffer through the agony of trying." She pushed herself away from the table.

He also stood, and stepped forward as if to stop her from leaving the kitchen. "But given the other options—"

"I know which one I'll take." Despite everything he'd said, she couldn't believe in an all-powerful, irreversible curse. They could find a solution, but only if he believed it could be found. Stepping around the table, she caught him off guard, and pulled his head down for a heated kiss. She opened her heart, her soul, and her mind to him, pouring her love through the kiss, desperation shattering any thoughts of restraint.

He wrapped his arms around her, drawing her tight against him, even as his mouth claimed hers in searing response. He kissed her with all the hunger in his soul, trembling with the restrained passion he fought to contain. His mingled fear and desire coursed through her, scalding her thoughts with the heat of his emotion.

He jerked his head back, breaking the kiss and breaking their contact. She barely felt the cold air of the kitchen on her skin as he pushed her away, devastated by the chill left behind in her lonely, solitary thoughts.

"Damn it, Rebecca! You know better than to do that."

"Yes, I do. And so do you. But that wasn't enough, was it?" She advanced on him, forcing him to walk backwards across the kitchen as he tried to keep a space between them. "And knowledge will never be enough to keep us apart. Because what we feel for each other is too strong to be denied. You're the other half of my whole. We can not be separated. And any attempt to keep us apart is doomed to failure."

He rubbed a hand over his face. He was as physically perfect and healthy as ever, but his resigned expression and dull eyes made him seem old and broken. "You may be right. In which case, you'll have to leave."

"No!" Rebecca clenched her fists. Her strategy had backfired. Now she'd have to work doubly hard to convince him of her real intent.

"It's for your own good," he told her. The dreaded phrase snapped her already strained self-control.

"My own good?" She stalked across the kitchen, knocking the chairs out of her way. "And who are you to decide what is best for me? Who are you to decide what I should do? Is it because you don't think I'm a mature adult, capable of making reasoned decisions on my own? After all, you've had over a hundred years of accumulated wisdom and experience, compared to my few decades."

Desmond held out his hands, trying to placate her. At the same time, he backed away, glancing nervously from side to side. "Rebecca. Darling. You're overwrought."

"Overwrought? Overwrought! Next you'll tell me I'm overreacting."

"But you are."

"Really?" She stopped and struck a casual pose, leaning back on her elbows against the counter. "Then by all means, enlighten me. Somehow I'd gotten the impression that you wanted me to rip out my heart and stomp it into the ground, on the theory that this would make me happy. But if I'm wrong, I'm willing to listen. So talk."

Desmond cleared his throat, unsure of what to say. She'd taken his words and twisted them, making them into something completely opposite of what he'd intended. Of course he only wanted her happiness. But she had to see that her only chance for happiness lay in being separate from him, no matter how much the separation hurt him.

She tapped her foot, reminding him that the time she was allowing him for explanations was fast running out.

"Can we start by listing what we agree on?" he asked hopefully. Maybe if he could figure out where her reasoning had jumped the track, he could get them back in accord.

"Sure. We agree that there are two possibilities for our future: stay together or split up."

"Rebecca, I'm not asking you to leave because I want to be rid of you. That's the farthest thing from my mind. I love you. I adore you. Which is why I can't risk your life this way. I would live with you for the rest of your life, if you would let me. But you're the one who insisted you couldn't do that."

"But what kind of a life would it be without you?"

"Any life is precious. And it needn't be forever. After you've mastered your mental control—"

"You said that would take thirty-five years! You want me to wait until I'm a senior citizen before coming back to you? At that point, making love to you would probably still be fatal. I'd have a heart attack from the unexpected activity."

An invisible fist punched through his chest and squeezed his heart. He couldn't draw a breath, and couldn't hear past the high-pitched whine in his ears. Time had once again played him for a fool. His beautiful, passionate wife would leave, never to return. Even if she came back after she'd honed her mental skills, it would be another woman, bearing her name and her time-ravaged face, who returned to him. His darling Rebecca would never come back.

He shook his head, forcing himself back to the here and now. "The important thing is that you'd be safe. You'd have a life, even if it didn't include me."

"You just don't get it, do you?" She closed her eyes, and screwed up her face in concentration. And then the waves of mental images hit him.

Rebecca, returning to her apartment. A series of friends and acquaintances, each of whom she tried to mentally reach out to, searching for the connection she'd found with him. Each failure made her that much more bitter and alone. She funneled her energy into her work, producing probing and insightful articles and reports. Until she started to report things known only to the people she interviewed, that her burgeoning telepathic gifts had pulled during the interview. Unable to tell the difference between the two types of hearing, she exposed secrets her subjects intended to hide. People no longer wanted her to interview them. After a few complaints and threats of lawsuits, her editors no longer trusted her reports. Her career started a long decline, culminating in her expulsion from the most disreputable of the tabloid rags. Her beautiful chestnut hair had turned gray from the constant stress, and her pixieish face had turned pinched and drawn from worry. Harsh lines scored her countenance, and her clothing hung from her emaciated body. She returned to her apartment, now a dingy walkup in a dangerous part of town, and tried to drown her sorrows in the alcohol that blunted her too-sharp perceptions. Then she walked into the bedroom and opened the nightstand drawer, reaching inside for the gun she kept there....

He broke their mental contact, opening his eyes to search her pale white face. She met his gaze with her direct gray stare.

"Do you—" His voice broke, to his chagrin, and he started again. "Do you really expect it to be like that?"

"Yes. Or worse. You said your curse would kill me if you admitted you loved me. Well, even if I leave, it will. The knowledge that I loved and was loved, and threw it all away, will eat at me until I can't bear to go on."

He righted one of the chairs she'd knocked over earlier, and sat down. He wanted to protect her, to keep her safe, and to ensure her happiness, even at his own expense. But he'd thought returning her to her previous life would carry no risks. A cold dread snaked through his stomach.

"There's a way to prevent that. If you returned to your old life exactly the way that you left it, with your mental powers dormant...." He swallowed and looked away, unable to even finish the suggestion. But if saving her required sacrificing her memories and love of him, he would do it.

"Pretend the last few weeks didn't happen?" she whispered in stunned disbelief. "Wipe them out of existence, along with everything that happened during them? Destroy our love, as if it never was?"

"If that's what it takes to protect you—"

"Then the cost is too high."

"But—"

"No."

They stared at each other, stalemated. Not for the first time, she had him completely at a loss for words. Finally, she broke the silence.

"You keep saying you want to protect me. That's sweet, and very noble of you, but you forgot to ask me one very important question. You never asked if I *wanted* to be protected. And Desmond, I don't. I'm a fighter. I don't want to sit on the sidelines where it's safe. I want to be playing the game."

He sighed and rubbed the back of his neck where a tension headache was forming. Everything she said made sense, but—

"I can't do it. I can't risk taking your life. It goes against everything—"

"You said you'd never take anything that wasn't freely offered, didn't you?"

He nodded, unable to answer. There was only one reason she'd ask that question now, and he had the irrational hope that if he didn't speak, she wouldn't either. He was wrong.

"Then I offer you my life, freely and without hesitation." Her eyes hardened into chips of granite. "But I refuse to let you take my hope. I refuse to let you take my dreams."

"Rebecca, please. Reconsider."

"No. I've made my position clear. What are you going to do about it?"

He stared into her eyes, searching for any sign that she might weaken. Two chips of diamond glittered back at him. She would not be moved.

He loved her more in that instant than he ever had. And she was right. He couldn't live without her.

He would have to keep from infecting her. If he failed, he would watch her die in his arms, knowing he'd caused her death. She'd given him no other choice.

"What am I going to do about it? What can I do?" He sighed. "I'm going to love you. Forever."

He held out his hand. Without hesitation, she placed her hand in his. He opened his thoughts to her, unconcerned when she stepped closer and wrapped her arms around his neck. He was not projecting any feelings of bloodlust. His mind was too filled with the wonder of her love.

Chapter 19

HAND IN HAND, they walked into Desmond's bedroom. The bedroom that belonged to both of them, now.

Desmond stopped in the middle of the room, and turned Rebecca to face him. "I love you."

Now that the words had been said, he could not stop himself from repeating them. He slowly opened her blouse, pausing after each button to kiss the newly revealed flesh, and to tell her again that he loved her. By the time her blouse and bra had fallen to the floor, she was flushed with passion and swaying beneath his touch.

Her fingers fumbled with his shirt, and he shrugged it off. They embraced, chest to chest and cheek to cheek, as he stroked her silken back, and she trailed feathered caresses up and down his spine.

She nestled closer, lightly kissing his ear, and whispered, "Mmm. This is nice. And you thought we couldn't touch."

He wasn't sure why the blood lust was dormant, but he didn't intend to waste the opportunity. Holding her close, reveling in their love, he felt like he stood in a gilded moment forever set apart from the stream of time.

"I love you," he whispered again.

She shivered at the words, and slid her hands up to tangle in his hair. "I love you, too. Now kiss me."

He chuckled at her sweet demand, and fitted his lips to hers. She melted beneath him. Pulling his head down, she intensified the kiss, even as he slid his hands under the waistband of her jeans to press her closer, against his arousal.

A gentle fire was building inside him, but he felt no urgency. He could stand here forever, caressing Rebecca and celebrating their love.

Wanting more freedom for his explorations, he undid the button and zipper on her jeans, and pushed her pants over her hips. She wriggled out of them with a shimmy that temporarily stole his breath. Then he undid his own pants. Tilting his head back, he sighed in pleasure as she guided the clothing past his arousal and slid it to the floor.

Soon they were completely naked, heated flesh pressed to heated flesh, and still he drifted in a haze of happiness, willing to stay in her arms forever.

She sighed, and nibbled his lips with delicate kisses. "Tell me that you brought the condoms home from Las Vegas."

"I did." He dusted her lips with butterfly kisses. "Did you want me to get them?"

"Yes, please."

He chuckled. "So polite."

"Of course I am, when you're being so very, very nice to me."

"I can be better," he whispered.

"That's why we need the condoms."

Reluctantly, he pulled away from her. She pursed her lips in an adorable little pout, and rubbed her arms.

"It's cold without you."

"Get under the covers. I'll be back in a minute."

He opened the closet door, and quickly found the box he'd thrown in his suitcase. Turning, he was struck by the sight of Rebecca in his bed. The black satin comforter and ebony headboard accentuated her creamy skin and gray eyes, and the dark green sheets and pillows seemed made for her lustrous chestnut hair. Passion flushed her cheeks, and her kiss-swollen lips beckoned him back to sample their sweet honey.

"You are so beautiful," he said.

"You're not bad yourself. But you'd look a whole lot better close up."

Desmond laughed, and soon joined her beneath the covers. She immediately nestled close to him.

"Mmm. You're so nice and warm," she purred.

He stroked her back, pressing her closer, and guided her arms around his neck. "You don't feel cold to me."

"That's because you make me so hot." She giggled. "I can't believe I just said that."

Because of his altered metabolism, he was no judge of proper body temperature. Still, he brushed the back of his hand against her forehead. It did seem a little warmer than he expected. Were her cheeks delicately flushed from passion, or from fever?

He clutched her in a tight embrace, burying his face in her lemon scented hair. He never should have told her he loved her.

"You do seem a little warm," he said, finally. "I'll get the thermometer so we'll know for sure."

"Now?" she wailed.

The romantic moment had succumbed to dread. She couldn't be sick. He must be wrong. But he had to know. "Now."

As he pushed aside the covers and got out of bed, she shivered. He tucked the thick comforter around her, alarmed at the way she burrowed under it. Her voice muffled by bedding, she mumbled, "Hurry back."

He raced through the living room to Gillian's bathroom, and flung open the medicine cabinet. The thermometer sat on the second shelf, along with a bottle of Children's Tylenol. Desmond grabbed both, filled a plastic cup with water, and hurried back to Rebecca.

While he was gone, she'd curled into a tight ball beneath the covers. Leaving his things on the night stand, he slipped into the bed beside her, and gathered her trembling body close to his warmth. She wrapped her arms around him and twined her legs with his.

Her shivers slowly subsided. When she eased herself away from him to find a more comfortable position, he asked, "Better?"

"I'm warmer now. But I feel funny. All wiggly."

His heart turned to lead. Picking up the thermometer from the night stand, he said, "Let's check your temperature. All right?"

"Do I have to come out from under the covers?"

"No."

"Then okay."

When he opened the covers, she curled a little closer to him, but only shivered once. Placing the thermometer beneath her tongue like an obedient patient, she drowsed against his chest. He silently counted off the agonizingly long seconds, then pulled the thermometer out. She didn't open her eyes.

"Well?" she murmured.

"You're running a low-grade fever."

"Low-grade? Nope. I only have premium, A-1 quality fevers. Never settle for second best." She tried to smother a giggle, but it escaped.

"No, I meant...never mind."

He lifted her to a sitting position, and guided the cup of water to her lips. She sipped it, took the Children's Tylenol he offered her, and swallowed the rest of the water. The comforter fell from her shoulders, but she didn't seem to mind. Was her fever abating or getting worse?

"Rebecca?"

"Mmm?"

"I love you."

"You don't have to sound so sad about it. I love you, too."

His only answer was to wrap his arms around her and cradle her against his chest. She was burning up.

"Rebecca, I am so, so sorry."

He buried his face in her hair, lost in an agony of recrimination. Philippe had tried to warn him, but he hadn't listened. He'd let his desires overwhelm his good sense. He should have sent Rebecca on her way as soon as the bone marrow transplant was through, or let her recover on her own in the hospital. He never should have made love to her. And he definitely should have never said he loved her, and called down the power of his curse on her.

She shifted in his arms, her eyelids fluttering and then opening. "Desmond?"

"Yes?" He hardly dared to breathe.

"I'm sick, aren't I? With the neukocytes."

"Yes. My curse is killing you."

"Don't be ridiculous." Her voice, though weak, held it's familiar tone.

He blinked. "But—"

"How is this curse supposed to be killing me?"

"You said it yourself, you're sick."

"I have a fever. My body's immune system is fighting off an infection."

"But that infection is my cursed blood."

"Desmond, listen to me. I don't know how you and Philippe got to be like you are. A Voodoo curse is as good an explanation as any. But everything after that has happened according to scientific principles. What is this institute for if not to research the science behind your condition? Why does your daughter get shots if you can't fight the curse?"

Her words cut through the fog of fear that had surrounded him, letting him think rationally about the situation. "The only time you could have become infected is last night. So the neukocytes were in your system already, before I told you I loved you. I didn't invoke the curse."

She nodded. "Now you've got it."

"And if your sickness is a natural, physical reaction, it can be cured."

"Yes."

His momentary optimism deserted him. "But we don't know how

to cure it."

"But you can fight it."

"If it's similar to Gillian's reaction." He tightened his hold on Rebecca, giving her a fierce hug, then disentangled himself and climbed out of the bed. "There are plenty of needles in the kitchen. I'll take a sample of your blood to Doctor Chen. He can have an answer in a few hours."

"Good idea."

He hurried to the kitchen, the apartment's floors cold on his bare feet, the air chill on his bare skin. Grabbing a needle from Gillian's supply, he checked the clock. Gillian and Mrs. Waters weren't due home for another four hours. Good. The last thing he needed was for his housekeeper to see him running naked around the house.

He raced back to Rebecca's side. She held out her arm, looking away as the needle pierced her skin. The reservoir of the needle filled quickly with blood. Pressing her other thumb to the spot, he withdrew the needle.

"Hold down on it until it stops bleeding. I'll take this to Doctor Chen right away."

"Could you bring me a pen and some paper?"

"You want to work while I'm gone?"

Her eyes shadowed. "I have to do something."

"I'll get it for you. Anything else?"

An impish smile lit her face. "Yes. Put on some pants."

REBECCA CROSSED out the last sentence, and frowned at the letter she was trying to compose. She remembered Olivia's letter in her nightstand, and shivered at the eerie parallel. She wasn't cursed. She wasn't going to die.

But just in case...Sighing, she picked up a new sheet of paper, and began again.

Dear Mom,

I'm sorry it's taken me so long to come around to your point of view. You only ever wanted what was best for me, and thought an imaginary hero made a better father for a little girl than a fallible man. When my father came back, you had no way of knowing if he'd stay, or be frightened into leaving again. And so you didn't take the chance. For you, the promise of love wasn't worth the risk. Then, and now, I'm willing to risk everything. That doesn't make either of us wrong, just

*different. I hope you can forgive what I said and did when I left, and
that I can see you again. There's someone very special that I'd like you
to meet. And if anything happens to me before we have that chance,
remember that I thought love was worth the risk, and am happy with
the decisions I've made.*

Rebecca read the letter again. That was as good as it was going to
get. She was too tired to try any more.

She gathered up the other papers into a loose pile and pushed
them onto the floor. Her mother's letter, she folded neatly, then wrote
what she knew of her mother's address on the back. She set it and her
pen on the nightstand.

Burrowing beneath the covers, she let her eyes drift closed. She
hoped Desmond would return soon.

"ARE YOU CERTAIN?" Desmond asked.

"They're the same," Doctor Chen repeated, laying two colored
charts on the desk in front of him. Two identical colored charts.

The doctor tapped the rightmost chart. "This is the analysis of
your wife's blood, okay?"

He slid the other chart beneath it, where it lined up perfectly.
"This is an analysis of the blood cells I created before your daughter's
transplant, to prove a child of yours could act as a bone marrow donor."

"But what does that mean for Rebecca?"

"It means her blood chemistry is stable, like yours or Philippe's."

"She'll live?"

"Yes." Doctor Chen held up a hand, cutting off Desmond's
jubilation. "At least, if she survives rejection sickness."

Rejection sickness. The specter that haunted each of Gillian's
transplants. Rebecca's body was trying to purge itself of the tainted
blood.

"What can I do?" he whispered.

"Keep her fever down. If it gets too high, bring her to the
hospital."

Desmond thanked Doctor Chen for his good work, and hurried
home to be with Rebecca. As he keyed the card reader outside his door,
a wave of weakness hit him. He clutched the door frame, and staggered
inside.

The room seemed wavy and out of focus. He blinked his eyes, but
it didn't help. He rubbed his hand across his face. When he brought it

away, it was damp. His face was covered in sweat.

His curse was in full force. He was sharing her death.

"No!" he croaked. He would not lose her now. Not when they were so close.

He made his way to the bedroom and threw open the door. Rebecca lay under a mound of bedding, her face streaked with sweat. She moaned softly and twitched at the covers, her head rolling from side to side in mute denial of her sickness.

He had to lower her fever. Now. He couldn't wait to get her to the hospital.

The room spun about him. He swayed, but stayed on his feet. His weakness didn't matter. He had to save Rebecca.

Stumbling into the bathroom, he caught the edge of the sink to keep from falling. He fumbled with the cold water tap, finally twisting it open, and drenched a towel in the tepid water. Letting the water run until it turned glacial, he filled a cup then gulped it down. His parched throat cried out for more, and he drained three cups before filling one for Rebecca.

The cold and the moisture braced him, and he returned to her steady on his feet. Kneeling beside the bed, so that his body heat would not add to her discomfort, he bathed her face and torso with the wet towel. Rebecca's restless thrashing stilled somewhat, and he lifted her up enough to wet her lips with the cup of water. Even in her fevered state, she recognized what he was doing, and reached for the cup with both hands.

Swallowing the water in greedy gulps, she continued to suck at the cup even after she'd drained it dry. He pulled it away, easily overwhelming her feeble resistance, and placed a corner of the towel over her lips instead. She sucked the moisture from the already warm towel, and he hurried back to the bathroom to get a fresh towel and a full glass of water.

When he returned, not half a minute later, she was writhing on the bed. Her breath came in short pants, punctuated by growling moans. He rushed to her side, placing a hand on her forehead to discover how high her fever had risen.

Struggling to hold her head still, he ended up winding his arm around her neck in a half-nelson. Pinning her in place, he retrieved the cup he'd set down and lifted it to her lips. She stopped fighting long enough to swallow all the water, and he took advantage of the pause to throw the new towel around her. Her blistering heat scorched it in seconds.

His efforts weren't enough. Her fever was still climbing faster than he could offset it. He needed a faster way to cool her.

The tub! Disentangling himself from her, he ran back to the bathroom, this time throwing wide the spigot in the tub, filling it with a cascade of lukewarm water. He turned back to the bedroom, and stopped in horror.

Rebecca had pushed herself into a seated position, cringing against the headboard, as she stared around her with wild-eyed terror. Her hands moved in a blur before her face, swatting and swiping at something only she could see. With a cry, she began desperately clawing at her arms and chest.

He raced toward her, frantic to stop her before she injured herself. Before he'd crossed half the room, she suddenly stopped, her eyes growing wide as she stared at a spot a few feet above the foot of the bed. A beatific smile spread across her face, a chilling contrast to her flushed skin and sweat-matted hair.

"Daddy," she breathed. "You came for me."

"No!" Desmond bellowed, as if he could enforce his will by sheer volume alone. Grabbing Rebecca around the waist, he hauled her towards the bathroom.

She pounded his shoulders and kicked his shins, but he barely felt it. No bodily harm could match the searing pain slicing through his heart. He pulled her toward the bathroom by instinct alone, his vision blackening as his ears filled with the beating wings of a thousand birds.

"No. Let me go," she whimpered. "Let me go. I have to go. Daddy!"

He plunged her into the water, heedless of the shock to her system.

"Never! You aren't cursed. You will not die!"

Her eyes rolled back in her head and she sagged limp in his arms. He pulled her body from the tub, frantic to find a heartbeat. Her heart raced within her chest, but she showed no other sign of life.

Kneeling on the slick tile beside her body, Desmond captured her hands between his. He was losing her. He wasn't good enough. He couldn't save her. She was going to die, and it would all be his fault, not because he had cursed her, but because he'd waited too long to get help bringing her fever down.

The black emptiness of an eternity without her yawned before him, an endless existence with no hope of life.

And then her fingers tightened on his hand.

He dared to open his eyes. The harsh scarlet streaking her face had faded to a soft rose, and her chest rose and fell evenly. Her mouth was closed, although a faint smile tilted at the corners, and her eyelashes rested lightly against her cheeks in normal slumber.

He squeezed his eyes shut and took a breath so deep, he thought it would shatter his chest. "I love you," he breathed.

Careful not to jostle her, he slid his arms beneath her and lifted her up. She mumbled in her sleep, and curved toward his chest, nestling her head against his shoulder. He'd never seen or felt anything so wonderful. Placing her reverently onto the bed, he sat at her side and watched her sleep.

Her fever hadn't completely abated, and he continued to bathe her with tepid water. But she'd survived the worst of it. She would live. All she needed now was time.

He laughed. Time. She had all she needed, now.

VOICES AT THE door, and the sound of a keycard in the lock, broke his concentration. Gillian was home from her picnic. She mustn't be allowed to see Rebecca like this. Not so soon after losing her mother.

He grabbed his robe and threw it on. He reached the door just as it opened.

"Daddy!" Gillian squealed and launched herself at him. He caught her, crushing her to him in a tighter-than-usual embrace, and let her cascade of happy thoughts wash over him. His wife and his daughter. He had them both. And after coming so close to losing both of them, the sudden rush of joy staggered him.

He could even restore his friendship with Philippe. After all, Rebecca's reaction to learning Desmond was cursed had been the exact opposite of Philippe's prediction. Philippe had never been one to stand on pride, though. He'd admit he was wrong. The future had never seemed brighter.

Desmond struggled to maintain his composure, and act normally.

"Did you have a nice picnic, sweetheart?"

"We had fun! We went outside in the sun, and sat on warm rocks, and picked flowers, and fed squirrels." A montage of thought-pictures accompanied her words.

"And did you enjoy it, Mrs. Waters?"

"We had a lovely time. How was your wedding?" She tried not to look at his bathrobe and obvious exhaustion, drawing the natural conclusion.

"Wonderful. Rebecca looked radiant. Unfortunately, she also came down with something while we were in Las Vegas. She's been running a pretty high fever the last few hours."

"Nothing serious, I hope."

He didn't answer. How could he? Instead, he asked, "Would you mind watching Gillian one more day?"

"But Daddy," Gillian started to protest.

"You're only just getting well again. I'm not taking any chances with you."

"But I live here. Make her leave."

"Sweetheart, Rebecca lives here, too, now."

As if on cue, the door to his bedroom opened and Rebecca walked out, wrapped sarong-style in a sheet.

"Is there anything to eat in this house? I'm starved," she croaked.

"Rebecca," he whispered, hardly daring to believe she was really there. Her chestnut hair hung in bedraggled, sweat-soaked strands around her pinched and drawn face. But her fever had broken. She'd never looked lovelier. And now that she'd passed the critical point, the neukocytes in her blood stream would be healing her with as much speed as they'd previously made her ill.

"Mrs. Lacroix, I'm glad you're feeling better." Mrs. Waters bustled past him into the kitchen. "You just tell me what you want, now, and I'll bring you in a tray. Some nice soup, perhaps? A sandwich?"

"That sounds great. Maybe two sandwiches. I'm really hungry."

Gillian poked Desmond's shoulder. "I wanna help."

"You want to help make a sandwich for Rebecca?" He didn't think he'd understood her correctly, but Gillian nodded. Thought-pictures of when she'd been sick, and the people she'd cared about had tended her, flashed through his mind. Mixed in were dim memories of her mother's illness, when Gillian had been an infant.

He set her down with a light kiss on her forehead. His family. It was more than he'd dared to hope for, more than he'd ever believed. And because of Rebecca, he had it all.

"Go ahead and help Mrs. Waters. Rebecca will like that."

Gillian laughed and pelted into the kitchen.

"Why will I like that?" Rebecca asked, arching her eyebrow.

"First of all, because you're starving." He walked across the room, feasting his eyes on her. He'd been so afraid of losing her. Now that she was here to stay, he didn't think he'd ever be able to get enough of her. Lifting her into his arms, he carried her back into their room. "Second, because even though you're getting better, you still need rest, and I'm putting you to bed."

He laid her gently on the bed, then fluffed the pillows behind her head. Going over to the dresser, he picked up a hair brush, then came back and sat beside her. As he smoothed the brush through her hair, she closed her eyes and sighed in contentment.

"Any other reasons?"

"Yes." He leaned down and touched her lips with a kiss. "Because I'm putting you to bed, and you don't need that much rest."

She laughed, and wound her arms around his neck.

"You're right. I think I'll like that very much."

~ * ~

Jennifer Dunne

JENNIFER DUNNE wrote her first "book" at the age of four, telling the story of a lost little girl and a helpful elephant. She was all set for a career in the literary arts, to begin in that far off misty future after kindergarten – then she discovered a book about "the new math" on the coffee table, and fell in love with numbers instead. After getting a degree in math, followed by a masters awarded for teaching a computer how to take relationship building into account for negotiations, she joined IBM and devoted herself to doing neat things with computers, all the time continuing to write romance stories as a way of balancing so much logical brain activity. Much to her surprise, and despite everything her mother had always warned her about, people were actually willing to pay her for these stories.

Combining her love of science with her love of romance, Jennifer became the driving force behind the Science Fiction Romance newsletter, tirelessly working to promote books mixing these elements, and the two-term president of RWA's Fantasy, Futuristic and Paranormal chapter. Her first book, the science fiction romance RAVEN'S HEART, won the EPPIE Award for best science fiction original ebook.

Visit Jennifer's website at: www.jenniferdunne.com

Printed in the United States
5004